Friendship and Fortitude

A Pride and Prejudice Variation

Amelia Westerly

Copyright © 2024 Song Sparrow Press

All rights reserved

The characters and events portrayed in this book are fictitious. Any similarity to real persons, living or dead, is coincidental and not intended by the author.

No part of this book may be reproduced, or stored in a retrieval system, or transmitted in any form or by any means, electronic, mechanical, photocopying, recording, or otherwise, without express written permission of the publisher.

ISBN-13: 9798325716959

Cover design by: Song Sparrow Press
Printed in the United States of America

Chapter Thirty-nine	302
Chapter Forty	311
Epilogue	320
Thank You	333
Other Books by Amelia Westerly	335
Other Books from Song Sparrow Press	337
About the Author	339

Chapter One

In the summer of 1812, on the road to Ramsgate

The roofs and streets of Ramsgate were coming into view, and the faintest hint of salt was perceptible in the air when it happened. With a loud cracking noise, a hard jolt, and a strong oath from the coachman, the left rear wheel of Mr Darcy's carriage broke, bringing the carriage to an abrupt halt.

Mr Darcy responded with admirable calm, stepping down from the carriage and looking over the damage. To ascertain the state of the vehicle was the work of moments. There must have been some hidden flaw in the material that, upon hitting a slight obstacle in the road, had given way at its weakest point. There could be no question of a quick repair, for even the spokes were badly cracked. Indeed, though the morning was a capital one for travelling, the weather clear, the air fresh, and everything fine and pleasing, there was no help for it.

"We'll not be on our way again for quite some time," Mr Darcy observed to John the coachman.

He shook his head ruefully. "No, sir. It can't be repaired — we'll have to get a new one. I'm dreadfully sorry, sir. I know how anxious you were to see Miss Darcy."

Where many a gentleman would have been offended by such free speaking in his servants, Mr Darcy considered it a compliment, the surest proof of their loyalty and fond feeling for the Darcy family.

"So I am indeed," Mr Darcy agreed, "but it can't be helped. There is nothing much to be done but make our way to the nearest inn and inquire after a wainwright. I hope the horses were not injured in the accident?"

"Oh, no, sir," John reassured him. "They are right as rain, I am happy to say, and ready to go on as soon as ever the coach can."

"Then all is well, and I am sure the delay is of little significance."

In later days, Mr Darcy would come to remember those words, and to bitterly regret that he had ever spoken them. It was not yet too late. If he had been animated by some strange sense of worry or haste, he might even then have taken one of the horses, ridden into Ramsgate, and been in time.

Yet he had no inkling of what was about to occur and thought only of how best to reassure his faithful servant and protect his horses. If he arrived at Ramsgate and greeted Georgiana in two or three days after the carriage was fixed, it would not much matter. She would run to greet him with the same joyful smile as ever, the same pleasure in his surprise visit. She would doubtless have learned a new piece on the pianoforte to play for him, and he could surprise her with the present of new sheet music he had carefully hidden away in his valise.

Mr Darcy did not know, and would not learn until it was too late, that Mr Wickham was even then persuading Georgiana to leave for Gretna Green with him. A few days — perhaps only a day — would have made all the difference in the world. If he had only arrived in time, if he had only been there, surely Georgiana would have confided all to him, and he could have saved her.

Instead, he would arrive in Ramsgate three days later, all happy confidence and joy at the prospect of seeing his little sister. The coach would rattle over the cobblestone streets towards the lodging house where he had left her with Mrs Younge, and he would not know until it was too late that she was already gone.

Gone to Scotland, and beyond redemption.

—

At almost the same moment that Mr Darcy

was reassuring John the coachman, Georgiana was drawing her hand out of Mr Wickham's gentle grasp with an apologetic smile and privately thinking of her own foolishness. She had actually thought George Wickham was flirting with her, when it was the most obvious thing in the world that he was simply being a good friend.

"Of course I shall call you George again, as I did when we were children," Georgiana said brightly, though with an effort. It would be too shameful if Wickham suspected her infatuation with him. Of all things, to take on so because a handsome man was as kind to her as he had been when she was a child! It was simply too mortifying.

An objective observer might have pointed out that when Georgiana had been a child, Mr Wickham had already been a man grown, but it is all but impossible for a young lady of sixteen to believe that she is, in fact, still very near to the years of childhood.

Mr Wickham smiled at her. "I am glad to hear it, Georgiana, for I do not know that my poor heart could bear it if we were ever to lose the intimacy that has all my life been so precious to me." He paused a moment. "You are dearer to me than perhaps you know."

At such a proof of feeling, Georgiana could not stop herself from blushing. Yet even still, her shyness and modesty led her to believe him to be speaking merely of friendship.

"Yes, we are fortunate to have always been such good friends," she agreed shyly. "And I hope that we always will be."

So gently that she did not think to prevent it, Mr Wickham took her hand again, cradling it tenderly in both of his. "Oh, Georgiana — my Georgiana — am I really nothing more than a friend to you?"

She darted a shocked glance at him, flushing brightly. He seemed as though he meant — as though he must mean — but that was obviously impossible. It was impossible that George Wickham, quite the best-looking and most charming man she had ever met, could be interested in *her*. Georgiana Darcy, gawky and awkward, with nothing more than a little talent for the pianoforte to recommend her — were there not two score of women more beautiful and talented than she who would marry him in an instant?

If Georgiana had been only a little older, she would have realised that a dowry of £30,000 is, in fact, a significant inducement to marriage. But at sixteen, shy, modest, and with little concept of wealth, the thought did not even enter her head.

"Do you mean...I can hardly believe that you mean..." Georgiana's voice failed her. At last, she took courage, and spoke again. "I can hardly believe that you would be interested in me. You, who are everything charming!"

Mr Wickham laughed a triumphant laugh,

although Georgiana thought it was merely a happy one. "No, my dear, no, it is you who is everything charming. Please, Georgiana, do not toy with my heart. Do I have a chance, then? Could you ever think of me so?"

"I could. I could, indeed," Georgiana said, so low it was nearly a whisper.

He clasped her hands more tightly than ever. "Then — oh Georgiana, my Georgiana — would you even consent to be my wife?"

Tears came to her eyes at the romance of it all. "Yes, George. I will marry you," she said, picturing herself as the heroine in her favourite gothic novel. It seemed almost too perfect to be true. She had not thought that she, quiet girl that she was, could ever have such a moment.

Though Georgiana was afraid of what Mrs Younge might have to say, her companion's approbation quickly reassured her. Georgiana had expected her to object, or at least to insist that Mr Darcy ought to give his blessing to the engagement. Yet Mrs Younge seemed not to have the least hesitation or doubt in giving her approval and support. On the contrary, she urged them to leave for Scotland as soon as possible, that their happiness might begin without delay. Everything seemed to move about her in a whirlwind, and when she spoke of the necessity of communicating the joyful news to her brother, both her companion and her fiancé negated the idea so quickly and yet in such cheerful terms that it seemed a foregone conclusion. To Scotland they would go, because poor dear Wickham could not bear to wait now that their happiness could begin immediately. And though Georgiana began to feel a terrible sense of dread, she told herself that she was being a silly girl, and said nothing to stop it.

Chapter Two

Pemberley

Mr Darcy clasped the letter in shaking hands. Though he had already read it several times over, he read it once again. Perhaps he hoped the words might somehow change, or perhaps he felt he deserved to feel every bit of the suffering it caused him.

Gretna Green, 13 July, 1812
My dear brother-in-law,

With what joy do I write to tell you of my marriage to Georgiana! Your little sister is the most charming wife. A little shy, of course, but as I have known her all my life, I do not mind that. Scotland is lovely at this time of year.

Now, brother mine, to the meat of the matter

– dear Georgiana's dowry of £30,000. You will kindly release it to me as her husband, that I may keep her in the style that she — and I — deserve.

Regards,

George Wickham

P.S. Georgie sends her love, but I'm afraid I shan't send on the letter she wrote for you until I hear word from you about her dowry.

—

It was bad — it could hardly be worse. His failure as her guardian, as her brother, was complete. Though he and Colonel Fitzwilliam had chased after them as soon as the loss was realised, though he had made Mrs Younge tell what she knew, it had all been too late. Even the relief of duelling Wickham, which Colonel Fitzwilliam had most urgently wished to do, was denied them. Mr Darcy had absolutely refused to allow it, for it could only deepen his sister's suffering. By now, Georgiana might know how she had been deceived, but he would pray that she did not. That Wickham might still treat her kindly, might make the marriage as good and gentle as one begun on such a foundation of deception could be, was the only hope that Mr Darcy could imagine. Even Georgiana's fortune would be lost, for he did not for a moment imagine that Wickham would use it judiciously and well. In the hands of such a wastrel, even £30,000 might come to nothing. Then Georgiana would suffer the privations of poverty, on top of every other misery she would face as the wife of such a man.

Mr Darcy stopped a moment, frozen almost stiff by a sudden thought. It would not save Georgiana from the misery of an unfit marriage, of having a weak and unprincipled husband. Nothing could do that now. There was only one thing now that he could preserve for Georgiana — her fortune. A small thing, if everything to Wickham, but he might yet use it to ransom his sister some measure of security.

With a heavy heart and a slow quill, Mr Darcy wrote a letter.

—

Pemberley, 18 July 1812
Wickham,

If you had intended for our relationship to proceed with any degree of even pretended civility, you would not have withheld Georgiana's letter from me. Let us therefore at least have the relief of honesty.

I will not take the trouble of rebuking you. You know the goodness and innocence of Georgiana's heart as well as I do myself; you know what I think of this marriage to a girl of sixteen, and doubtless you know how completely you have revenged yourself upon me. I will not dissemble; you have triumphed over me indeed.

Perhaps you will forgive me for pointing out that you have also committed something of a tactical error. Georgiana's fortune was not set down in our father's will, legally committed to be turned over to her husband as soon as she was married. On the contrary. Our father always intended for her to have a fortune of £30,000, but he left the means and method to his successor as her guardian — namely to me.

If I wished, Wickham, I could cut you off without so much as a farthing. However, I will not do so. I will grant you an ample allowance, paid each month on the condition of Georgiana's continued wellbeing. If I one day come to feel fully satisfied of Georgiana's happiness with you and your continued respectability, I shall then — and only then — make over the balance of it to Georgiana, in her own name.

Do not retaliate against her, Wickham. I had the greatest difficulty in convincing the Colonel that killing you would only deepen her misery. If we hear that you have hurt her in any way, I shall not make the effort again.

Sincerely,
Fitzwilliam Darcy

—

The letter was slowly written, but quickly sent, for it represented the best protection that Mr

Darcy could afford his sister. Feeling the stupor of misery coming even more deeply upon him, Mr Darcy realised that civility and friendship bade him write a second letter.

Pemberley, 18 July 1812
Bingley,

Please accept my apologies, but I will not be able to join you in viewing your new leasehold as we had planned — not at any time in the coming months. My visit to Ramsgate ended in disaster. Wickham has taken Georgiana to Gretna Green. My dear friend, I am sure you can guess the rest, and will be at no loss to imagine what appallingly bad company I would be at this time. I shall not inflict myself upon you and your sisters. You will have to view the prospective property without me. I hope it is everything pleasing, and that your stay in Hertfordshire will be all you might wish.

Sincere regards,
Darcy

Time seemed to pass strangely in the halls of Pemberley. Mr Darcy found he was sometimes in his bedchamber, sometimes in his study, sometimes in the library, without entirely recalling having moved from one to the other, or having the least idea what he had come there to do. The business of running Pemberley, of resolving disputes and making provision for the poor, was a relief, yet even after hours at his desk, he found he could not recall what he had done, and must hope that years of experience had allowed him to do it justly and well all the same. Time seemed a nothingness suffused with misery.

As Mr Darcy was sitting blankly in his study some days later, he heard an odd noise coming from the halls. It was Mrs Reynolds. Naturally, to hear the voice of his housekeeper was no unusual occurrence. However, to hear her voice raised in exasperated protest was all but unheard of.

" — now then, Mr Bingley, you are a good friend of the master and there's no denying it, but he is not at home, I say! He has given me the clearest instructions that he is not at home."

"Please forgive me, Mrs Reynolds," Mr Bingley replied firmly. His tone was gentle, and yet more determined than Mr Darcy had ever heard from his friend before. "I am being abominably rude, I know, and yet you must allow me to have my way. I am convinced that your master needs a friend now if any man ever needed one, and if I must be abominably rude to comfort my friend, then rude I shall be."

Mrs Reynolds seemed to make some reply, her

protests somewhat quieted, but it was too late. A moment later, Mr Bingley pushed open the door and hurried to Mr Darcy's side.

"I am sorry, Darcy," was all he said at first. "I am so very, very sorry."

For a long moment, Mr Darcy shut his eyes, ashamed of the hot feeling of tears that had come into them at his friend's sympathy. His voice was a little rough from disuse when he spoke.

"What are you doing here, Bingley? Why are you not in Hertfordshire even now? You ought to be admiring your new property."

"I have given it up," Mr Bingley announced, without the slightest appearance of regret. "What ought I to do in Hertfordshire, when a friend needed me in Derbyshire? Come now, Darcy, I am convinced that you do. We shall go travelling together, and it will not make things a whit better, but it will give you something else to think about."

Mr Darcy blinked at him in astonishment. "Bingley, you cannot mean it. I know how you have looked forward to having a place in the country, how often you have spoken of it. Surely you cannot have given up Netherfield Park after all this."

"I have, and I tell you I feel not a particle of regret over it," Mr Bingley announced. "Come now, my old friend. Doubtless there are pleasant people and pretty girls to be met with in Hertfordshire, but so there are in every corner of the world. In the end, what have I to lose by not going to Netherfield?

There will be other estates, or perhaps I shall find the one I mean to buy at last on some fine day during our travels."

With this cheerful speech, he grasped his friend's forearms and lightly tugged him up from his chair, making his implacable determination perfectly clear. Mr Darcy followed him, still half numb, as Mr Bingley made free of the master bedchamber and ordered his valet to begin packing for a journey.

He closed his eyes for a long moment, conscious of an almost painful gratitude. To be freed from the anguish of his own company, to be allotted a span of time in which a good friend might make all the little choices of everyday life, was a blessing devoutly to be wished.

I shall not forget my failure to protect you, Georgiana, Mr Darcy silently promised his sister. *I shall never forget it. But I shall go for a little while until I am again able to be of any use to you. Until I can look myself in the face again.*

Chapter Three

Longbourn

Though Mr Bingley had been entirely sincere in his protestations that it could make no difference whether he took Netherfield Park or any other estate equally well situated and available under equally favourable terms, he was, in fact, entirely mistaken. Had Mr Bingley taken Netherfield Park, he — who always had a quick eye for a lovely face — would certainly have noticed the prettiest girl in the neighbourhood. Being a man of good and steady understanding as well as good humour and lively manners, he would have also quickly noticed that Jane Bennet, the woman behind the lovely face, was in fact as kind, virtuous, and steady as she was beautiful. And, as Jane Bennet's mother was as avid a matchmaker as any woman in the kingdom, local rumour would have already established them as well on the way to having an understanding.

Instead, Mr Bingley did not let Netherfield Park, and Jane Bennet did not meet the man with the happiest manners of her acquaintance — or, at least, she did not meet him at that time.

Not long after Mr Bingley broke the intended lease of Netherfield Park, Jane Bennet's father received a rather curious letter.

"My dear," he inquired of his wife some time after opening and receiving it, for Mr Bennet was not attentive in his communications, "my dear, I have a most unusual housekeeping problem to put before you."

"Oh! Mr Bennet," his wife began. "Surely you will not suggest that we give over the second drawing room to bookshelves once again? I have told you before, it cannot be done. Your books must remain within the confines of your own study, which I am sure is no difficult arrangement. And indeed, surely you do not really want your valuable books to be out among the family things."

"It is not about my books," Mr Bennet replied. "The question with which you are to be faced is, how are you to host a man for whom you have repeatedly voiced a most heated dislike?"

"Mr Bennet, I daresay I have not the least notion of what you are speaking. Nor could anyone expect me to, when you talk so wild!"

"Indeed, it is a troublesome question," Mr Bennet said solemnly, enjoying his wife's confusion. "One does not know quite how to act."

"Perhaps Mama would know better how to

act, Papa, if you were to tell us rather more clearly what you mean," his second daughter Elizabeth said smilingly. "I must admit to some curiosity myself."

At this, Mr Bennet relented, for though his behaviour towards his wife was not well-calculated to inspire tender devotion or raise her admittedly rather silly mind towards higher things, he was not a cruel man, and Elizabeth was his favourite daughter.

"Very well, my dear," he said with a chuckle. "If even your wit cannot penetrate my meaning, I have been too obtuse indeed. I am speaking of your cousin, Mr Collins, who is next in the entail and shall inherit Longbourn when I am gone."

"Oh! That scoundrel!" Mrs Bennet exclaimed at once. "I shall never forgive him, never, and I do not see how the man can live with himself. To go about intending to turn us out of our home as soon as you are cold in your grave, and him a clergyman, too!"

"I see now what you meant by 'heated dislike,'" Elizabeth commented, "but Father, do you really mean that he is coming to stay with us?"

"I do, indeed. He arrives in four days." With this, Mr Bennet handed Elizabeth a letter. She scanned it curiously.

"His manner of expressing himself is certainly...unusual," Elizabeth said at last. No milder form of description came to mind, for the personality expressed through his letter inviting himself to their home was one that she could not look forward to meeting.

"Unusual indeed," Mr Bennet agreed with relish. "I expect the visit to be most diverting."

As Elizabeth did not share her father's enjoyment of foolishness, she excused herself to join her oldest sister. Jane pointed out all the goodness of wishing to be known to their family, smoothed over everything that was awkward or ungainly in Mr Collin's letter, and did her best to put her sister into a better frame of mind for the visit.

"Jane, Jane, it is enough, it is quite enough," Elizabeth protested laughingly. "Save your consolations for Mama, for she needs them much more than I do. I may not expect to meet a sensible man in our cousin, but neither do I have any objection to his visit."

"Do you think I ought to attempt it?" Jane asked seriously. "Mama has been so intent, so nearly violent in her objections, that I thought I would have little chance of success. But if I may improve her present comfort or her future civility towards our cousin once he arrives, I suppose it is my duty."

"I would not call it your duty," Elizabeth replied, "but if you can succeed in bringing Mama into a better frame of mind, I am sure it would be an improvement to the comfort of us all, particularly Mama herself."

At this, Jane left her sister with a smile and a pat on the hand, and went to make the attempt.

Her success was rather better than the general run of those who attempt to change another's mind, for Jane was wont to make such attempts so gently and so rationally that her listener could find no way to take offence.

Jane's labour was soon to bear fruit, for her cousin arrived at Longbourn at the very hour of the very day his letter had specified. Mrs Bennet's greeting to him was nearly civil, and upon receiving hints of his intention to make amends for the monstrous injustice of the entail, it became actually welcoming.

Poor Jane! Had Mr Bingley only taken Netherfield Park, he would certainly by this point have noticed her beauty, and given rise to high hopes in her mother and much more modest ones in the lady herself. But it was not to be. And so, when her cousin Mr Collins gave certain hints about his intentions to Mrs Bennet, her answer was rather different from what it might otherwise have been.

"In fact, Mrs Bennet," Mr Collins said in high self-satisfaction, at the conclusion of a long speech, "I came here intending to find a bride from among your daughters, that she might become mistress of Longbourn after Mr Bennet's death, and upon finding your daughters so charming and accomplished, I am more confident of my intention than ever. I think it a thing highly to be desired in a clergyman to listen for the will of Providence, and I fancy that the desirableness of these arrangements shows that I have done so."

Mrs Bennet was too thrilled by the prospect of a suitor for her girls to have any attention for this rather curious piece of theology. "Oh, Mr Collins," she said breathlessly, "why, what a delightful thing for you to think of, and I am sure I should be glad to have any of the girls mistress of Longbourn. Why, just think, how well they know all the neighbours and all the servants, and everything about it! You should both have an easy life, indeed. I think you may choose any of the girls, just as you like. Jane is my beauty, of course, but Mr Bennet has always thought Lizzy the cleverest. And Mary is the best at the pianoforte, and she studies marvellously, which you might appreciate, being a clergyman yourself. And dear Kitty is a fine artist, and of course I must put in a good word for my Lydia. She is rather young, of course, but such high spirits! She is a dear girl, indeed."

Being rather overwhelmed by this wealth of commendations, Mr Collins did not at first know how to reply. After taking a moment to collect himself, he cleared his throat. "You do me honour, madam — indeed, you do me great honour. I may say that I have a high view of the rights of seniority, and in view of this, perhaps I would do best to speak to Miss Bennet. After all, it would not be entirely desirable if the younger girls were to be placed over their oldest sister. Indeed, this would not be conducive to family feeling, and I find that as a clergyman, I ought to be particularly careful in promoting this blessing for all within my sphere of influence."

"What a good man you are, Mr Collins," Mrs Bennet gushed, her earlier opinion of him as the wicked thief of Longbourn entirely forgotten. "Yes, indeed, I shall inform Jane that your courtship has my entire approbation, and I am sure you shall get on well together."

Armed with such support as this, it did not take Mr Collins long to speak with his intended. Taking the first opportunity of a morning walk around the grounds of Longbourn, he approached Jane with a confidential tone that took her rather by surprise.

"May I join you, Miss Bennet?" Mr Collins said, hurrying up to where Jane stooped over the lavender bushes, her arms full of fragrant stems.

"Certainly, Mr Collins," Jane replied with a polite smile. Her cousin had already made it quite clear at supper the previous night that his company was not to be desired. Yet it was not in Jane's nature to be unnecessarily rude to anyone.

"Perhaps I might assist you," he offered gallantly, holding his arms out to receive the lavender.

"It would be a shame to mar your coat, Mr Collins," Jane demurred. "I have purposely worn one of my oldest dresses, so that the stems and their juices do not stain a newer one."

"There is no need to fret, I do not regard it in the least," Mr Collins insisted, "for my noble patroness, Lady Catherine de Bourgh, has conferred a most valuable living upon me, and so I am thankfully relieved from the necessity of considering such little things. And, of course, the inheritance that is to come upon me — that is not entirely to be wished, and yet naturally I cannot regret it —"

"You are speaking of the entail, I believe," Jane said, wishing to free him from the conversational difficulties in which he had entangled himself. As Mr Collins even yet held out his arms to receive the lavender, Jane relented and placed the bundle in them. Yet almost in the instant he received the flowers, Mr Collin's clumsy grasp sent half the bundle tumbling to the lawn.

"I am dreadfully sorry, Miss Bennet," Mr Collins gasped in alarm, and sent the rest of the bouquet falling to earth in his attempt to retrieve the first half. Seeing Jane kneel to retrieve them, he knelt down as well, only to send their foreheads smacking into each other as both reached to retrieve the scattered lavender.

Despite his profession, Mr Collins only just swallowed down an oath at the pain that shot through his head, while Jane exclaimed a sharp "Oh!" Abandoning the lavender as a bad job, she stood again, taking a deep breath to calm herself. Though keeping her face carefully serious to protect her cousin's dignity, Jane was conscious of a private amusement. The anticipation of how Lizzy would laugh once she had sufficient privacy to tell her sister of the absurd encounter was more than worth the lingering pain in her head.

"Do not worry about the lavender, Mr Collins," Jane said kindly. "It is of little matter. I am gathering it for the still room, but as you can see, there is no shortage of the plant. We are fortunate that a flower of such worth and beauty grows in such abundance."

"You interest yourself in the running of Longbourn, then?" Mr Collins inquired attentively.

Jane gave him a friendly smile. "I do. Our mother is training me in all that I will need to run a house of my own one day. There is a great deal to it, but I must say that I find the work of the still room particularly interesting. There is so much that plants can do for us."

"Indeed, Miss Bennet, but there is something else I wished to speak to you about," Mr Collins said. "I hope we will laugh over this foolish accident in years to come, for it has only confirmed to me my first intention upon entering this house. Namely, Miss Bennet, I wish for you to be my wife."

"I — I beg your pardon?" Jane said in dismay.

"Your modesty, Miss Bennet, has perhaps led you to misunderstand me. And indeed, I suppose I should explain how it is that I came to Longbourn to seek a wife. Firstly, allow me to reassure you. I have come with the full knowledge and support of my patroness, Lady Catherine de Bourgh. Perhaps it is unnecessary for me to say so, for naturally I could not think of seeking a wife without her blessing."

"Naturally," Jane echoed weakly, wondering if the blow to her head had confused her senses.

"I have long felt the difficulties in my inheriting Longbourn, since this necessarily results in depriving you and your honoured mother and sisters of the property. However, the law is the law, and I could not do otherwise than obey it."

Jane privately felt this was rather much, as Mr Collins's nobility could not be expected to extend to giving up the inheritance of Longbourn, whatever his respect or lack thereof for legal principles. However, she said nothing, and he quickly went on.

"I therefore resolved to venture to Longbourn and choose a bride from among you and your sisters. And you, Miss Bennet, being equally first in birth and beauty" — here Mr Collins swept a bow that attempted gallantry, but was merely rather awkward — were my choice, and I hoped you will consent to being the companion of my future life, and the future mistress of Longbourn. Naturally, I am aware that your dowry is small, and I promise you I shall never mention it again once we are wed."

"I do not know what to say," Jane finally replied, as the pause threatened to become awkward. "I am conscious of the honour you do me, Mr Collins, and yet I confess that the suddenness of this declaration is too much for me. If you would give me the indulgence of some time to collect my thoughts, cousin, I should be honoured to give you my answer two days hence."

Though Jane was half fearing and half hoping to offend him, Mr Collins did not look at all concerned. "Naturally, Miss Bennet, naturally. Your modesty would not allow you to make an immediate reply. I understand completely. Go to your mother and father, my dear, and ask for their approbation. I am certain that, once you are assured of their support, I shall receive a favourable answer."

Thankfully, Jane found that no reply to this was required, as Mr Collins strode jovially off before she could make one. In the confusion of the moment, she hardly knew whether to laugh or cry. Marriage to Mr Collins! The thought was appalling. And yet, did she not owe it to her family? In a single stroke, it would take away all threat of being sent away from Longbourn to starve in the hedgerows. And all it would cost was the slow, grinding misery of marriage to a man she could never respect.

Chapter Four

The appointed two days passed slowly and then seemed to have disappeared in an instant. Jane rather feared that Mr Collins would try to woo her, but to her equal relief and disgust, he clearly considered her already won. Evidentially, his vanity could not conceive of any reason for refusing him.

In one sense, he was right, for it was a most eligible match in a prudential light. At her darkest moments, Jane did not believe she had the right to refuse it. Did she not owe it to her mother and sisters to secure their comfort forever? For her own, she had not the slightest temptation to say yes. Even if the most perfect foreknowledge would have said that no other offer would ever be made to her, Jane was certain that she would be happier in genteel poverty or honest work than as the wife of Mr Collins, even if being so meant she would also be mistress of Longbourn. If it had been only that she did not love him, the answer would be plain enough. She must and would have accepted a sensible man, even without that most cherished good of promised love. But to wed a man whom she could not respect, whose conversation must ever be an embarrassment and a bore to her, whose company would wear away at her own self-respect — only the strictest sense of duty could bring her to consider it.

At that thought, Jane was back to the beginning again, to the absolute necessity of marrying him to secure her family's future. Yet the next moment brought all the misery of such a life before her mind's eye once again, and to marry Mr Collins seemed more impossible than it was inevitable. Jane made the decision again and again, first for one side and then the other, not knowing how she could bear to live with either.

On the second evening, when it seemed impossible to bear the weight alone any longer, Jane was sitting distracted and miserable in the drawing room. The rest of her family seemed much the same as ever. Her father had gone off to seek a little peace in his private study, though as Mr Collins had immediately followed him, peace might be in rather short supply. Mary was practicing the piano, repeating the same difficult sequence of notes over and over again, and their mother was instructing Lydia and Kitty, who were not listening to a word of it. Elizabeth, who had been reading a book, suddenly shut it and came over to her.

"Come away with me a moment, Jane," she said in a decided tone.

Jane had no temptation to deny her. Though

she knew she must make a decision, the chance to escape her thoughts for a little while was a blessing. She followed her sister down the corridor, so that they would not be overheard by anyone in the drawing room or the study.

"I do not wish to pry," Elizabeth began gently, "but I am convinced that something is weighing painfully on your mind."

Jane opened her mouth to deny it, as she knew she ought to, and found instead that she had started to cry. Telling herself not to be absurd, she blotted her eyes and desperately sought her composure.

"I had meant to deny it," Jane said ruefully, when she had at last composed herself enough for speech, "but I do not think that would be convincing."

"No," Elizabeth said with a chuckle. "No, I am afraid it would not be convincing at all."

"Well, then," Jane said, sighing, "I shall tell you a little of it. I am not sure what I ought to do."

Elizabeth looked at her with her dark eyes, saying nothing. Seeing that open, gentle gaze, Jane felt the words almost tugged out of her.

"Mr Collins has proposed to me. I asked for two days to decide my answer, and I must give it to him tomorrow."

"Is the answer so uncertain, then?" Elizabeth asked gently.

"It is. You cannot suppose that I wish to marry

him, Lizzy."

"No. I did not think you did."

Jane was grateful for her sister's carefully quiet manner, for she did not think she could have borne it if Elizabeth had put her in the position of having to defend a choice she badly did not want to make. At last, Jane sighed. "If it were not for the matter of the entail, I would not consider it. He is not at all what I would wish for in a husband. Yet to secure all our family's comfort, our safety, even the assurance that we may remain together after our father's death — is it not my duty to secure all this?"

"Surely it is not your duty," Elizabeth said. "I do not think it can be any woman's duty to marry a man, if she does not wish it."

Jane had begun some reply, she hardly knew what, when they heard the drawing room door open. In another moment, Mrs Bennet had bustled up to them and was urging them back into the drawing room, where it transpired that Mr Collins had returned and proposed to read to them all. The two eldest Bennet girls rather wished they had not been recalled to take part in the amusement, but there was no helping matters. He would read, in a patronising, over-enunciated tone that rendered the dry work of morality he had chosen still less engaging. The hour seemed late long before the evening mercifully drew to a close.

Though Jane had thought all the rest of the family ignorant of her predicament, her mother must have been privy to some part of it, for on the appointed day, she bustled all the rest of the family out of the parlour, leaving Mr Collins and Jane sitting alone together in some astonishment. Mr Collins immediately turned to Jane with a look of smug satisfaction.

"Well, then, Miss Bennet. It has been two days, and I am sure you have found time for consulting with your parents in the interval, as a dutiful daughter ought to do. Naturally, they will have removed any concerns you may have had. Do you have an answer for me?"

Even a woman of Jane's mild temper must have been angered at such proof of complacency. In that moment, even while rebuking herself for her selfishness, Jane knew what her answer must be. She could not stomach any other.

"Yes, Mr Collins, I do," Jane answered him steadily. "I have thought over my duty most carefully these past two days. I have spent much time in prayer, and in the end, I have come to an answer. I am most grateful for your generous attentions, but I must decline them, for I am certain that we would make each other desperately unhappy."

Though soft and low, Jane's voice was so decided that Mr Collins was caught short in the midst of congratulating himself. "Why — that is —" he sputtered.

Jane went on remorselessly. "Mr Collins, I see

much to respect in you. Your desire to select a bride from among my sisters and I, as a protection for our future, is truly noble. Naturally, I have the greatest respect for your profession. But I do not feel that basic sympathy between us which I hold to be essential between a man and wife. In our brief acquaintance, it has become clear to me that we disagree on almost all matters of conduct and propriety beyond the most essential and inarguable. Mr Collins, I could not be the wife that you deserve, however much I tried, and I believe I should be miserable in the attempt."

Here Jane stopped, half astonished that she had said so much. But it was necessary — the complacency of his expression, and the inordinately long time it had remained on his face even after she had begun, showed it to be necessary.

It was some time before Mr Collins's astonishment would allow him to speak, but his hurt pride would not permit him to remain still. "Very well. I see you have made your decision," he said stiffly. "It may be for ill. The time may come indeed when you regret having rejected such an offer, but it is done. We shall not speak of it again."

And with that, he left the room, leaving Jane behind him. She almost fell into a chair, resting her head on her hands. To offer any man such an insult was painful indeed, but she could not wish it undone. Each moment of his company only showed more and more clearly what she would have suffered had she agreed to become his wife.

A soft knocking came from the open doorframe, and Elizabeth poked her head into the room. "He is gone to the Lucas's, to stay for supper," Elizabeth announced with a small smile.

"That is a relief," Jane admitted. "Oh, Lizzy, I could not do it. I thought it through, over and over, and many times decided I must accept him, but in the end, I could not do it."

Her sister simply shook her head. "I did not think you would."

"Oh, Lizzy, how can you take it so calmly?" Jane cried out. "I would have made us all safe for ever. Indeed, I would not blame you if you never spoke to me again, after I have acted so selfishly. I have thrown aside all duty to my family, and I cannot even feel much remorse that I have done so."

"Hardly," Elizabeth said with a laugh. "Oh, Jane, you ought to know me better than that. I would never have spoken to you again if you had taken him — or at least, I could have never spoken to you with the same confidence in your honour and good sense that I have enjoyed all our lives. Duty? What duty could there have been in marrying a man you could not respect? No, Jane, you have acted rightly. I know that to my heart."

"It does me good to hear you," Jane said almost in a whisper, feeling all the strain of the past days rushing in on her. Elizabeth came to her, arms extended, and Jane stood to all but fall into them.

"Now, I do not say that all members of our family shall be equally well satisfied," Elizabeth said cheerfully into her sister's ear. "I expect that our mother shall be horrified."

The sisters laughed a little ruefully, for their mother's probable reaction was all too easy to envision. But both felt too much relief, as of disaster nearly averted, to feel much concern over any future ills.

Chapter Five

Though Jane and Elizabeth would have liked to enjoy a peaceful family supper as a respite from Mr Collins, it was not to be. He had informed Mrs Bennet of Jane's refusal as almost his last communication on the way to Lucas Lodge, and she had not stopped wailing in dismay since the door had closed behind him.

"Jane, Jane, whatever can you be thinking?" Mrs Bennet sobbed over the first remove. "I had not thought *you*, of all my daughters, to be so undutiful, so unfeeling. My poor nerves! I shall perish under the strain, I know I shall, and then I shall not be there to help when Mr Bennet dies and you are all turned out to starve in the hedgerows."

Elizabeth had a little trouble suppressing her mirth at this hyperbole, but was at least able to turn her laugh into a cough. Jane sent her a quelling look.

"I am sorry, Mama," she said. Her voice was soft, but utterly unwavering. "I know how much it would have meant to you — how much it would have meant to us all — to have Longbourn remain within the family. I assure you, I thought it over carefully. But in the end, I found I could not respect Mr Collins, and I am sure that to marry without respect is wicked."

"Besides that," Elizabeth added, "Jane would have been utterly miserable, and it would have made me miserable to see her so. Do you not think so, Mama?"

Mrs Bennet appeared torn at this, for even her flexible judgement could not really imagine Mr Collins to be the sort of man who could ever make Jane happy.

Mr Bennet cleared his throat. "No one has yet asked what I, your poor father, think of the matter."

"I am sorry I did not ask your advice, Papa," Jane said quickly, "but I was sure I did not feel for him even the simple approbation that is surely the most basic requirement for marriage, and I did not think I could marry him even if you bid me to do so."

"How can you speak so to your father, child?" Mrs Bennet exclaimed in astonishment. "I am really ashamed of you. I shall speak to Mr Collins and tell him you have changed your mind, and you will accept him, I tell you here and now."

"You will not do any such thing, Mrs Bennet," her husband told her with some asperity. "I have not yet given my opinion of Jane's suitor."

"Well, then!" she told him with a toss of her head. "I beg you will tell us, and let Jane know what her parents think of what she has done."

Mr Bennet looked his oldest daughter in the eyes. An unusually soft smile came over his face. "Jane, I am proud of you," he began. Mrs Bennet gave a shriek of dismay, but was quickly quieted by the stern look given her by her husband.

Mr Bennet went on. "Jane, I am proud of you, for while we have all known your beauty and your good temper, your old father has never been quite sure that you had the fortitude to do what was difficult, to displease others when it is necessary. I have now seen that you can indeed be disobliging and indomitable when it is necessary, and the knowledge pleases me excessively. My dear, now that I know you can say 'no' when it is called for, I am certain you will be a very happy woman."

Jane smiled brilliantly at her father's praise, though her eyes were bright with tears. Elizabeth could not help laughing at his delivery, though the message touched her heart as deeply as it had touched her sister. Mary looked rather surprised at what their father had said, and the younger girls were not attending at all, being occupied in whispering to each other.

"Thank you, Father," Jane said. Her low, clear voice seemed to put a pin in the conversation, and supper passed off rather peacefully after all.

After supper, Mr Bennet left for his study with an expression of great relief, while the ladies went to their evening amusements of books, needlework, and conversation. They had not long since removed to the drawing room when they heard the housekeeper, Mrs Hill, open the front door and admit their wayward cousin.

Jane and Elizabeth exchanged a look that spoke eloquently of dismay. They had time for no more commentary than this before Mr Collins entered the room.

"Good evening, Mrs Bennet, Mr Bennet, young ladies," he said. His look paused on Jane with an attempt at frostiness that made him look rather as though he had found the Lucas's supper indigestible.

Much to Elizabeth's surprise, Mr Collins then favoured her with a broad smile. Cautiously, she smiled back. It was perhaps a good sign that he could so quickly be friendly with Jane's closest sister, for surely he must know that Jane had told her everything. Perhaps the rest of Mr Collins's visit would not be so unpleasant, after all.

The next moments proved Elizabeth very wrong indeed.

"If you would allow me, Mrs Bennet," Mr Collins announced in a lofty tone, "I should like the favour of a few words alone with your daughter Elizabeth."

Merciful confusion lasted only an instant before Elizabeth realised what he must be about. Yet it was impossible — surely no man could ever imagine —

"Why yes, of course," Mrs Bennet replied promptly. "I was just telling the other girls that I had something particular to show them upstairs. Come along now, girls."

That her sisters had arrived at the same conclusion as Elizabeth herself was made obvious by their expressions. Lydia wore a look of gleeful hilarity, clearly already relishing the idea of repeating the story about Meryton, while Kitty seemed torn between curiosity and shock. Mary bore a look of disapproval, while Jane looked almost as horrified as Elizabeth felt.

The eldest Miss Bennet took a quick deep breath and faced her mother. "Perhaps I ought to stay, Mama," she announced bravely. "I think perhaps Lizzy would rather that I stay."

"Yes indeed, I would much rather," Elizabeth quickly seconded. "Do let Jane stay, Mama. Mr Collins can have nothing to say to me that he could not say before my sister."

For a moment, she had hope that the stratagem might yet work. Then Mrs Bennet opened her mouth.

"Now, now, Jane, this is no time to be petty and jealous. Let Lizzy have her turn, for certainly —"

Jane rushed to the door, following her mother out and shutting it behind them before any more could be heard. Little as Elizabeth liked being left alone with Mr Collins, she was heartily grateful that her sister had spared them at least that humiliation.

"I hope you will not be angry with your sister, Cousin Elizabeth," Mr Collins said with rather elaborate sanctimony, "for it is only natural that she should be somewhat reluctant to see such an opportunity go another way. I imagine you have guessed what it is I have to say — namely that I wish to make you, Cousin Elizabeth, mistress of Longbourn and the partner of my future life. Almost as soon as I entered the house — that is, as soon as I recovered from my misunderstanding of your sister's character — I singled you out as the only woman I could ever marry."

Elizabeth had never before realised that such desperate fury could be so deeply wedded to an almost irresistible impulse to hilarity. Mr Collins was in every way abominable. She knew not what appalled her most, the absurd slight on Jane's character, the dishonest attempt at gallantry, or the idea that she might ever marry such a man.

No, that is not quite true, Elizabeth thought grimly. *There is in fact no contest which idea appals me most.*

Mr Collins had continued speaking without waiting for a reply. "As I told your sister, I ought perhaps to explain my reasons for seeking the wedded state at this time, and particularly for attempting to find my bride at Longbourn. Firstly, let me assure you that my right noble patroness, the Lady Catherine de Bourgh, approves of my being married. 'Mr Collins,' she said to me, 'Mr Collins, if your wife is a reasonably genteel sort of person, I shall certainly acknowledge her.' What graciousness! What generosity! And I assure you, the lady has many favours within her gift."

Elizabeth pinched the bridge of her nose, attempting to swallow down a great billow of hilarity, for she earnestly wished to bring the encounter to as quick an end as possible. For a moment, she considered saving Mr Collin's feelings by saying that she could never wound her sister by accepting a man Jane had rejected. Yet a brief consideration of the insults and absurdities that Mr Collins heaped on each fresh utterance made her decide another way. The man deserved no such courtesy.

Elizabeth cleared her throat. "When a lady receives a proposal of marriage, I believe it is customary for her to thank the gentleman, whatever her own feelings may be. It is natural to feel gratitude in return for the compliment of sincere affection, and if I felt any, I would certainly owe you my thanks. But I am certain that I do not. It is absurd, Mr Collins. It is in every way absurd. You certainly do not like me — not in any real sense. Mr Collins, you proposed to my sister Jane two days ago! I thank you for wishing to provide for my sisters and I, but I shall not marry you. I cannot marry you. My conviction on this matter is absolute, and so I bid you goodbye."

Mr Collins's jaw gaped wider and wider as Elizabeth went on. By the end of her little speech, he resembled a trout freshly plucked from the lake. But if Elizabeth had imagined that such plain-speaking as this would convince the man, she found she was mistaken.

"Now then, Miss Elizabeth, I think you have not considered what your father might have to say about the matter," Mr Collins gasped. "Once you have spoken to him, I am sure you will see things rather differently."

Though her hand was already on the door handle, Elizabeth paused and turned back. She gave him a mild smile.

"Perhaps you ought to speak to my father, Mr Collins," Elizabeth said. She gave a small flutter of her eyelashes and looked modestly at the floor. "You may tell him you wish to marry me, and that I have refused you. And if he responds to my refusal with anything but the heartiest approbation of my choice, I shall give you fifty pounds."

With Mr Collins sputtering behind her — she believed it was something about the evils of wagers and how he had never been so insulted in all his life — Elizabeth let the door click shut and hurried away. At last, she could give in to the temptation to laughter.

How absurd, how utterly absurd! She would rather her first proposal had not been so wholly insulting, but at least she might laugh over the affair. Better still, Mr Collins's visit was due to end in only a few day's time, and if she were lucky, she might never see him again.

Chapter Six

Three years later: the summer of 1815, in a rented townhouse in Edinburgh

"Good afternoon, Mr Tiller," Georgiana Wickham said with a bright smile. The gentleman bowed and greeted her. He sat down across the desk in her study, as was his custom. Though the room was rather small, the door was always left open, out of comfort as much as concern for propriety, and the windows were angled well to take advantage of the sunlight.

"Well, Mrs Wickham, the draft has arrived in your account on time," Mr Tiller began.

She nodded. "As it always does."

"Of course. Mr Darcy is most conscientious," Mr Tiller said. There was an awkward pause, for Georgiana's brother was as little mentioned by either as they could reasonably contrive. Mr Tiller, who had been a manager of affairs at Pemberley since Georgiana was a girl, had come to Edinburgh not long after the Wickhams had settled there, and had been of the greatest use to a young woman not accustomed to the affairs of the world. Shortly after she had wed, when Georgiana had gained the first, dim sense of Mr Wickham's true character, she had realised with a shock that it would not be her part to simply learn from and be guided by her husband, as she had always assumed it would be. If their affairs were to be conducted on a basis of dignity and honour, she would have to take an active role in arranging them. That Mr Tiller had been in Scotland and willing to provide tutelage at such a stage had been the greatest blessing in the world to a young woman increasingly aware of the vulnerability of her position, and one for which she could never sufficiently express her gratitude.

The Georgiana of nineteen thought differently from how the innocent girl of sixteen had been wont to do. This, though he had not known how to formulate it, had in fact been Mr Darcy's greatest fear — that marriage to an unfit, dissolute lout would corrupt all that was good and beautiful in his sister's character.

In fact, it had happened rather differently. There are doubtless many women who would be entirely sunk under the misery of marriage to a man who intended only to use them. Considering Georgiana's gentle nature, it was not even unreasonable to fear that she might be one of them. But it was not so.

Ever since the guardianship of Georgiana had first come upon him, Mr Darcy had been most anxious that the good principles their father had always emphasised ought to be shared with her — that, at least to the extent of his powers, all the goodness and benevolence of their late honoured father ought to remain alive in the lessons he would have shared with his youngest child, had he lived to do so. He had succeeded beyond his expectations, for when Georgiana at last understood what her husband was, and with what selfishness he had pursued her, the realisation did not sink her. Though regretting more than ever what an innocent failure of judgement had cost her, she did not retreat into dissolution and vain pursuits, as Mr Wickham's influence might have led her to do; she did not even fall into despair.

Instead, Georgiana had done everything in her power to restore her life to happiness and respectability. Mr Wickham had never allowed her to see the exchange of letters between himself and Mr Darcy, no doubt out of a certain reluctance to let his bride know the full extent of his wickedness. Georgiana had therefore been left to interpret her brother's failure to release her dowry as best she might. At length and after much thought, she had settled upon a deep and abiding anger with her. The explanation seemed entirely plausible, for Georgiana strongly felt herself to deserve it. Had she not ignored all the principles he had so carefully taught her? Had she not selfishly grieved the man who had been as much a father as a brother to her? Little wonder if he could not bear to write directly to her or see her, and did not feel that her husband ought to have the liberty of her full dowry. It was no more than she deserved.

In fact, Georgiana misunderstood both herself and her brother rather badly. Herself, in how much she ought to be blamed for falling prey to a fortune-hunter when she was just sixteen, and her brother, in supposing that he would ever hold her responsible for the actions of another, or that he could have remained angry with her even had a far greater degree of culpability been her own. The monthly allowance was not the most he could bring himself to do, as Georgiana rather supposed it was, but the least.

Mr Tiller being close to hand, he had become her mentor, to guide and teach her as he had taught her brother before her. Thanks to his capable instruction, Georgiana had soon taken on the management of the monthly income. Over the past three years, she had gradually taken on a greater and greater portion of running their affairs. Mr Wickham meant well, Georgiana supposed, but when he had directed their spending, the rather generous monthly income had somehow always run short before the next instalment was to arrive. With careful diplomacy, Georgiana had taken over first one part of the household affairs, and then another, until they were no longer living above their means. As Mr Wickham was a rather languid man, whose only cares were his own convenience and that the general opinion of him should be good, he was willing enough to let her do it, since he did not wish to take the trouble himself.

In Mr Wickham's name, Georgiana had taken a little house in Edinburgh, where they might live in reasonably good style at little expense. For all Mr Wickham liked to talk of the many friends left behind in England, there were rather more individuals he was eager not to meet again, making their continued residence in Scotland a most eligible plan. For her part, Georgiana sometimes found herself fighting back an almost unendurable longing for Derbyshire, and for her brother. But since Fitzwilliam seemed to wish never to see her again, it was better to remain far away. She could at least spare him that much.

Mr Tiller showed her the latest numbers from her — or rather, Wickham's — account, and they looked over the columns of figures together. With rueful gratitude, Georgiana thought it was good the allowance was a generous one, for she really could not make do with less. Though she practiced all possible economies in her dress and personal expenses, though the house was not large and the servants not many, there was always some unexpected expense of gambling debts or meals out incurred by her husband that ate up what little she might have otherwise hoped to save.

Suddenly, a violent noise came from the front of the house. After sharing a shocked glance, Mr Tiller and Georgiana began hurrying towards it. It sounded as though the front door had been opened with such violence it was nearly torn from its hinges, and there was a crowd of men's voices in the hallway.

At the nearest landing before the entryway, Mr Tiller turned to Georgiana with an expression of concern. "Perhaps it would be better for you to remain here, Mrs Wickham," he suggested quietly. "I shall find out what is the matter, and I believe you will be able to hear all that transpires at this slight distance."

"I think that would be for the best," Georgiana gratefully agreed. Though it pained her to admit it even silently, the company kept by her husband was not always genteel. Finding out what had occurred might indeed be a task better left to the joint efforts of Mr Tiller and her housekeeper.

Mrs Evens had already reached the front door, and her exclamations of surprise added to the general din. With a look of concern and an avuncular squeeze of her hand, Mr Tiller left her, hurrying to join the fray.

"Now then, what is this? What on earth has happened?" Mr Tiller inquired, in a tone of such calm emphasis that it cut right across the din.

There was a confused attempt at an

explanation by several male voices. Gradually, Georgiana could hear the voice of Mr Wickham's particular friend, a Mr Denny, rising above the others.

"There was a bet — oh, how I wish we had never entered in to such a foolish wager!" Mr Denny exclaimed. Thankful that she was unobserved, Georgiana closed her eyes in exasperation. All too often, there had been a wager, something started in drink and ending in foolishness and thoughtlessness of the worst type. Mr Denny was explaining the wager, at least to such an extent as it could be explained to anyone whose spirits were not unduly exalted by strong drink, which was not much. They had the idea of racing tradesmen's wagons down the Royal Mile. They had thought it the funniest thing in the world. They had no idea there could be any harm in it — indeed, no one could have thought there could be any harm in it.

Georgiana was torn between humiliation at the degradation of her husband's conduct and resignation, assuming that the next words would speak of a wager lost and money to be paid, damage done to the wagons or buildings or both and yet a greater sum owed to repair them, when Denny's next words at once put an entirely different complexion on the matter and explained the wealth of panic in his voice.

"—and then he fell from the driver's seat, directly into the path of the horses," Denny finished, his voice hollow with grief and despair.

"Have you not called the apothecary?" Mr Tiller asked sharply, and Georgiana was running, running towards them as though she might prevent the answer, but Mr Denny was already speaking.

"No, I did not," Mr Denny said quietly, his voice strained. "By the time I reached him, his heart had already stopped."

Georgiana came to an abrupt halt, and the men parted before her, clearing the path to Mr Wickham.

His handsome face was entirely undamaged, and free from even the smallest stain of blood. Yet there could be no doubt of his fate. All the animation had gone out of it, to be replaced by a strange, stiff slackness. His waistcoat was soaked black with blood.

"He is dead," Georgiana said, looking down at her late husband. She felt herself wrapped in numbness, as though a door were closed between her and all that transpired. Death seemed an impossibility. It could not have claimed Wickham, who was all that was lively and engaged.

Yet in that moment, Georgiana felt herself to be a wicked creature. Grief she did feel, grief for all that was lost and wasted in Wickham's abruptly ended life, but she could not pretend that it made up the greater part of her feelings. It was but a minor note in her heart, one that threatened to be lost amid a guilty chorus of relief.

I am free. I am free. I shall never be shamed by my husband's actions again. Oh, I thank God that I am free.

Chapter Seven

The autumn of 1815; Longbourn

Elizabeth Bennet grasped her father's hand tightly, as though she could thereby communicate all her love and all her sorrow. The words of the apothecary had only confirmed what she already knew to be true — her beloved father was not long for the world.

"Elizabeth, my Lizzy," Mr Bennet gasped weakly. "I am sorry — so very sorry to leave you in such a state."

"Hush, Father, do not worry," Elizabeth urged him. "All will be well in the end." In the bleakness of her private thoughts, she thought he was right to worry. Since he and Mrs Bennet had never produced a male heir, Longbourn would go to the odious Mr Collins. With no dowries and few connections, his five daughters were in a pitiable state indeed. But if there was any way she could soothe her father's pain of mind, even with a judicious untruth, she would do so.

Mr Bennet coughed out a shaky laugh. "My dear, you are not a good liar."

"Father, it is not a lie," Elizabeth insisted. "I admit I am frightened — of course I am. And of course I wish you were well and hale. But it will come right in the end. We shall not starve in the hedgerows. We have our uncles to help us, and good neighbours, and our health. Father, we shall find a way. I promise you that."

His eyes were shining with tears that sprung equally from guilt and from relief. "Oh, Lizzy. I am so sorry that I have left you all this to do, and even to reassure me into the bargain. And yet I am glad to believe down to my toes that you are capable of doing it."

"Not I, Father," Elizabeth said, her smile carefully even for his sake, "not I, but we. With Jane's wisdom and Mary's hard work, we older girls will do it together."

The relief her words brought to his face stayed even when another of the vicious, heaving attacks of coughing wracked his body. Elizabeth left his bedside then. The apothecary had begun his futile efforts, and it would not do to let her father see the tears that she could no longer keep from falling.

—

The funeral was not many days later, though

enough that the Gardiners had time to come from town. It was well that they had arrived before Mr Bennet breathed his last, for it took all that Jane and Mrs Gardiner could do to somewhat quiet Mrs Bennet.

When Jane at last left their mother and joined Elizabeth in their shared room, she looked haggard and pale. "Poor Mother," she said simply. "To have such grief for Father, and such fear for herself, too."

"She might remember that you have the same grief, and the same fear, too," Elizabeth replied ruefully.

"But I do not," Jane said softly. "Of course I miss Father, and I am afraid. But it is not the same in the least. We are young and strong, Lizzy. That makes all the difference in the world."

"I said something rather like that to Father," Elizabeth slowly admitted. "It was the best I could think of to comfort him. But I must confess that I do not feel it to be true, not in my heart. I feel rather more like a lost child."

Wordlessly, Jane went to her sister and caught her up in a tight embrace. Elizabeth dropped her head onto her sister's shoulder, grateful beyond measure to lean on another's strength, if only for a moment.

"Oh, Jane," she said at last. "We shall find a way, I know we shall. But at the moment, I am entirely at a loss for what it shall be."

—

The next morning's post brought, if not a reprieve from their grief, at least something of a distraction, for it contained a letter from their cousin, Mr Collins. Though the gentleman's letters could not be expected to contain much in the way of heart's ease, they could at least be relied upon for a diversion.

—

Hunsford, Kent, 15th October 1815
Dear Ma'am,
Please allow me to express my deepest condolences on the death of your husband, my cousin Mr Bennet. In the midst of your grief, I hope you may find comfort and joy in the knowledge that he is with our Lord in heaven, free from all sorrow and pain.
My noble patroness, Lady Catherine de Bourgh, has informed me that I ought to make my way to Longbourn at an early date, to take the burden of running the estate from your shoulders as quickly as it may be done. You may therefore expect me at Longbourn a fortnight hence. Naturally, I shall not expect you and the girls to leave it so quickly, and you may inform Miss Bennet and Miss Elizabeth Bennet

that I have entirely forgotten any conversations that may have taken place between us three years ago, and I do not by any means hold a grudge, or wish to call to mind any regrets.

Sincerely,
William Collins

"As ever, he is an oddity," Elizabeth said ruefully.

"And to think that we might have been safe forever! Jane, how could you have been so selfish?" their mother cried out, and burst into a fresh fit of tears. "And Elizabeth, too! I cannot think how I have raised such ungrateful daughters."

Elizabeth patted her sister reassuringly on the shoulder. "For my part, Jane, I think the last passages of that letter make the correctness of your decision more certain than ever. I certainly feel no regret for mine."

"Thank you, Lizzy," Jane said gratefully. Her gratitude was not only for the support, necessary as it was in the face of their mother's dismay, but also for expressing what she had felt herself, but not had the words to convey. To have written such a letter, at such a time, and to still feel and convey resentment against two young women who had just lost their father, for having declined his proposals three years prior! Starving in the hedgerows looked remarkably palatable in comparison to marriage with such a man.

"However, he is right in one respect," Elizabeth went on briskly. "We do need to formulate a plan of some sort for our future, or we shall regret it, indeed. I think we ought to begin on the project as soon as Mr Gardiner returns."

"That will not be long," Jane remarked. "He has only gone to see about matters down in the farm. I should think he must be nearly finished by this time."

Elizabeth nodded. "Good. Now then, between you, and I, and Uncle Gardiner, I am sure we can think of what is to be done."

"I should like to join you," Mary said firmly. Her elder sisters startled slightly at her comment, for they had not realised she was in the room.

Jane recovered first. "Then so you shall, and Kitty and Lydia too. Indeed, we all must be concerned in deciding how we are to live from now on."

Looking at the steadiness of Jane's expression and the determination on Mary's face, Elizabeth felt a rush of pride in both her sisters. "We will find a way," she said, extending her hands to them both. Each grasped one tightly in promised determination. "I am certain of it."

Chapter Eight

When Mr Gardiner had returned from the farm and had time to freshen himself, the family took to the drawing room to make their plans over a cup of tea. Even Mrs Bennet seemed caught up in the spirit of determination and optimism, for though her tears still flowed, she kept them quiet to avoid interrupting the meeting, and her face showed as much grief as ever, but rather less despair.

For her part, Elizabeth thought they could not afford despair. The question of how best to make their way in the world had occupied all her thoughts of late. It was no easy question to solve. Six women, all brought up to be gentlewomen. How could they earn their own keep? Marriage was surely a lady's pleasantest preservative from want, and yet one could not find a suitable husband simply by wishing it might be so. No; husbands did not appear on command. They would have to find a solution that relied on no one but themselves.

After much thought, she had at last reached a decision. Elizabeth felt the more confident in it for its very uncertainty and compromise. It was an imperfect solution, but she did not think she would have trusted any perfect one. Now, if only she could convince the others of its practicality. As Elizabeth looked around the drawing room and saw her family in all their fear and confusion, she took a deep breath and began.

"The situation stands thus," Elizabeth said crisply. "We shall lose Longbourn, and though Mr Collins will allow us to stay for a time, it cannot form any part of our plans for the future. Mother has five thousand pounds secured to herself, and to us after her passing."

Here, Mr Gardiner cleared his throat. "Though I am afraid your father could not save much, there is some money, and some valuable goods that are not comprehended in the entail — your father's books, for example. I believe this will come to perhaps two thousand pounds in all."

Elizabeth nodded. "Already it is not so bad. Now, uncle, much as you might wish to protect us, I know you could not support us all. But do you think you could take in Jane? She would be the best of all of us at watching the children, and she would be the most likely to find a husband through your introduction to London society."

At this suggestion, a clamour broke out. The loudest voice was Jane's, protesting that by no means should she, the eldest, have the safest and most comfortable place. But silent though they were, Mr Gardiner's nod and look of pride at Elizabeth spoke far louder.

"It is sound — you know it is sound, Jane," Elizabeth said, gentle and firm in equal measure. "Our nieces and nephews love you the best of all of us, and you are the most likely to benefit through greater access to society. It is not only for your good, either, for we would all benefit if you were to marry a man of consequence."

These arguments were too sound to protest, and Jane reluctantly fell silent. There was another argument which Elizabeth felt to be still more pressing, but this she chose to keep silent for the time.

"Mother, am I right in thinking you would not wish to leave the neighbourhood, if that were possible?" Elizabeth asked gently.

Mrs Bennet made an effort to compose herself and equal the efforts at bravery made by her daughters. "Yes, I should prefer to remain. But my dear girls, you must know that I would go anywhere or do anything that might secure your comfort, if only my poor nerves were equal to it."

Kitty, who sat nearest their mother, gave her a quick, light hug. "We know, Mama, and I am sure we are grateful for it."

At this, Jane and Elizabeth exchanged a quick glance of surprise, impressed that their little sister had overcome her tendency towards sullenness to place such emphasis on their mother's feelings.

Kitty was growing up into a fine young woman, greatly altered from the near-hoyden she had been only a few years before.

Mr Gardiner spoke up. "Fanny, if you would like to remain in Meryton, what of our sister and Mr Phillips?"

"If we paid our room and board," Kitty said thoughtfully, "I am sure that Aunt and Uncle Phillips could take in Mama and Lydia and I, all three. I believe they would enjoy the company, and not think it a burden in the least. And I own I should like to stay with Mama, if I could."

"Just think, to be in Meryton proper!" Lydia cried out. "We would hear all the latest news every day, and perhaps we would have some to tell Aunt Phillips, instead of the other way around."

Inappropriate as Lydia's heedlessness was at such a time, her levity was at least a relief to everyone's spirits, as they all enjoyed a moment of hearty laughter at her eagerness.

"I shall speak to my brother-in-law, then, and see if that may be," Mr Gardiner said decisively. "Though I should not wish to speak for him, I rather think that he will have no objection. Indeed, I know our sister dearly loves the company of her nieces. And that is four of the six of you well settled. We must now speak of Elizabeth and Mary."

Here, Elizabeth bit her lip and turned to her younger sister. "Mary, I ought perhaps to have spoken with you alone first. But it is my settled belief that you and I ought to find respectable work."

Everyone else in the room cried out in protest, but Mary did not look at all distressed. On the contrary, she was nodding thoughtfully, and a small smile had begun on her face.

"You have studied so diligently, Mary, that you would be an ideal governess," Elizabeth continued. "Just think, you could teach the children piano as well. For my part, I cannot believe that anyone would want me as a teacher, for I do not have half your application. I rather think, however, that I might find respectable employment as a companion to an older lady."

"I should like that," Mary said thoughtfully, "and you would be sought after as a companion indeed, if only they knew how easy you are to confide in."

"What — I beg your pardon?" Elizabeth said in confusion.

"You are, you know. Is it not a fact that you have often received other people's secrets almost without trying? I know I have told you many things that I had firmly intended to keep to myself."

Elizabeth knew not what to say. In astonishment, she saw Jane was nodding with a fond smile, and all her family seemed to agree. Thinking back, she remembered many instances of times when others had taken her into their confidence. It had always seemed only natural to her, yet perhaps there was something to the idea that not everyone was so often a recipient of unburdened hearts.

"It is true, Lizzy, you have a special talent for listening," Mrs Gardiner said. "I have often observed it. I should greatly like to keep you with me, but if you must go out into the world, I think you could not do better than to be a lady's companion."

With an effort, Elizabeth regained her composure. "Very well then," she said. "I think I am right in saying that this plan will not overtax either our little means or that of our family?"

"Yes, indeed, Lizzy," Mr Gardiner said warmly. "If Mr Phillips agrees, as I am sure he will, this will be an excellent plan. Your mother and sisters will be kept in very reasonable comfort, without the expense of renting their own house, and we shall think it nothing to keep Jane with us."

Mrs Gardiner stepped in firmly. "It would be best for you and Mary to come to London with us until you can find good places," she said, "for your uncle can help you do it, and he will speak to the families and make sure they know you are not someone to be trifled with."

Mr Gardiner nodded. "Yes, indeed. Do you know, I think this plan may even allow for a little savings, by and by, to add to your own comforts and those of your mother. I think it is a highly eligible plan."

Elizabeth smiled, though a little sadly. "It is just as I told Father," she said. "I said it would all come right in the end, and indeed I believe it shall."

Chapter Nine

That night, Elizabeth retired to her room with considerable relief. Though the discussion of what their little family ought to do to secure their futures had gone more smoothly than she had dared to hope, it had nonetheless left her exhausted. Much as she hoped to go to bed without much conversation or preferably even without much thought, one glance at Jane's face as she shut the door behind her showed it was not to be.

"Now, Lizzy," Jane said firmly, "I am sure there was more to your plans than what you told us all. Indeed, you must have, for I shall not accept being given greater comfort than my mother and all my dear sisters without a reason."

"That is going a bit far, do not you think?" Elizabeth protested. "After all, you will be working for your keep, albeit the pleasant work of caring for our dear cousins, and Mama and Kitty and Lydia will not."

Jane smiled at her sister, but refused to yield. "Do not attempt to distract me, Lizzy. I will and must know what you are thinking."

Elizabeth sighed. "Oh, very well. I was in earnest in everything I said, for you are indeed the best fitted of us to care for our cousins, and the most likely to benefit from the wider circle of society to be had in London. If any of us can marry to advantage under such circumstances, surely it will be you."

"And?" Jane prodded her.

"And I would be afraid for you in a stranger's house, as I am not afraid for myself or for Mary," Elizabeth admitted. Jane waited in silence until Elizabeth could bring herself to continue. The wait was of some duration, for it was not an easy subject to discuss.

"You are so beautiful, Jane, and so soft-spoken. If you were to work as a governess, many a woman would be reluctant to bring you into her home, lest her husband's eye fall upon you. And once you had found a position, I would fear for you to be so unprotected. Mary and I can both speak up stoutly when we need to. Indeed, I am fierce enough when the circumstances require it."

"Surely you cannot think that I would allow anyone to take liberties," Jane protested.

"I have not the least doubt of your morals or your good sense — you know I have not. But of your ability to answer rudeness with rudeness of your own when it is called for, I have grave doubts indeed. You are too apt to make allowances for everybody, Jane, and in such a case, it simply will not do."

Jane sat heavily down on the bed. Elizabeth grieved to see her sister's face, for her expression was dreadfully unhappy. "And yet you and Mary are to run such risks? It cannot be, Lizzy. It must not be. We must find another way."

"No, Jane," Elizabeth said quietly. "I truly believe that this is best. We cannot ask either of our uncles to take us all in. How could we? Uncle Phillips will have as much as he can do if he takes in Mama and our two youngest sisters, and Uncle Gardiner has already a household of six to care for. It is not wrong for Mary and I as it would be for you, not if we take good care in choosing our employers. We shall have useful employment, and we shall know ourselves to be doing good for our family. I see nothing wrong in that."

Jane was shaking her head, tears in her eyes, and yet Elizabeth could see that her protests were already over. As she had herself, Jane must accept the necessity.

"Lizzy, I have always known that we must be parted one day. But I always imagined that it would be leavened by the happiness of marriage. I can hardly bear that we should be parted by such necessity."

"It is too soon to despair," Elizabeth said gently. "Who are we to say that we shall be nursemaids and companions all our days? Perhaps you shall meet a charming gentleman in London, and I shall fall in love with my employer's nephew."

"I shall hope it may be so," Jane said, and though her expression was still subdued, a species of hope was beginning in her eyes.

Chapter Ten

Edinburgh

"You have made your decision, then?" Mr Tiller inquired diffidently.

Georgiana nodded. "Yes, I am ready."

Though the words were said as confidently as she could make them, it would not have taken a keen observer to perceive the hesitation in Georgiana's tone. She and Mr Tiller both stared down at the letter from Mr Darcy as though it might explode, or perhaps leap off the desk to bite them. Being merely inanimate paper and simple ink, it did nothing of the kind. Yet for all the measured phrases it contained, a wild beast could not have been viewed with more trepidation.

Georgiana swallowed. "It is clear enough, I think. I must come to London and meet with him if I am to take the money intended for my dowry into my own hands."

"I do not think Mr Darcy intended his letter to

be taken in such a way," Mr Tiller protested. "Indeed, I am persuaded he merely meant to express his hope that you would choose to visit him. I do not believe any conditionality of your property was implied."

"Perhaps not," Georgiana said softly. Though she was not really convinced, she had no wish to argue with Mr Tiller, who had only ever tried to help her. "Yet if there is any chance of it, I cannot take the risk."

Though she already knew it almost by heart, Georgiana scanned over the even, precisely written lines once again.

—

Pemberley, 27 October 1815
Dear Mrs Wickham,

Please allow me to express my condolences on the death of Mr Wickham. My thoughts are with you at this most difficult time.

Of course, the monthly allowance shall be continued as long as you wish it. But when you are ready, I hope you will consider a visit to England, that we may discuss the question of your inheritance. The Exchange has been profitable over the past three years, and the fortune of £30,000 our father intended for you has grown considerably. Naturally, there is no call to hurry. Yet when you feel yourself able to come to London, we may discuss how you wish to direct your household in the future, and to what extent you wish the management of your money to come into your own hands. You know you will always have a home with me, if you wish it.

Your brother,
Fitzwilliam Darcy

"Is it not plain enough?" Georgiana said, a little grimly. Her tone did not wobble, for she absolutely forbade it. "He would do anything rather than speak to me again, but he feels it is his duty. As for making the money over to me, he feels the deepest reluctance in trusting me with such a sum, but that, too, he feels to be a matter of justice."

"I do not think that is it at all," Mr Tiller protested.

"Then why is there not one word of fondness, one intimation that he might wish to see me? I cannot blame him. After I behaved so foolishly, so slightingly, to one who was almost a father to me, it is no more than I deserve."

Yet Georgiana was painfully mistaken, for if Mr Darcy had had any notion of his words being taken in such a way, he would have gone to great lengths to avoid it. Though Mr Tiller was about to say as much, he reluctantly stopped short. The young widow lacked a crucial piece of information about her brother's feelings and wishes — namely, that Mr Tiller had not come to Edinburgh by chance, but rather upon Mr Darcy's earnest pleas and under his employment, so that Georgiana would have from another the help and advice Mr Darcy did not think his sister would accept from the brother who had failed her. In the absence of such crucial knowledge, Mr Tiller did not think she would believe him.

"That is all water under the bridge now," Mr Tiller instead replied, "and in any case, whatever the motive, I think your decision is a good one. Indeed, if I were to advise you, it would be to make the trip to London. I should have mentioned it before, in fact — Mr Darcy has also sent a travelling allowance." Here Mr Tiller named a prodigious sum, one that would have allowed a rather larger party to make the journey in the utmost comfort.

Georgiana sat back a moment, considering the proposition. It had been a long time since she had travelled. Indeed, it must be fully three years, for she had not left Scotland once she had come to it. She had not even left Edinburgh since arriving there from Gretna Green. How was she to do it, now that she had neither a brother nor a husband to attend her? The journey was a long one, and she would need to stop at many inns along the way. There was the threat to her reputation, the difficulties of arranging everything — it was hardly to be thought of.

With a start, Georgiana realised she was

looking at the question entirely wrongly. She was not the innocent young unmarried girl she had been before. On the contrary, she was a wealthy widow, and as such, a figure rather more similar to her formidable aunt, Lady Catherine de Bourgh, than to her own younger self. She would travel in her own coach, with her own servants, as Lady Catherine did. If anyone looked askance at such freedom in a woman so young, either her widow's black or her heavy purse would be her answer. It could and would be done — indeed, it must be done.

All of her internal arguments had taken no more than an instant. "You think, then, that I would be capable of managing my own money?" Georgiana asked Mr Tiller. That gentleman having a wife and daughters of his own, he did not miss the subtle glint in her eyes that spoke of the willingness and, in fact, eagerness to be convinced of it.

Mr Tiller smiled at her. "You have done admirably. I would have no fears for you — no, indeed, I would not. You will, of course, have to take great care against fortune-hunters, for one does not see such a sum in the hands of a marriageable woman every day. And if you do not choose to stay with your brother, I would advise you to collect a household about you in some other way, for it would be better that you are not alone."

"That is certainly true," Georgiana said thoughtfully. "Yet I would not inflict myself on my brother after all this time, and still less when he would feel it a duty, whatever his own preference might be. I would rather have a household of my own."

"A hired companion, then," Mr Tiller said promptly. "Then you will have company always with you, and you will avoid many dangers of reputation that might otherwise be incurred by so young a widow."

"My last companion was a Mrs Younge," Georgiana said, a little absent-mindedly. "I hope my next shall be rather more prepared to make my interests her own."

—

Excerpt from The Times, 31 October 1815

WANTED, a Companion for a newly widowed Lady. This Lady, finding that she must travel from Edinburgh and reside for a time in London, is desirous of a woman of good character and excellent conversation to reside with her. Such a companion must not object to frequent playing of the pianoforte by the Lady; it is desirable but not necessary that she should play herself. Accompanying the Lady to Meetings of Business shall be no small part in this rôle. Pay to be discussed. Interested candidates shall be received for interviews in Mayfair beginning a fortnight hence.

— Mrs W

Chapter Eleven

London, November 4, 1815

Dear Mrs W

    I read your advertisement in The Times with great interest, as, in consequence of my Father's death, I am in search of work as a Lady's Companion. I hope that my character is good; my conversation is as excellent as application and interest can make it. If you wish to speak of the pianoforte with a companion possessed of much enthusiasm and only a little skill, such a one am I. To accompany you to Meetings of Business would be a matter of great interest to me. If you select me for an interview, my Uncle Gardiner shall accompany me to meet you. I reside with him in Cheapside.

Best regards,
Miss Elizabeth Bennet

Georgiana neatly separated the responses to her advertisement into piles on her desk. To the left, a pile of unappealing responses, some too strident, some too diffident, and a few that seemed not to have read, or at least not to have understood her requirements. In the centre, a pile of letters without serious flaws, being neither overbearing nor ingratiating, and having at least mentioned an interest in the pianoforte. On the right, there was a single letter — the one that had made her smile. Though prudence caused Georgiana to shuffle it back into the centre pile, honesty forced her to admit that she hoped Miss Elizabeth Bennet would be as suitable as her letter suggested. She had not thought to request a witty companion, yet if anyone could raise her heart under the circumstances, it was a blessing not lightly to be dismissed.

Nothing could be easier than imagining how Mr Tiller would have advised her had he come to London instead of remaining in Edinburgh. Placing prudence above all, he would have advised her to interview Mrs Browne, perhaps, a widow of forty-five who had assisted her late husband in running a shop, but wished to come to London to be nearer her daughter. She had ample experience in business, and might provide beneficial advice. Mr Tiller would doubtless have preferred a Mrs Rodney as well. She had been a companion to a succession of young girls, each of whom she had left on the occasion of their advantageous marriages. Yes, prudent choices there were many, but none whose letters spoke of spirit, of possible friendship, as Miss Bennet's did. Though there were significant disadvantages to be reckoned with in hiring an unmarried companion, rather than an older widow, Georgiana could not bring herself to omit granting Miss Bennet the interview. Imprudent as it might be, she would have her interview along with the others.

The next task, to respond to the letters and propose meeting times to the candidates, was quickly accomplished. When the letters had been dispatched to the post, Georgiana breathed a sigh of relief. For a time, at least, there were no more decisions to be made. She would enjoy the sensation while it lasted, for it would not last long.

—

In a certain house in Cheapside, another young lady was likewise weighing a number of uncertain options. Mary Bennet, however, was of a different mind, and would have considered it almost sinful to weigh any considerations above that of prudence.

"I should greatly like to have your guidance, Uncle Gardiner, Aunt Gardiner," Mary said a little bashfully, "but really, I think I have almost made my mind up that it shall be one of these two. The Calder family of Lyme, or the Stopford family of London. I

FRIENDSHIP AND FORTITUDE

should be obliged if you would look over the letters and give me the benefit of your wisdom."

"Of course, Mary," Mrs Gardiner said at once, and took the letters from her niece's hands. She kept one and gave the other to her husband.

Mary had been most diligent in answering the advertisements that had appeared each day. While Elizabeth had given the task her best efforts, her sister had sent out nearly twice as many responses, a condition partially due to the number of advertisements placed for governesses as opposed to companions, and partially due to the particularity of the two sisters. Mary placed each advertisement she saw before Uncle Gardiner, and if he saw no danger or impropriety in it, she responded. Elizabeth likewise sought her uncle's guidance, but she was not so unselective as her sister, and rejected several notices for what they seemed to say of the writer's temper and character.

Mary's hard work and relative lack of fastidiousness had paid off. If Elizabeth had received a trickle of responses, Mary had a flood. Surely at least a few would offer her the position of governess in truth, and one would be worthy of accepting.

At last, their aunt and uncle had finished reading through both letters. "I see nothing amiss with either family," Aunt Gardiner began. "Do you, my dear?"

"No — not at all. I should not be afraid to trust our Mary to either of them, if the final interview goes as well."

"Then I shall write to them directly," Mary replied with a broad smile.

It all seemed to run as though on wheels. All Mr Gardiner's inquiries about both families were most favourable. They were generally known, though not too generally, and liked by all who knew them. Elizabeth rather hoped that Mary would choose the Stopfords, for the thought of her younger sister away in Lyme was rather a fearful one. If she remained in London, she would at least have Jane and the Gardiners, even if Elizabeth had to go elsewhere to find employment.

Sensible as the desire was, it was not to be. Upon being interviewed by the two families, Mary felt such a decided preference for the Calders that Elizabeth could not bring herself to make the argument for London, for it was sensible, and there was a risk Mary might have listened to it despite a clear and rational desire to do otherwise. Mr Calder was a pastor, and his wife was a deeply devout woman. This, combined with their great warmth and friendliness, would have been attractive to Mary even in itself, but there was a still greater incentive to take the post in the two children to whom she would be governess.

The boy was bright and eager for instruction; the girl likewise, and passionately fond of the pianoforte to boot. They liked Mary even on a first meeting, and she them. The terms of payment and lodging were all so reasonable that Uncle Gardiner had not the least trouble in coming to an agreement on Mary's behalf.

It seemed all too soon that the arrangements were complete. On the day she got into the Calder's carriage to begin the journey to Lyme, Mary was too excited to weep, but her sisters wept for her. Mary left them with a kiss and a cheerful word, making her way in the world without seeming to have the slightest doubt.

Jane and Elizabeth remained on the stoop even after their aunt and uncle had gone inside, seeming to understand their need for a little solitude.

"I did not think it would be Mary who had to go away all alone," Elizabeth said at last.

Jane gave a rueful smile. "I know you did not. You thought it would be you."

Elizabeth sighed. "I confess I did. I did not realise how much this plan asked of you, Jane. It is not easy to see a younger sister leave."

Jane gave her little sister a quick hug. "No, indeed it is not."

Chapter Twelve

Over her time in London, Elizabeth had greeted the arrival of the post with rapidly evolving feelings. At first, there had been only normal interest. When Mary had received her post, a little anxiety for her sister and great eagerness to hear of how she fared had been added. There was the great excitement of waiting for a reply when she had first responded to the advertisements posted in *The Times*, and, as time went by without success, more than a little despondency at each successive disappointment.

Oh, there had been interviews. One elderly lady had rejected Elizabeth as looking too lively and too seemingly inclined to answer back. Elizabeth could not much regret the loss, for it certainly would not have been a comfortable home. Mr Gardiner had swiftly vetoed another potential employer. At his brisk excuses and explanations that they must go, Elizabeth had been greatly surprised, for the lady whom she would have kept company seemed pleasant. But on looking up, she had caught a certain glint in the eye of her would-be employer's husband, and Mr Gardiner's reasoning was made unimpeachably and unpleasantly clear.

Some of her letters had been rejected, while others had not been answered at all. Though Mr and Mrs Gardiner were all kindness and waved away any idea of her being a burden, Elizabeth knew it could not go on forever. They would never ask her to leave, but she would be placing a real strain on their purse. To house one of the Bennet sisters when they could not pay was a great kindness; to take two, for all their aunt and uncle attempted to deny it, would be, in truth, an imposition.

All this, though true, did not entirely explain how much Elizabeth wished to hear back from Mrs W. There was something in the advertisement that had appealed to her. Perhaps it was the modesty of her wishes, or her evident fondness for the pianoforte, or the mysterious Meetings of Business, which had an intriguing sound quite appealing to Elizabeth's curiosity. The address in Mayfair, too, was some inducement, for it spoke of someone who could easily afford a companion's wages and keep.

Added all together, it was making it rather difficult for Elizabeth to keep her wise resolutions about not growing too hopeful, or depending on any one job in particular. It took all Jane could do in the way of gentle reminders, soft pats, and a listening ear to keep her sister in tolerable spirits until a reply might come.

At last, it did. Elizabeth read the reply, which established Mrs W as a Mrs Wickham, offered interview times, and gave the address of the townhouse in question in a tone of friendly politeness and no excessive formality, in a spirit almost of jubilation. She quickly found her uncle and handed him the note.

Mr Gardiner scanned it, nodding approvingly. "Yes, good. I cannot make the time offered on Tuesday, for I must meet with a supplier, but either of the other two would suit me. Have you a preference, Lizzy?"

Elizabeth answered in favour of the earlier date, and Mr Gardiner agreed to her suggestion that she ought to write confirming the appointment at once.

Thankfully, there were only a few days to wait, for Elizabeth could not seem to settle down to anything. Though it was nothing like a last chance to find a position — after all, she might go on answering advertisements for as long as there was a paper to print them — Elizabeth earnestly hoped that she need seek no longer.

On the appointed day, Elizabeth accompanied Mr Gardiner to his offices, that they might take the carriage to Mayfair without returning home. While Mr Gardiner worked, she attempted to occupy herself with a book, though even the gothic thrills of Mrs Radcliff's latest work could not entirely hold her attention.

At last, Mr Gardiner closed his ledgers and said that they might go. Elizabeth had never been more grateful for her uncle's careful habit of punctuality, for she did not think she could have borne arriving late.

As the carriage drew up to the steps of the Mayfair townhouse, Elizabeth carefully straightened her spine and took a deep breath to strengthen her composure. In some respects, Mayfair was not so different from Cheapside, after all. The avenues were broader and the houses larger, but Uncle Gardiner's home was every bit as tidy and well-maintained as the one before her.

The butler who opened the door to them made them welcome and quickly showed the way to the drawing room, where Mrs Wickham was to receive them. It was a rather curious room, divided into two parts connected by a pair of wide double doors which presently stood ajar. The sitting area occupied the nearer part, while the second half of the space was arranged as a music room, complete with a pianoforte gleaming with polish.

"Mr Gardiner and his niece, Miss Elizabeth Bennet," he announced to the woman in widow's black. She had risen from the pianoforte on their entering the room and made an elegant contribution to the formal bows. In the first nervousness of meeting, Elizabeth noted only that her dress was fine and her hair thick and free from even the slightest touch of grey. Mrs Wickham was not a beautiful woman, but her figure was slim and graceful, her smile tentative but friendly.

She was also young, astonishingly young. Elizabeth thought with blank astonishment that she must be younger than herself. If she were to guess, she did not think her any older than Kitty. Yet this woman was not only already married but already widowed.

"I am pleased to meet you, Miss Bennet, Mr Gardiner," Mrs Wickham said. Her voice was soft, and her eyes met Elizabeth's only for a moment before glancing away. With a sudden shock, Elizabeth realised that the young widow was as ill at ease in the meeting as she was, or perhaps more so. Everything suggested that Mrs Wickham was naturally shy, and that, thank the Heavens, was a difficulty Elizabeth did not share.

"I am pleased to meet you, Mrs Wickham, and delighted that you offered me the interview," Elizabeth said, infusing her voice with as much warmth as she could manage. Her efforts were rewarded by seeing Mrs Wickham smile more naturally and seem to grow a little more at ease. It was a soft, girlish smile, one without an edge of calculation.

Mr Gardiner cleared his throat. "My niece has shared your letter with me, Mrs Wickham. I am sorry to hear of your loss. I believe you did not have a companion in Edinburgh?"

Mrs Wickham shook her head. "No, I never

did," she said softly. "But now that I am come to London, it is not fitting for me to live alone. Beyond this, I feel myself to be greatly in need of daily society. I fear I should be lonely if I lived entirely by myself."

"I would not know what to do with myself, living alone," Elizabeth said lightly. "I am one of five sisters, Mrs Wickham, and in such circumstances, one has neither the benefits nor the difficulties of solitude."

"Five sisters!" Mrs Wickham exclaimed. "I must own I envy you. I should have liked to have a sister."

"It has much to recommend it," Elizabeth agreed. "Take my eldest sister, Jane, for example. She is the dearest creature. I can only recommend having such a sister to anyone lucky enough to do so."

Mrs Wickham laughed — or rather, for the sound was as light and girlish as she was herself, Mrs Wickham giggled. "I asked for a good conversationalist, and I must say, Miss Bennet, you are more than I ever could have expected to find. Are you sure you shall not object to my playing the pianoforte for hours on end?"

"Anyone you hire shall not object to that, Mrs Wickham," Elizabeth pointed out, a little astonished. "I do not think you could find a hired companion in this city who would think it her place to object to such a thing. But to answer your question properly, no, I certainly would not. Though you will be disappointed if you hope to find in me a skilled performer, I greatly enjoy the instrument. I am sure I should enjoy listening to you play."

"Would you — if you do not mind, I mean — would you be so good as to play something for me now?" Mrs Wickham asked.

Elizabeth found the request did not entirely surprise her, for the advertisement had clearly shown how important it was to the lady. "I should be delighted," she replied firmly, and went to the instrument. After a little thought, she chose to play Bach's Prelude in C-Major from The Well-Tempered Clavier. The rippling pattern of the notes, streaming by like water in a river or rain on a windowpane, was ever a pleasure to her, and the piece was not so difficult that she would struggle to play it with composure. Elizabeth had no intention of trying to recommend herself by pretending she was more skilled than was really the case.

Though there are more relaxing circumstances in which to play the pianoforte than when one's future employment may depend upon the results, Elizabeth knew better than to spoil her listener's enjoyment in hearing her by neglecting her own enjoyment in playing. Music is joy, after all, or it is nothing. The result was tuneful and pleasing, if nothing anyone would have mistaken for the work of a master musician, and the applause Elizabeth received at its conclusion was sincere.

"Delightful!" Mrs Wickham cried. "It is a pleasure to hear you. I greatly enjoy hearing beautiful playing."

Elizabeth laughed without thinking. "Beautiful playing? I think you are rather too generous, Mrs Wickham. Surely you must have heard how I mistimed the notes in the fourth stanza, and how I slurred my way through the more difficult sections."

"From a technical standpoint, certainly there were things an instructor might point out to you for correction," Mrs Wickham said almost impatiently, "but you have such style in playing, such enjoyment in the music, that one does not notice it at all. Truly, it was lovely."

"I will not argue with you, then," Elizabeth replied lightly. "I am only too glad that your standards of playing are not more stringent, for while I do like to play and sing, no one would ever mistake me for a true proficient. Will not you play, Mrs Wickham? I should dearly like to hear it."

It was perhaps rather impudent of Elizabeth to make such a request of her potential employer, but the young woman did not appear to think it odd. "Why, yes — if you wish it," Mrs Wickham agreed readily enough, though sounding rather shy. "I do love to play the pianoforte."

"Then indeed you must give us the pleasure of hearing you," Elizabeth urged her, with Mr Gardiner adding his polite agreement.

Mrs Wickham moved to the pianoforte and sat down, hesitating a little. Elizabeth was rather curious to see how skilled the lady would be. She would have had the advantage of good instructors, of course. Yet as Elizabeth knew all too well, nothing could make up for the lack of application when one had it not. Many a wealthy lady spoke of her enthusiasm for the pianoforte in order to raise her status in the eyes of society rather than from any genuine love of the instrument. Though such pretence was not uncommon, Elizabeth could not have much respect for it. To hear Mrs Wickham play would therefore provide valuable insight into her character.

At last, she made her selection, stretched her hands, and began. Elizabeth caught her breath. She had recognised the piece almost from the first notes — it was the aria to Bach's Goldberg Variations. The piece was too difficult for Elizabeth to even think of playing, but she was familiar with it from hearing Mary, a far more technical pianist, make the attempt. When Mary had first tried to play the piece, it was halting and uneven, and she was forced to stop and begin again, often with an exclamation of frustration. After many months, she had improved, and could play the whole thing through, though still with many a sour note or error in timing.

When Mrs Wickham played, the listener forgot the difficulty of the piece, and remembered only the beauty. She did not attempt to play quickly, as Mary sometimes did when she wished to impress an audience. On the contrary, Mrs Wickham gave almost the impression of lingering over the notes, as though she wished to give each one time to express its fullest beauty.

The effect was spellbinding. Each note seemed to draw the listener deeper in, and unbidden, Elizabeth found herself adrift in grief, feeling all the loss of her father and her home afresh.

Though her listeners would not have minded if Mrs Wickham had performed the Variations in their entirety, so delightful was her playing, she stopped after only the aria. Mr Gardiner seemed to be as swept away by the music as Elizabeth, for there was a moment's pause before either realised the music was at an end, and applauded with all their hearts.

"I shall never object to hearing you play, not when you play like that," Elizabeth informed Mrs Wickham.

Elizabeth was on the point of reproaching herself for speaking as though the position had already been offered to her when Mrs Wickham's reaction made any such reproach unnecessary.

Her smile was as bright and warm as any paid companion could wish to see. "You will take the position, then? I am glad to hear it, for I think we should get on wonderfully well."

Mr Gardiner cleared his throat. "If you will both forgive me, perhaps we ought to talk over some practical matters, to make sure that we are all as well agreed on other concerns."

"Yes, indeed," Mrs Wickham agreed. "You must excuse me, for I am afraid I have little experience at hiring anybody. Now, I shall wish my companion to live here, in the second guest bedroom, which would be made over to you entirely, Miss Bennet. You may see it, if you like."

"Please, I should like that very much," Elizabeth agreed.

"Shall we go now?" Mrs Wickham suggested, and without waiting for a reply, she rose from the piano and led them from the room. Mr Gardiner and Elizabeth exchanged a look of surprise, for they both would have expected a woman of such means to have her housekeeper show them the room, instead of doing it herself.

She is young, which no doubt accounts for it, Elizabeth told herself with a mental shrug, and followed Mrs Wickham and her uncle through the halls.

"This would be yours," Mrs Wickham said, and gestured them inside.

"Oh, my," Elizabeth said without thinking. She had not imagined that she would be offered anything half so nice. The room was as large as the one she presently shared with Jane, if not somewhat larger. A broad window let in what sunlight the grey London skies offered, and a desk was placed before it, where she might look out as she wrote her letters.

A small shelf held several books and items of bric-à-brac, and a chaise lounge stretched along one wall. All the furnishings were done up in pale wood and shades of green. Elizabeth had rarely seen a room so exactly to her own tastes.

"Do you like it?" Mrs Wickham asked, a little anxiously.

"I do. I like it very much indeed," Elizabeth replied.

"I am glad to hear it," she replied with a shy smile. When Elizabeth and Mr Gardiner had looked their fill, the party returned to the drawing room and sat down.

Mrs Wickham looked earnestly from Mr Gardiner to Elizabeth. "I hope you will find my proposed terms of employment fair. I had advice from Mr Tiller, my man of business, in determining what to offer." She then named a sum of payment, what time Elizabeth might have to herself, and notice periods on either side. All her conditions were notable only in being the spirit of generosity.

Mr Gardiner said as much. "I have come along to look after my niece's interests, Mrs Wickham, but you have left me with little to do. I cannot in good conscience negotiate with such an offer as that."

"Good," Mrs Wickham said firmly. "I wish the arrangements to be favourable on both sides, and I hope Miss Bennet shall be as pleased with them as I am." She hesitated a moment. "There is one more matter that we ought to discuss. It is the fact that

Miss Bennet is only a little older than I am myself, and unmarried."

"I must own, I did not expect so young a lady to be hiring a companion," Elizabeth replied.

Mrs Wickham nodded. "I never thought of it when my husband lived. And I had intended to hire a rather older companion, a widowed lady, much as I had when I was a girl."

If Elizabeth knew her uncle, he was thinking that Mrs Wickham still was no more than a girl, but thankfully, Mr Gardiner was far too well-mannered to say any such thing out loud. Elizabeth was grateful for it, for certainly Mr Bennet would not have hesitated to point it out.

Mrs Wickham went on. "However, the older women I interviewed did not suit me. I welcome the opinions of a companion, as we all can benefit from another's judgement, but I will not be dictated to as I was when my companion was still almost in the role of governess to me. Neither do I wish to hire someone who will only say 'Yes, Ma'am,' and 'No, Ma'am.' I am afraid I tend to be a little shy myself, and two of us in one household would really be too much. I should so much like to have my companion be a friend, and that I believe you and I could have, Miss Bennet."

Elizabeth smiled. "I thought the same thing."

Mrs Wickham smiled back, though her smile seemed to falter after a moment. "I will come to the point, then. Though it is a great deal to ask,

Miss Bennet, might we present you socially as a Mrs Smith instead? You are already wearing mourning, and the social position of two widows would be rather easier than that of a very young widow almost as the guardian of an unmarried woman."

Elizabeth bit her lip. "I must own that I do not care for the idea of deceiving anyone."

"I understand," Mrs Wickham said quickly, "but I am afraid it is rather important, for we would draw an undesirable degree of attention as a widow of nineteen and an unmarried woman only a little older. However, if you really feel you cannot, of course I would not blame you. Perhaps you might take a day or two to think it over and discuss it with your aunt and uncle?"

"I, too, have serious reservations about this idea, Mrs Wickham," Mr Gardiner said quietly. "It might have severe consequences for my niece's reputation, and how could such a thing even be done? Would not your own family and friends be sure to learn the truth sooner or later?"

"Oh! They would learn it sooner, for I did not mean to suggest that we would or could conceal it from everyone," Mrs Wickham exclaimed. "I think all my nearest family ought to know the truth. It is only society at large that I propose to mislead a little."

Mr Gardiner did not appear convinced, although his expression shaded from grim towards merely thoughtful. "If you will allow me, my dear," he said to Elizabeth, "I think you ought to take the time Mrs Wickham has offered to think it over, and to discuss this proposal with your aunt. Though in all other respects, it is a most eligible position, I am not sure you ought to misrepresent yourself in such a way."

"Yes — yes, I shall think it over, and give you my answer, Mrs Wickham," Elizabeth readily agreed. She was eager to gain the reprieve, for she did not know what her answer ought to be. She could easily understand Mrs Wickham's request, for in truth, Elizabeth's age made her less than ideal to provide chaperonage for a widow still younger than herself. For the young Mrs Wickham to be more worldly than her companion would look almost absurd, and would be sure to draw some censure from society. Still, Elizabeth hesitated. The idea of deceit was most unpleasant, and if Mrs Wickham had intended her to conceal her real identity from everyone around her, she would not have considered it. Yet if all those most concerned in the matter knew the truth — if the situation was so eligible, and Elizabeth could not find another half so good — if Mrs Wickham truly needed a friend, as Elizabeth suspected she did —

Temptation warred with prudence, and Elizabeth was not sure which ought to win.

Chapter Thirteen

"Say no," Jane said promptly. "Really, Lizzy, you must not do it. It would be shameful to use a name that is not your own."

"I do not consider it lightly," Elizabeth protested. "Mrs Wickham does not wish to conceal it from everyone, only from the wider circle of society, into which she mixes rather rarely. As a mere hired companion, I would attract so little interest that I cannot imagine it being much of a problem."

"Lizzy, you know you may stay with us as long as you need to," Mrs Gardiner said gently from her seat on the sofa. Her needle never ceased moving in and out of the embroidery frame, leaving the delicate fronds of a fern done in green silk behind it. "Truly, if work as a companion does not arrive this week, or this month, or even this year, you are not to think another moment about it."

Elizabeth rose and crossed the room to sit beside her aunt. "That is good of you, aunt," Elizabeth said firmly, "but it is not quite so simple. Am I to be a burden on you all my life? It cannot be. You have four children, and each pound sterling you spend on my keep is one less that you have for them."

"Your plan was for me to stay here, Lizzy," Jane said with some asperity. "Surely it is not so different. I am not more deserving of a home than you are."

"Nor are Kitty and Lydia, but we must all have a place, and we made our plans to give each a place as well-suited as possible," Elizabeth exclaimed. She paused a moment and sighed. "Forgive me. That may be true, but there is no need to grow so heated about it."

Jane patted her hand in token of forgiveness and gave her sister a gentle smile. Under the influence of that smile, Elizabeth felt her emotions relaxing out of the tight knot into which they seemed to have gathered. With greater ease came greater understanding.

"Tell me, aunt," Elizabeth requested. "Do you think it would be immoral to conceal my name, or only imprudent?"

"My concerns are all on the side of prudence and caution," Mrs Gardiner replied promptly. "I do not see it as a moral question, not when all most concerned in the matter would know the truth. But Lizzy, think for a moment. What if you were to meet someone and fall in love with him? Would not that involve the most terrible difficulties?"

"No, I think not," Elizabeth said slowly. "Let us indeed imagine that I have come to feel the most tender affection and regard for a man. Would I not then simply tell him the truth? I cannot imagine that any man would be so displeased to find he was marrying a maiden without a dowry instead of a widow poor through ill luck."

"There is something to what you say," Mrs Gardiner admitted. "But what if your true name were revealed at some unfortunate moment? Would that not cause a most unpleasant scandal?"

"It is unpleasant to think of, but I do not suppose the risk to be great. I am a person of no interest in London, and not likely to become one. And beyond that, everyone who knows me here will already know the truth. I certainly am not afraid that you, or Mr Gardiner, or Jane will tell my secret."

"Lizzy, are you truly set on going through with this?" Jane asked. "Please, you must not be hasty."

Elizabeth paused. "Set on it — no, certainly not. If you forbid me, my dear aunt and uncle, or even if you most earnestly advise me that I ought not to do it, I will not set myself against your greater experience and wisdom. If you truly think it would be wrong of me, you need only say so, and that will be an end to the matter. I would be foolhardy indeed to defy an aunt and uncle who have been everything kind to me, and have always sought only the best for me."

"Oh, Lizzy," Mrs Gardiner said, a little teary-eyed from listening to this speech. Mr Gardiner was no less affected, for he walked over to Elizabeth and patted her gently on the shoulder.

"You are a good girl, Elizabeth," he said, his voice a little hoarse. "A good girl indeed. Now, let us talk seriously. You have said that you will let yourself be guided by your aunt and I, but if you were to decide yourself, I believe you would wish to take the position, even under the name of Mrs Smith. Is this correct, Elizabeth?"

"Yes," Elizabeth said plainly. "I cannot entirely explain it, for my desire to accept the position is not solely based on wishing to make such a good salary and have such a pleasant room, or even on concern that I might not find another position nearly so eligible. Somehow, I feel that Mrs Wickham needs me. I should like to be a good friend to her."

Mr and Mrs Gardiner exchanged a long look. It was not the first time Elizabeth had marvelled at their ability to communicate without words, and wondered if she might ever find someone with whom she could do the same.

"Very well, Lizzy," Mr Gardiner said at last. "If you want the position, you shall have it. I think you ought to write to Mrs Wickham directly, and let her know the good news."

At finally gaining her uncle's approbation, Elizabeth felt a surge of such wild elation that she at once knew her decision to be the right one. Come what may, Elizabeth Bennet — or rather, Mrs Elizabeth Smith — would be Mrs Wickham's hired companion. For the first time in her life, she would live among strangers and earn her own money.

Elizabeth only hoped she was up to the task.

Chapter Fourteen

Elizabeth's first morning in her new employer's townhouse dawned clear and fine. She woke rather slowly, and for the first, disorienting moments, she did not remember where she was. That it was not her bedroom at Longbourn was immediately obvious, but nor was it the familiar guest bedroom at her Uncle Gardiner's home, lately grown more familiar to her than ever.

As wakefulness finely stole over her entirely, Elizabeth laughed under her breath at her own foolishness. Of course, she was in her bedroom at her new employer's London townhouse, only half an hour by coach from her uncle's home, and yet a world away.

She was lucky to be in the habit of waking early, for it would never do for a companion to keep her employer waiting. Throwing back the covers, Elizabeth briskly crossed the room to the wardrobe and readied herself for the day ahead. She chose her favourite day dress, one with a subtle line of Spanish lace at the hem, washed her face, and put her hair up neatly. When she walked briskly to the breakfast table, Elizabeth was pleased to find she had arrived before Mrs Wickham. Her first day showed every promise of starting well.

She had not been seated for long before Mrs Wickham joined her at the table. "Good morning, Mrs Smith," her employer said with a shy smile.

"Good morning, Mrs Wickham," Elizabeth replied with all the warmth she could pair to suitable deference. Before an awkward silence could fall, she continued, "Have you any plans for the day?"

Thankfully for her composure, Georgiana had anticipated the question. It would surely be one of the more difficult parts of having a hired companion, to give orders to one who was almost a social equal. Matters had been simpler when she was a girl. It had been her place to listen and be guided, and while her preference might have weight, it had never been her place to tell her companion what ought to be done. Matters now were entirely otherwise. For all Elizabeth was four years older than herself, her role was to provide friendly company, not to be a teacher and guardian.

Georgiana had therefore prepared her answer in advance. "I thought that we might have a quiet day at home today," she replied. "I shall not be at home to visitors this morning, for I wish to practise the pianoforte. I shall tell you when I am done, for you are free to use the instrument whenever I am not, you know."

"That is a generous offer," Elizabeth replied, "and I only hope that I have not misled you about the state of my own playing. I am afraid you may find my application sadly lacking compared to yours."

"Perhaps we may return to the instrument together in the afternoon, then," Georgiana said eagerly. "I am sure I shall not be disappointed, for there is always much enjoyment to be found in the differences between musicians — in what one person likes and another does not, I mean. I do not believe I have ever met a practitioner from whom I could not learn."

Elizabeth laughed. "That is more a credit to your own love of music than to others' skill, I believe."

Georgiana shook her head lightly in repudiation of the compliment. "Perhaps, perhaps," she said lightly. "In the afternoon, then?"

"I shall be delighted," Elizabeth replied. "Would you like me to sit elsewhere while you practise?"

"You must do just as you like," Georgiana replied. "I am not very self-conscious when I am practicing, for I am all too apt to forget anyone else is present at all. Or if you would like to go anywhere, I shall instruct the coachman to take you."

"That is generous, but I believe I shall stay and write some letters. I have three sisters beyond Jane, and I owe each of them a letter."

Georgiana inclined her head, but her smile seemed a trifle forced, and a shadow had fallen across her face. Behind an even smile, Elizabeth furiously tried to work out what had caused her pain in so ordinary a response.

"It is good of you to be so careful in writing them," Georgiana said at last. "It is a sad thing when siblings do not speak."

Elizabeth sat up. For all there was finality in her employer's tone, it was merely the finality of politeness. It was obvious to Elizabeth that she wished for the relief of frankness — devoutly wished for it, and did not know it was to be had.

"That would be difficult, indeed," Elizabeth said slowly. "Yet it can happen easily. My sister Mary and I have not always understood each other well, for we are of very different natures. Misunderstandings seem to occur so easily! Perhaps you have known something of what I speak."

Elizabeth sometimes wished Mary had never opened her eyes to her gift of unlocking others' secrets, for once known, it could not be unknown again. Neither could she ever return to the innocence of ignorance, of thinking that everyone was the recipient of as many painful secrets and confessions as she was herself. Yet the change had, perhaps, still been all for the good, for it had allowed her to realise what she had not before — that, in fact, she had many techniques for loosening a tongue that desperately wanted to be freed. To illustrate that one would listen without judgement, would understand the emotion to be shared, was one of the most fundamental techniques. It worked here as well as it generally did.

Georgiana's voice wobbled a little as she replied. "I wish it were only a misunderstanding in my case, but it is not so. My brother's distrust of me is entirely my own fault."

Elizabeth felt rather as though she had missed a step in descending a staircase — the alarming sensation of the ground abruptly disappearing beneath her was disquietingly similar.

"Your brother?" Elizabeth inquired neutrally, feeling that the only thing was to allow her employer to decide how much — or perhaps how little — she wished to reveal.

But though the years of her marriage had brought an unusual degree of self-possession and control to Georgiana, she was still a girl of nineteen. Older and wiser heads than hers had told all that weighed on their hearts when caught in Elizabeth's clear, unflinching gaze.

"My brother, Fitzwilliam Darcy. It is my fault that we are estranged," Georgiana said heavily. "My brother was my guardian, you see. He was everything to me — protected me, taught me, loved me. And I repaid him by running away to Gretna Green."

"To marry the late Mr Wickham," Elizabeth

prompted.

Georgiana nodded, gulped, and went on. "I knew myself to be doing wrong and yet I did it anyway. I knew my brother would not approve, and indeed he did not. My dowry was left to me conditionally, and in token of my foolishness, he did not release it to Mr Wickham, but gave us a monthly allowance instead."

"I see," Elizabeth replied, with her best attempt at neutrality. When anyone had a difficult history to get off their chest, it was best to allow them to present it as they wished, and keep her own thoughts and reactions to herself. However, it was sometimes cruelly difficult. Elizabeth wished she could have given the absent brother a piece of her mind, for it was perfectly obvious that Georgiana had been to blame for none of it. Oh, doubtless she had been foolish. What girl of sixteen is not? But the late Mr Wickham had surely been far more to blame that she. The absent Mr Darcy was a fool if he could not see that.

And then, adding error on top of error, he had actually withheld his sister's dowry! Elizabeth did not see how he could have done it without falling over in shame. He had probably told himself that it was only fair, after the way his sister had disobliged him, but Elizabeth begged to differ. In her view, it nearly disqualified him from being considered an honest man.

Georgiana had noticed none of her difficulties.

"He never visited me in Edinburgh. Of course he would not, while my husband was living. And when he died, he asked me to come to London, that we might talk over what was to be done about my dowry. It is intact, you see, or rather it has grown, for he kept it in the Exchange all this time. I hoped that he would have forgiven me, but he has not. He did not write one word in his letter beyond what was necessary and proper for a letter of condolence."

"He intends to make the balance over to you, then?" Elizabeth inquired. If so, he was at least an honest man. She could not say must more for him, but she would at least give him that.

"It seems so. Likely I must demonstrate to him that I am able to manage it, but this I hope to do. I have had the management of the accounts these past three years, and an excellent teacher to help me do it." Georgiana blushed. "Excuse me. I have been terribly foolish, telling you all these things."

"On the contrary, I am glad that we are already beginning to know each other so well, for a setting of strict formality really would not suit me," Elizabeth protested. She paused a moment, weighing how much more she ought to say. At last, she decided that after Georgiana's openhearted confession, she ought to do her best to be equally open. "As my employer and the superior in consequence, it really ought to be for you to suggest, but I hope you will forgive me a little rudeness. What would you think of using our first names with each other, at least when we are at home?"

"I should like that very much," Georgiana replied. "We shall be Elizabeth and Georgiana, then, and I shall feel much the better for it."

Elizabeth laughed. "I confess it will be a relief to me, for Mrs Smith still does not feel at all like my name."

Georgiana laughed with her. "I hope you will not forget to answer to it when we are in company."

"No, indeed I shall not. I shall consider it to be the first condition of my employment: when in company, I am Mrs Smith."

"No, not that," Georgiana protested. "Let it be the second condition of your employment, for the first condition must be the duty of being a good friend to me." She smiled. "As, indeed, you have already shown yourself to be."

Elizabeth jestingly raised her teacup. "To friendship."

The two women raised their teacups to each other in a laughing toast, each surprised to find how much she already felt herself to be at home.

Chapter Fifteen

One morning not long after, the two ladies were seated together in the drawing room after breakfast, chatting as easily as though they had known each other for years.

"Now that I am a little more familiar with your habits," Elizabeth said, "I confess I am rather surprised you take no instruction in the pianoforte, for you practise more constantly than any woman I have ever known. But then, perhaps you left your teacher behind you in Edinburgh."

But Georgiana was shaking her head with a slightly rueful expression. "No, I am afraid I did not. I had instruction when I was a girl, of course. I was fortunate in my teachers. But I have not engaged an instructor these three years together — not since my marriage."

"Your husband did not approve?" Elizabeth inquired, trying to hide her shock.

"No, nothing like that," Georgiana protested. "My late husband had the easiest temper in the world. It was only that he was not...I hardly know the right word…he was not methodical, I shall say, in his business dealings. I had a piano, for I cannot live without one, but I found it better not to enter upon the additional expense."

Looking at their lavish surroundings, Elizabeth found this rather difficult to understand, but she would not have pressed on a subject that was obviously distressing to her friend for the world. Instead, she turned the subject to more cheerful matters. "Perhaps you may engage an instructor now," Elizabeth suggested.

Georgiana brightened, obviously glad that the subject had been dropped. "It is strange that I have not thought of it before, but I shall — indeed, I shall. There is nothing I would rather spend money on than music."

"I thought it must be so, for I noticed that you have had the piano tuned, though I believe you have been in residence here only a short while."

"For that, I do not deserve the credit," Georgiana replied. A shadow of some strange emotion passed over her face, disappearing before Elizabeth could identify it. "It was my brother's doing. He hired this house for me when I informed him I would not trespass on his privacy and had a piano brought and tuned before I ever entered the place."

"That was kind of him," Elizabeth commented, closely watching Georgiana's face. She was not entirely sure that her employer's brother had meant it as a kindness, for kindness made no part of the impression she had formed of him. More likely, it had been an implied rebuke, a reminder of all the indebtedness Georgiana so clearly felt. He probably wished for his sister to feel indebted to him, and had been at pains to secure the impression. It would make it easier to sway her to his wishes, and when a fortune of such size was in play, what was the investment of a piano and a man to tune it, or even of hiring a London townhouse?

"It was kind," was all Georgiana said in reply, before turning away to accept the cards which the butler was then bringing to her on a silver tray. "Thank you, Benson," she said, a little absently. The man bowed and left the room.

"What is it?" Elizabeth cried aloud, for Georgiana had gone quite pale.

"It is nothing — do not be alarmed. It is only that my cousin, Colonel Fitzwilliam, has left his card. He is waiting for my answer now, and I must decide whether to visit with him."

"Is he such an awful figure, then?" Elizabeth asked.

"No, not at all. He is the kindest man in the world, very sensible, and with charming manners. You would like him. I am sure you would."

"Then I do not quite understand your difficulties," Elizabeth said gently.

"I have not seen him these three years

together. He was my guardian, along with my brother, and has nearly as much right to be angry with me."

"Perhaps you ought to admit him," Elizabeth said. "It would at least be an end to fearing that he might be angry." Privately, Elizabeth hoped he would not be. It did not seem unreasonable to expect, for if the Colonel was as sensible and kind as Georgiana portrayed him, he could not possibly be angry with her for actions taken at the tender age of sixteen, and which had hurt her more than anyone.

"I do not know — I cannot say," Georgiana said, almost stammering. "Perhaps I owe it to him."

"Now, that is going too far," Elizabeth replied, "for I am sure you do not owe it to anyone to be at home when you do not choose to be. Yet if you will forgive me for offering my opinion when you have not asked for it, I think you would do better to admit him. After all, he cannot chide you before a stranger, and I shall be present."

"You are right in that," Georgiana said. She took a deep breath to calm herself before summoning the butler with the silver bell that sat in readiness on an end table. While they waited for his arrival, she turned to Elizabeth and said lightly, "I had not thought before of putting my companion to such a use, but I believe you are correct. It is sometimes most valuable to have an unknown party to a family meeting."

"I am glad to be of service," Elizabeth replied.

As the butler was even then entering the room, she said nothing more.

"Please admit Colonel Fitzwilliam, if he is still waiting below," Georgiana instructed him.

He bowed. "Straightaway, ma'am."

"Thank you, Benson," Georgiana said a little breathlessly, and they sat down to await news of whether the Colonel had remained to be admitted.

It was not a long wait, nor one ended by the return of Benson, for Colonel Fitzwilliam actually entered the room before him, approaching them almost at a run.

"Georgiana, my dear!" Colonel Fitzwilliam cried aloud, and in defiance of all good breeding, he did not pause to bow or be introduced to Elizabeth, but crossed the room without delay and embraced Georgiana tightly. After a long moment, he held her out at arm's length.

There were tears in his eyes when he spoke. "It has been too long, cousin — much too long."

Georgiana's eyes were also bright with tears. "I did not think you would want to see me. I thought you were angry with me. You had every right to be angry with me."

He was shaking his head. "All this time, I hoped I had been wrong to think so poorly of Wickham — that perhaps your marriage was a good one, after all. Tell me, Georgiana, was I right to let Darcy talk me out of duelling him? He said it would only make things worse for you."

"I would not have had you duel for the world, for he was a soldier too, and might have killed you," Georgiana whispered. For a moment, they still clasped arms and looked into each other's faces, seeing the changes three years had brought. The Colonel was perhaps a little older, with a few lines brought by the strain of his profession and long hours outdoors, but was really hardly changed. Georgiana was no longer the shy girl of sixteen, but in composure and experience undoubtedly a woman.

The Colonel recovered first. "I am afraid we are being abominably rude, cousin," he remarked. "Will you not introduce me to your friend?"

"I should be delighted," Georgiana said, regaining her composure with some difficulty. "Elizabeth, this is my cousin, Colonel Fitzwilliam. Cousin, this is my companion, Mrs Smith."

"It is a pleasure to meet you, Colonel," Elizabeth remarked with much truth, for the reunion had been deeply affecting.

"And I am glad to meet you, Mrs Smith," Colonel Fitzwilliam returned. "I hope you and I will be good friends, for now that we are reunited, I intend to visit my cousin as often as she will have me."

Elizabeth smiled at him. "I am sure I would be delighted."

He smiled back at her. "As will I."

Elizabeth might have been surprised to know how truly he meant it, for by the time their visit concluded — at fully twice the polite half hour, and none of those present thought it over-long — Colonel Fitzwilliam was already thinking what a shame it was that the widowed Mrs Smith self-evidently had no fortune. Barring this one flaw, she was everything charming, but the lack of money is the only flaw that a younger son cannot afford to overlook. All the same, while knowing he could not think of her seriously, Elizabeth's presence would add yet another savour to that of visiting his cousin.

Beyond this, there was the joy of seeing how her companionship had lightened Georgiana's heart. Short as the duration of Mrs Smith's employment had been, the two already laughed together like old friends.

Colonel Fitzwilliam had no shortage of time to think about all the pains and charms of the visit, for upon leaving the house, he made his way directly to Mr Darcy's townhouse, knowing how desperate his cousin was for news of his sister. As Mr Darcy was out, but expected back directly, the butler escorted him into his master's study to await his return.

When the door closed behind him, Colonel Fitzwilliam sighed, relieved that he might spend a few moments unobserved. His memories were both inevitable and painful, for it was in that very room that Mr Darcy had persuaded him not to duel Mr Wickham.

"I should like to see him killed as much as you would. Indeed, I would like to see him hanged," Mr Darcy had said three years ago, in a voice that was all the more convincing for its bitter, implacable calm. "But it will not do. It will not serve."

"You cannot mean it, Darcy," Colonel Fitzwilliam had protested. In that moment of bitter agony at their failure to protect Georgiana and fear at what she might be suffering, violence of any kind would have been an exquisite relief. Only knowing that Darcy suffered even more than he did himself could have held him back from accusing his cousin of cowardice, or worse.

"I do mean it," Mr Darcy said quietly. He crossed to the window and stood looking out at the street, as though he could look all the way to Gretna Green — or, perhaps, as though he could not bear to look his cousin in the face while he spoke. "You must not duel him, for it would make matters still worse for Georgiana if you did. If he killed you, it would break her heart. If you killed Wickham, you would not have mended matters for her. Under such a scandal, she could never marry again. No one in England would receive her."

"Do you mean we are to do nothing?" Colonel Fitzwilliam said incredulously.

"To our feelings, it will seem to be nothing. I have used money to put a leash on Wickham, and this, I hope, will restrain him from the worst forms of selfishness and licentious behaviour. But beyond this, yes, we will do nothing. We cannot duel him, or sue him, or even cut him socially, should we ever meet again. It will be the punishment for our failure, for all these things would only be a balm for our feelings, while Georgiana would pay the price. We do not matter now. Only what is best for Georgiana matters."

There was no argument that Colonel Fitzwilliam could make to that. "You are right," he said heavily. "I despise the fact with a passion, but you are right."

"I know," Mr Darcy said softly. "Oh, how I wish it were otherwise — but I know it is not."

A knock came at the door, and Colonel Fitzwilliam startled out of the grasp of his memories. Mr Darcy entered.

"You have seen her, then?" he asked without preamble.

Colonel Fitzwilliam nodded. "She is well, Darcy — better than we could have hoped."

His cousin sat down heavily in the chair behind the desk and turned away his face. "Thank God," he said, almost too softly to be heard. "Thank God that she is well."

Colonel Fitzwilliam swallowed down the lump in his throat and went on. "She played the pianoforte for me before I left. You will love to hear it, Darcy. She plays more beautifully than ever. And she did not blame me for what happened, not in the least. I do not think she much mourns him, Darcy, but neither was he cruel to her. Though she said little enough, that much seemed clear."

Mr Darcy nodded. "We chose well, then."

"You chose well, rather," Colonel Fitzwilliam said, freed at last from the bitterness of that choice. "I will not dissemble. You were entirely correct, much as I hated it at the time. Three years later, and her reputation, her character, her wealth are all intact. Georgiana is still only nineteen, with the world at her feet — though I do not think she is entirely aware of that yet. These three years have been painful ones, but they are ended now, for all of us."

"Not quite," Mr Darcy said, so quietly it seemed as though he spoke to himself. "She has not forgiven me yet. And I would not blame her if she never did."

Chapter Sixteen

It was fortunate that Georgiana and Elizabeth welcomed Colonel Fitzwilliam's company, for after his first visit, few days passed in which they did not meet. They returned the visit at the house of his father, the earl, in which Georgiana was all a-tremble in fear of judgement from another branch of her family, and which Elizabeth approached in amused curiosity to be admitted to the honour of meeting so high a branch of the nobility. The visit passed off well, with not a word said in criticism of Georgiana's recklessness as a girl or the dubious character of her late husband, and Mrs Smith was admitted by all to be a charming woman, most eligible as the companion to their dear Georgiana.

"Though," the Countess said after they had left, "I wish dear Georgiana had chosen a rather older companion. At only nineteen, it would be better if she had an older head to guide her. I do not believe Mrs Smith is above twenty-four!"

"I should not be surprised if Georgiana is in need of a new companion before many months have passed," the Earl agreed, "for Mrs Smith is a rather pretty sort of woman, and she will meet many eligible men going into society with our niece. Perhaps that was her design in accepting the position."

"I should not doubt it, my dear, for Mrs Smith told me a little of her history as we sat together. She has four sisters, all unmarried, and if she can marry to advantage, I, for one, would think it almost her duty."

Elizabeth, meanwhile, meant to forward her duty by saving as much as she could for the better preservation of her sisters and herself. As Georgiana supplied almost every need but that of clothing, and her wages were remarkably generous, her savings were increasing even beyond what she could have hoped. Though they did not approach what anyone would have considered a dowry, she at least had a small fund that could cushion the blow in the event of an emergency.

She had sent a few pounds back to Meryton for the benefit of her mother and younger sisters, for Kitty and particularly Lydia were sadly missing the luxury to which they were accustomed. Doting on her youngest daughter, Mrs Bennet had always thought nothing of giving Lydia a little pin money whenever she begged for it, but this it was no longer possible to do. By sending on some of her wages, Elizabeth might at least make their residence with Aunt and Uncle Phillips brightened by some small luxuries.

It was not many days since Kitty had last written, a good long newsy letter pleasantly full of nothing in particular. They were enjoying hearing all the Meryton gossip; their aunt and uncle were everything kind; all were in good health and spirits, and looking forward to the next assembly. Though not a word of it was any kind of surprise, Elizabeth was deeply grateful for the confirmation that she need not worry about one part of her family, at least. Kitty even had good news about Mrs Bennet's nerves, and how comparatively little she mentioned them. Though there was pain in thinking of Hertfordshire and of her father buried there, of Longbourn occupied by Mr Collins and her family separated, there was at least the pleasure of remembering the dear old familiar things of home.

Elizabeth had been even more relieved when Jane received a letter from Mary, one intended for both her older sisters. Of all the sisters, Mary's situation was by far the most precarious. While Elizabeth had also gone out to earn her keep among strangers, she had at least found a place in London, where she might see Jane each week, and where Mr Gardiner might easily be reached if any trouble came to her. At Lyme, Mary was separated from all her family. If she were not such a diligent correspondent, and if the news had not been uniformly good, Elizabeth felt she would have regretted her suggestion that Mary should work as a governess many times over.

Thankfully, Mary had never seemed at all dissatisfied with her lot. On the contrary, she had nothing but the best news to share of the family. Her home was pleasant, the children funny and attentive, and there was no need for concern. Mary had the same stern, rather affected tone in correspondence as conversation, so it might have been too much to call her happy, but she was, perhaps, content.

With a little smile, Elizabeth thought that 'perhaps content' was no bad description of her own inward state. She was of course grateful for the pleasant position she had found, for the great luxury of wages good enough to send a little to her family, and the still-more unlooked-for benefit of an employer who was also rapidly becoming a good friend. Yet all the pain of the past months could not so quickly pass away. Memories of her father would surface at the most unexpected moments. Elizabeth could not regret it. However painful, however difficult to be in company when such moments in broke upon her, they were still precious to her, in keeping Mr Bennet's memory alive and fresh. If the memory of what her father had said about a particular book or how he might have laughed at some witticism came coupled with grief at his loss, it was worth it.

Elizabeth had quickly learned that Georgiana's loss was a more complicated case, and perhaps more painful in denying her the purity of simple grief. Though the young widow always tried to be discrete in how she spoke of her late husband, it would not have taken a listening ear as open or a mind as discerning as Elizabeth's to see that the man had not been what he ought to have been. There must have been some good in him, to be sure. Georgiana spoke fondly of his warm and engaging manners. Yet it was evident in what she said, and still more in what she did not say, that he had not been a man of character and integrity.

It was this, perhaps, that made the greatest part of Georgiana's suffering — that it was impossible for her to remember the late Mr Wickham with respect. For this, however, neither Elizabeth's quick wit nor her soft heart had any answer. She could only listen to Georgiana, what little she chose to say, and comfort her as she could. Elizabeth hoped wryly that she did indeed have the gift of listening well that Mary had imputed for her, for she certainly had great need of it.

Chapter Seventeen

Though Georgiana's renewed acquaintance with her cousin and former guardian was doubtless good in itself, it had given Elizabeth one cause for unease on her employer's behalf. In the first flush of confidence and happiness after Colonel Fitzwilliam's first visit, and remembering the anxiety with which he had waited to be admitted, Georgiana had instructed the butler that, if Mr Darcy were to call upon her likewise, he was to be admitted at any time and without delay. Though Elizabeth said nothing, she thought it was a mistake. The best she could say for the decision was that it seemed unlikely ever to go into use, for from all she had heard of him, Elizabeth could not imagine Mr Darcy resuming the relationship so easily and genially as Colonel Fitzwilliam had done. Indeed, the Colonel seemed to be on extremely good terms with Mr Darcy, and he had not said the least word to imply that his cousin was likely to follow where he had led. If Mr Darcy did come, it would probably be upon an errand of business, or to summon Georgiana to a meeting at a time and place of maximal inconvenience.

Though Georgiana said nothing to confirm it, it was obvious that she hoped a reconciliation might come about through a letter, if not through a morning visit. Her eagerness at the arrival of the post, and her brave attempted concealment of dejection when no such letter appeared, would have wrung a harder heart that Elizabeth's. She really wished that Mr Darcy might have seen it, for even the coldest of brothers must have had pity on so dutiful a sister.

One morning, after the little scene of anticipation and disappointment had been repeated yet again, Elizabeth could not help but say something.

"Perhaps you might write to him yourself, Georgiana," she said gently. "He will have to see you sometime, you know, if there are matters of business to be arranged."

To her credit, Georgiana neither pretended ignorance nor grew angry at the hint. "You are right, I know you are right," she said with a sigh. "I will do so, if much more time elapses. But I would have so liked to have some sign that he forgives me, that our meeting may be that of brother and sister, and not that of mere creditor and supplicant."

It seemed very little to ask, Elizabeth thought privately, and yet from what she had heard of the man, it might yet be too much. "I hope it may be so," was all she said before turning to her own letters.

They were really well worth attending to, for Mary had written at last. She had sent one short missive, saying that her new place was all that had been promised, the family vastly kind, the children intelligent and eager to learn. Then, silence, with only the letter written to Jane to relieve her fears. Elizabeth's eagerness to learn what her sister had experienced in the interval was great. She quickly read the letter through.

Lyme, 21 November 1815
My dear Sister,

I hope you will forgive my tardiness in writing to you — I am happy to report that the cause is nothing more nor less than great busyness. I am well, and I had yesterday a letter saying that Mama, Kitty and Lydia are all likewise. Please write to me of Jane and yourself when you have a moment.

My situation in life is a happy one, for I greatly enjoy the work of a governess. The children mind me well, and when they are naughty, I tell them a little of Philosophy in a stern tone, and they are better again, for they do not like to hear of it. Samantha is progressing vastly well on the piano. I must practice diligently, or I shall not be able to keep ahead of her! My employers are most gracious, and do not mind my playing after the children are in bed in the least. Indeed, they often ask me to play a little to amuse them in the evenings, or when there is company to call.

I have played every evening of late, for their dear friend Admiral John Pellew is staying with them, and he is a great enthusiast of music. He is a delightful guest, for one could never tire of hearing his stories of far-off places and terrible battles. And a man of such sense and good breeding, I believe I have never before met. Even Father could not have found fault with his wit, Lizzy, nor would you find any fault with his character. I believe even Kitty and Lydia would like him, for he is quite handsome for an older gentleman, and, of course, he has a fine uniform. But it is silly of me to go on so, for no doubt you will never meet. I am afraid his visit is almost over. The children will be sorry when he goes, and so shall I.

You would like Lyme a great deal, for there are wonderful walks to be had here. You would walk by the sea, and along the cliffs, and along the Cobb, and be vastly happy all the while. I hope you may visit me one day, though I know not how.

With best regards from your sister,
Mary Bennet

—

Elizabeth read her sister's letter with much pleasure and no small portion of surprise, for it had a lightness that she had only rarely seen in Mary. After a second reading, concern joined her thoughts. It was a wonder she had not seen it before, so obvious was her sister's interest in Admiral Pellew. Yet that seemed a hopeless business, for an admiral must have a wide acquaintance and a decent fortune, or he could not have attained his rank. He was not likely to have serious designs on a young woman of so little wealth that she was working for her keep, and without even the blessing of extraordinary beauty. Elizabeth had never been so grateful for Mary's strict sense of propriety, for the situation might have been rather dangerous for a woman more persuadable.

"Oh!" Georgiana cried out in a tone of great frustration.

Elizabeth quickly hurried to her, but the cause of her employer's vexation was obvious before she had crossed half the room. Georgiana had caught the edge of the ink bottle on her sleeve and overturned it, to grievous effect. Her dress was seriously marred, and ink was dripping down the desk, coming ever closer to the beautiful Aubusson carpet.

"I cannot think how I came to be so clumsy," Georgiana said, voice tight, and rang the bell to summon the housekeeper, Mrs Johnson. It was not more than a few moments before she arrived with two maids in tow.

"If you will go to your room, ma'am, I

shall have your maid meet you there directly," Mrs Johnson suggested. "We shall have this cleaned up in a trice, for thankfully it has not touched the carpet yet."

"Thank you, Johnson," Georgiana said gratefully, and was off directly. Elizabeth watched her go, an odd smile twisting her face. She was thinking of how great a change a year had rendered in her situation. Though a companion was not a maid, she had moved towards the accident by reflex, for she was now on the other side of the great divide between the employers and the employed. A year ago, she too would have rung the bell for Hill. It would not have occurred to her then to clean anything herself. A Miss Elizabeth Bennet of Longbourn did not do any such thing. But, of course, a Mrs Elizabeth Smith of nowhere in particular was a different creature.

It was not long before the maids had erased any sign of the accident. Elizabeth remained in solitary possession of the room, for it would doubtless take some time for Georgiana to change and return. She was grateful for the chance to be with her own thoughts for a moment, without the necessity of presenting a pleasant face, the most constant duty of a companion. There was a strange sense of loss within her, compounded of her father, dead and gone, and her own former life, equally vanished.

At that moment, the butler entered, followed

by a tall man, simply but exquisitely dressed, with dark, wavy hair and a face equally notable for its handsomeness and its rather stern expression. "Mr Darcy, ma'am," Benson said, and left with a bow.

Elizabeth and Mr Darcy looked at each other in horror, for that strangers must not speak before being introduced was almost the first rule of good society. Yet to remain in silence for the uncertain interval until Georgiana returned was obviously impossible. Looking at Mr Darcy's face, Elizabeth felt she would have known who he was even if the butler had not announced him. His resemblance to Georgiana was clear, and though he was perhaps more handsome as a man than she beautiful as a woman, anyone might have known them as siblings.

The silence must be broken, and it must be Mr Darcy's place to do so, for he was by far the superior in consequence. Yet the man remained speechless, the lines of his face as stiff as though carved in stone. No doubt, Elizabeth thought with some asperity, he was torn at which was the more awful fate, to speak without an introduction, or to be forced into a *tête-à-tête* with a woman of so little significance.

—

Upon leaving his carriage before the townhouse he had rented for his sister, Mr Darcy exhaled slowly, carefully. He reminded himself that there was every reason to believe Georgiana would admit him, and little enough to fear that she would not. Though he must brace himself to find her deeply changed, though three years of marriage to Wickham might have left her opinions coarsened and her morals more loose, the change would have to be grievous indeed for the sweet, gentle girl of three years ago to refuse entry to her own brother. Especially when he was the one who paid the rents on her house.

Besides all this, she had admitted Fitzwilliam. Mr Darcy sighed and knocked on the door.

Thankfully, the interval before the butler appeared was short. Though Mr Darcy had interviewed and hired the man himself, he presented his card. He would never gain Georgiana's forgiveness by forcing himself back into her life, he thought ruefully.

Though Mr Darcy had expected Benson to leave with his card and return in some little time, with news either good or ill, he was to be surprised.

With a small, respectful smile, Benson nodded. "Very good, sir. Mrs Wickham has left me orders that she is at home to her brother at all times. Please follow me."

"Why, I — that is — thank you, Benson. Yes, of course," Mr Darcy replied, half stammering before he could master his astonishment. It was a proof of confidence and willingness to forgive such as he would not have dared to hope for, and for which he would have given much.

As he followed Benson to the drawing room, Mr Darcy's thoughts were far afield. He could not hope too much, must not presume too much. There was still a heartfelt apology to be made and Georgiana's forgiveness to be won. Yet everything declared Georgiana was at least willing to listen, which was almost more than he felt he deserved.

"Mr Darcy," Benson announced at the door to the drawing room, and with a bow, he departed.

But the person before him was not Georgiana. It was a woman, dark of hair and rather notably pretty, whom he had never seen before in his life. For the first long moment, Mr Darcy was only consumed with wondering at the strange absence of Georgiana, and whether she had left deliberately, as a show that she did not wish to speak with him after all. It was only in the next moment that the full awkwardness of the situation dawned on him. He could not speak with the woman, for there was no one to provide an introduction, and it would have been the height of ill breeding to begin speaking to her without one. Yet it was obviously equally impossible to remain alone in the room with her, perhaps for a quarter or even half an hour, in total silence. Without knowing where or why Georgiana had gone, it was impossible to know how long it might be before the introduction could be made. If it were only a brief time, it might be better to wait, that they could be introduced according to the full norms of society. Yet if it were a long one, speaking might be a lesser evil, and Mr Darcy was uncomfortably aware that the silence was already growing awkwardly long.

—

Looking at the stiff, appalled lines of Mr Darcy's face, Elizabeth had been rather tempted to let the silence draw out as long as it might. It would be a fitting punishment on him for his pride in refusing to speak with her.

With a rueful little smile, she thought the better of it. She would not, Elizabeth resolved, allow her behaviour to be dictated by his rudeness. On the contrary, she would do what she thought right, however Mr Darcy might scorn such a course of action.

"I believe we must make a little alteration to the usual rules of conversation, Mr Darcy," Elizabeth said lightly. "Please forgive me for speaking to you without an introduction, but it may be some time until your sister returns, and I feel that to remain entirely in silence would be the greater evil. Allow me to introduce myself. I am Mrs Smith. Mrs Wickham has hired me as her companion."

"That cannot be," Mr Darcy replied in surprise. Belatedly, he winced at his rudeness in such an answer, but it was all but unbelievable that

Georgiana's companion could be so young and attractive a woman. Young as Georgiana was herself, she ought to have chosen a comfortable, matronly woman, someone of great experience who could shield and protect her. Mrs Smith must have been widowed not long after her marriage, for she could not have been five-and-twenty.

Before he could excuse himself for his rude interjection, Elizabeth was replying.

"Indeed, it is so," Elizabeth told him. "May I ask the reason for your surprise? Surely it is not so surprising that your sister would wish to have some company always with her, after the recent loss of her husband."

"You must excuse me, Mrs Smith," Mr Darcy said, making an effort to recover himself. "I had already learned through my cousin, Colonel Fitzwilliam, that Georgiana had hired a companion, and I find her decision entirely logical. It is only that — if you will forgive me — you are very young. I imagine you cannot be more than a handful of years older than Georgiana herself." Realising how close he had come to the unpardonable rudeness of asking a lady's age, Mr Darcy flushed. But thankfully, Mrs Smith showed no offense.

"You are not mistaken, Mr Darcy. I am not yet four-and-twenty. But perhaps it is not entirely surprising that your sister preferred a companion near her own age. She and I may, perhaps, have more to speak of together than had she hired a woman of greater age and experience."

"I would not wish to suspend any pleasure of Georgiana's," Mr Darcy replied softly, and for the first time, Elizabeth looked at him in open surprise. He had not sounded much like the implacable, unforgiving brother who had abandoned a sister of only sixteen years to her fate.

"I am glad to hear it," she replied mildly, and they spent the remaining minutes of their private interview in mere commonplace pleasantries, each equally eager for the return of Georgiana, though for rather different reasons. Elizabeth had little wish to converse with a man so evidently stern and proud. For Georgiana's sake, she must hope that the relationship would be repaired, for it was evident that her employer wished it to be. If it were to be so, she would be in company with Mr Darcy frequently, and it would not do to be at odds with her employer's brother. Yet she had little liking for the man, and little wish to gain any. Georgiana might feel that her brother ought to be forgiven for his harsh judgement and stern distance of three years ago, but Elizabeth did not agree.

Mr Darcy, meanwhile, was wishing his sister had chosen a less pretty companion. Mrs Smith was not truly beautiful, of course. There were many faults of perfect symmetry in her face, and nothing of extraordinary loveliness in it. Yet she was so pleasing as a whole — so light and graceful in her figure, so witty and easy in conversation, so evidently possessing a quick mind and good judgement — that she was not entirely a good choice for a young widow so marriageable herself. Georgiana ought to have chosen a woman who could look after her, protect her, and certainly one who would have no thought of a second marriage. At that, Mr Darcy concealed a grimace, for he realised he ought to be careful around Mrs Smith himself. However sensible Mrs Smith might be, any woman in her circumstances would be apt to become a little over-ambitious in the face of such wealth and consequence as represented by Pemberley and the Darcy name. Not to mention that staying with his sister presented a considerable advantage of access, one that few women would waste.

There was a soft rustle of skirts by the door, and Georgiana entered, having changed the ink-stained gown for a fresh one.

Mr Darcy rose, and they exchanged bows as though they were strangers. Looking on, Elizabeth could hardly believe that this was the reunion after three years separation of a brother and sister. And Georgiana, in their most confidential conversations, had said he was almost a father to her.

"It is good to see you again, Georgiana," Mr Darcy remarked. "It has been far too long."

Georgiana nodded, looking shy. "I agree, brother. I am glad to see you." She sat down, indicating that Mr Darcy might sit as well, and he did so.

Though Elizabeth had intended to say as little as might be, to better facilitate the meeting of the siblings, its awkwardness convinced her she would do better to forward the conversation. Accordingly, she resolved to speak.

"I understand your estate is in Derbyshire, Mr Darcy. Are you fond of the countryside?"

He nodded. "Yes, indeed I am. London has, of course, the advantage of great culture and all the benefits of good society, but I confess I am never entirely at my ease away from Pemberley." With a brief hesitation, he turned to Georgiana. "Perhaps you might pay me a visit this spring?"

"I should like that very much," Georgiana replied, her voice slightly hoarse. Yet for all her evident willingness to accept the suggestion as a great compliment, Elizabeth could not see it as one. To suggest that his sister visit the family home at a time of his convenience and choosing was a sure a proof as Elizabeth could imagine that the man had no proper family feelings. To invite her at all seemed almost absurd, for was it not equally *her* childhood home? If the Darcy siblings had parents still living, she was sure they would have considered it so.

"You grew up at Pemberley, did not you, Georgiana?" Elizabeth remarked. At Mr Darcy's look of shock, she almost wished she had used the proper, cool address of 'Mrs Wickham' instead. But that was absurd. They had agreed to use their first names together, and Mr Darcy could think whatever he liked about it.

"Yes, I did, and I think there is no place more beautiful in the world," Georgiana said eagerly. From the smile on her face, it was evident that she was thinking of innocent childhood pleasures. "I should very much like to see Pemberley in the springtime again. Oh, how I have missed it! Edinburgh is a fine town, but there is nothing like the English countryside in spring."

"Then I shall count on your coming," Mr Darcy said. With only a little more warmth, Elizabeth thought, his smile might have been called pleased.

Then she remembered. If Georgiana was to go to Pemberley in the spring, then she must perforce as well. She had best accustom herself to Mr Darcy's society, for she would experience a great deal of it.

While she had been momentarily abstracted, the brother and sister were talking of the various beauties to be seen in and around Pemberley in spring, from the lush green leaves of an especially fine chestnut tree in the nearby town of Lambton to the first blossom of wildflowers throughout the grounds. Listening, Elizabeth admitted to herself that she was by no means disinclined to visit a place so evidently beautiful. If only it had a more congenial master!

By the time the visit wound to its conclusion, Mr Darcy had invited them to supper the week following, and Georgiana had quickly accepted. After a few more pleasantries had been exchanged, he took his leave, and the front door had scarcely closed behind him before Georgiana was grasping Elizabeth's hands and saying, "I can hardly believe it! He is not angry with me, he is not angry at all! He has forgiven me, though I know not how. How is such a thing to be believed?"

Elizabeth made all the appropriate noises of soothing agreement, and in her distracted state of mind, Georgiana noticed nothing wrong. Yet privately, Elizabeth thought of the departing Mr Darcy almost wrathfully. A simple morning visit and an invitation to supper, and Georgiana was almost aglow with gratitude. Did she not realise she deserved rather more than this?

Chapter Eighteen

Mr Darcy leaned his head against the wall of his carriage, thankful to be alone. He had cut the visit with Georgiana rather shorter than he might have wished, for if it had gone on much longer, he could not have avoided burdening her with all his grief and regret. And that, after all the weight his sister had carried in her short lifetime, was something he refused to do.

She forgave him — nothing could be more obvious than that Georgiana was willing to forgive him, though he knew not how. Mr Darcy did not feel himself to be deserving of forgiveness, not in the least. It was like her, very like her soft heart and good temper, to forgive him even when he did not deserve it.

He had not given her the full apology and explanation that he had meant to, but on the success of the first meeting, Mr Darcy was no longer sure that the course of action he had previously intended was wise.

Georgiana had evidently put the past

behind her, as much as such a thing could be done. Would it truly be a kindness to rake it all up again? Any apology would necessarily involve a discussion of Georgiana's conduct, and while her age and the innocence of her intentions ought to excuse her to any reasonable observer, it was still not such as she would wish to speak of — particularly not before a third party, if Mrs Smith was present. No, he would do better not to speak. If a decision must be made, let it be on the side of discretion over excessive candour, and for forgetting sins and omissions over unnecessarily remembering them.

It was, of course, a relief not to undergo such a meeting, with explanations and apologies that must be giving pain to both, yet Mr Darcy told himself that his own wishes carried little weight in the question. No — viewed through the lens of impartial conviction, it was equally desirable that he should say nothing. Wickham was dead, and the past was dead; let them remain so.

If, in making such a decision, Mr Darcy was giving rather more weight to his own fears and desires and rather less to pure logic than he supposed, he would not be the first man of good judgement and sound principles to do so.

—

Though Mr Darcy was rather tempted to

repeat his morning visit on the next day, he forbore. Manners dictated that Georgiana ought to be the next to visit him, and while he would not have dreamed of standing on such ceremony with a member of his own family in ordinary circumstances, it would not do to risk Georgiana's easy warmth and forgiveness by asking too much of her. He would wait and hope that she would choose to return the visit. If she did not, there was at least the supper to look forward to, when Colonel Fitzwilliam's easy, friendly manners would smooth out any roughness.

It was fortunate Fitzwilliam was free to do so, for the supper to which he had invited Georgiana and her companion had not existed before the moment in which he issued the invitation and she accepted it. Mr Darcy was not much in the habit of giving formal suppers.

"I am glad indeed that you are not otherwise engaged," he remarked to his cousin, "for the conversation would be a sad thing without you. I have never mastered the art of conversing easily with strangers, and while Georgiana's Mrs Smith seems a pleasant enough sort, I have not the least knowledge of who her people are or her interests or anything."

Fitzwilliam chuckled. "Well, naturally, Darcy. Those are the subjects that one typically learns through conversing with strangers, by which process one may turn them into acquaintances. Do you know, I have even heard that on some strange occasions, a friendship may result?"

Mr Darcy groaned at his cousin's teasing. "Come now, I am not so bad as all this. I will admit that I am a great deal too apt in general to be silent when the world would prefer that I speak, and to look stern when I ought to smile. But I will have you know that I do have friends."

"On the contrary, you have family, and you have *a* friend," Colonel Fitzwilliam corrected him, "for I do not believe I have heard you mention anyone but Bingley as a friend since we were boys."

Mr Darcy shrugged. "If that be so, I am still a fortunate man, for I would rather have Bingley than a dozen friends one bows to and gambles with and never thinks of otherwise."

"Perhaps you are right, at that," Colonel Fitzwilliam admitted. "I have not forgotten what he did for you three years ago. I ought to have known that you should not have been left by yourself, with all the grief of Georgiana's situation and how we failed her. I ought to have gone to you as he did — but I was angry that you would not allow me to duel him, and so I stayed away."

"You were grieving as much as I was," Mr Darcy said simply. "Perhaps I am her brother and more nearly a father to her, but I have never thought that you did not love her as I do, Fitzwilliam."

Colonel Fitzwilliam smiled a little ruefully. "I have missed her, Darcy. It's good to have Georgiana back again."

"I hope we will have her back in truth in the end," Darcy mused. "I shall stand on ceremony with her as long as I must, but not a moment longer. Perhaps we may yet live at Pemberley together again — at least until Georgiana chooses a second husband."

Colonel Fitzwilliam raised an eyebrow. "I thought you were going to offer her the opportunity to form her own establishment. Georgiana may not take it kindly if you revoke that choice."

Mr Darcy shook his head. "That, I shall not do. The money is Georgiana's, after all, and thanks to Mr Tiller's instruction, she is well able to handle it." He paused for a long moment, rising and walking to look out of the window. "But if I am honest — in my heart, I hope she will choose not to do so, or at least not to do so until she marries again. Georgiana and I spoke of Pemberley, Fitzwilliam. I am convinced that she loves it as much as ever — as much as I do."

Colonel Fitzwilliam smiled a little crookedly. "Then she loves it very much indeed. Now, cousin, let me tell you what I think you ought to do about your supper party…"

Chapter Nineteen

Though Elizabeth told Georgiana that she thought Mr Darcy's morning visit ought to be returned before the evening of the supper party, her young employer absolutely refused to do so.

"I own I should very much like to visit my brother," Georgiana said softly, "but it is too soon. I cannot be so quickly forgiven for so great a slight. He has invited me — rather, invited us — into his home on a specific date at a specific time, and I shall go then. I shall not risk intruding where I may not be wanted."

"Is this not carrying diffidence and respect for his wishes a little far?" Elizabeth protested. "If you had made a new acquaintance in the park or a friend's drawing room, you would not hesitate to call on them once they had first called on you."

"I suppose you are correct in point of etiquette," Georgiana replied, "but I have made no new acquaintances of my own these last three years, only those my husband introduced to me. As a girl, I was so shy that indeed I might not have returned a call made to me, unless my governess made me do it."

Elizabeth looked at her friend and employer for a moment in wonder. Georgiana's spirits were generally so good and so even that one could forget that she was a new widow, despite the mourning colours she wore. Her shyness and diffidence were still so great, it was almost a shock to realise it represented progress from the still greater uncertainty and insecurity from which she had suffered in her earlier youth.

"Well, I am not your governess, and it certainly is not my place to make you do anything," Elizabeth began merrily, making Georgiana laugh, "but as your friend, I would advise you to do it."

"I do not say that you are wrong," Georgiana began, "but all the same, I will not do so. If the supper goes well, and I think it would not be taken amiss, I shall call on him."

Though Elizabeth made no further attempts to persuade her employer, she continued to think the choice was a mistaken one. Though she could see little to like in Mr Darcy, he had not seemed so irrational or such a tyrant as to resent a visit made according to the strictest rules of etiquette. But she had said her piece, and having failed to convince Georgiana of the merits of her view, there was nothing more to be done.

On the appointed evening, they took the carriage to Mr Darcy's townhouse. Punctual as they were, they were not the first to arrive, for Colonel Fitzwilliam had preceded them. Anyone observing their greetings might have thought that the Colonel and Georgiana were brother and sister, and Mr Darcy was only a cousin, if they had judged by the ease and warmth of the one conversation, and the stiff formality of the other.

Colonel Fitzwilliam always seemed as pleased to talk with Elizabeth as he was with his cousin.

"It is a pleasure to see you again, Mrs Smith, a pleasure indeed. I must commend my cousin for selecting such an agreeable companion."

With a little shock, Elizabeth realised he was almost flirting with her. But, of course, they both knew that for an earl's son to propose to a working woman was quite impossible. Perhaps the Colonel felt safe, knowing that no hopes could be raised in her.

With a little laugh, Elizabeth smiled and shook her head at him. "You are quite the flatterer, Colonel. Perhaps I ought to commend Mrs Wickham for selecting such an agreeable cousin."

They both laughed at that and began talking about a concert to be held next week. Elizabeth was well prepared to discuss it, for Georgiana had spoken of little else in the morning hours since they had heard of it two days ago. It was in fact a matter of lively interest to her as well, for the soprano was said to be particularly expressive, and the pianist one of unusual skill.

After some time, Elizabeth began to feel a strange sensation of being watched. Looking up, she saw Mr Darcy watching them, as though he wished to join in the conversation, but knew not how. Elizabeth dismissed the impression. It was contrary to everything she had heard about the man to believe him so diffident. More likely, he was listening to them in judgement.

At last, Mr Darcy cleared his throat. "I should not wish to interfere with any plans of yours, sister, but should you like to go as a general party? I think it would add greatly to the enjoyment of the evening."

"Yes, I should like that of all things," Georgiana replied without hesitation. From the brilliance of her smile, it was clear that only further proof of her brother's wish for renewed closeness between them could have added to her pleasure in what was already an urgently anticipated event.

"Then I shall purchase the tickets," Mr Darcy announced. "Fitzwilliam, after what you have been saying, I need not ask if you are interested. Have you any prior engagement?"

"No, and indeed I shall be delighted to go with you," he replied.

At that moment, the last members of their supper party arrived and were announced — Mr Darcy's particular friend, Mr Bingley, and his sister, Miss Caroline Bingley. Elizabeth watched them with some interest, for one could ascertain a great deal about a man through the friends he chose. Pleasant as Colonel Fitzwilliam was, Mr Darcy certainly deserved no credit for having a civil and sensible cousin, but a man's friends were surer indications of his character.

If it were so, Elizabeth thought, Mr Bingley's friendship might bring a mixed report. Oh, the man was vastly agreeable, without a harsh or unkind word to say of anybody. He rather reminded Elizabeth of Jane in that respect. He was pleasant to talk to, as ready to speak to Elizabeth herself as to Georgiana, despite his evident wealth.

Yet the very ductility of his character was all too clear a match to Mr Darcy's evident desire to have everything his own way. Elizabeth thought wryly that she might have respected him more, had he had a less agreeable friend. It would at least speak to an ability to get along with those who did not always agree with him. Anybody could get along with Mr Bingley.

His sister was another story. After all but ignoring Elizabeth during the formal introductions, she at last turned to her and remarked, "I believe you mentioned hailing originally from Hertfordshire, Mrs Smith."

"Yes, that is so," Elizabeth agreed. "A delightful part of the country, though I am afraid I have not been able to see half so much of our beloved England as I would like."

"Travel is a broadening pursuit," Caroline Bingley replied. Elizabeth marvelled at the way she had managed to unite agreement with rude condescension with almost a species of admiration.

"Yes," Caroline Bingley went on, "it is wonderful how one's opinions change when one has seen more of the world. My brother once intended to lease an estate there, but it would have been a sad mistake. Hertfordshire may be very well in its way, but it is nothing at all to Derbyshire, I assure you. If you had ever had the privilege of seeing Pemberley, you would know that nothing can compare to it."

"Pemberley is Mr Darcy's home, is it not?" Elizabeth inquired innocently.

"Yes, naturally, and a more beautiful place, I am sure I have never seen."

"Then Mr Bingley might as well settle in Hertfordshire, or indeed anywhere, for by your account, the beauties of Derbyshire seem to be consolidated into Pemberley, and I am sure Mr Darcy would never sell it," Elizabeth said laughingly.

Mr Darcy and Mr Bingley, who had been speaking together and turned a little away, joined them at this.

"Sell Pemberley! No, indeed, I never would," Mr Darcy said. "However came this to be suggested?"

"It was not a suggestion, Mr Darcy, but a little joke," Elizabeth explained. "We were speaking of Derbyshire and Hertfordshire, each of which, I am sure, have their beauties."

"Hertfordshire is fine indeed," Mr Bingley

agreed enthusiastically. "Do you know, I once almost rented an estate there, in a town called Meryton?"

"In Meryton!" Elizabeth cried out in astonishment. "Your sister mentioned you had once contemplated renting an estate in Hertfordshire, but she did not mention the name of the town. Why, I grew up only a short walk from Meryton. I suppose that you would have leased Netherfield Park, Mr Bingley."

"Netherfield Park — that is the place," Mr Bingley agreed. "How odd to hear of it again, three years later! Do you know who took the place instead of me, Mrs Smith?"

"Yes, indeed, for it stood empty for some time, and unless there has been a change since I was in London, the same family has held it these past two years. They were well liked in the neighbourhood."

Mr Bingley replied pleasantly, and Elizabeth was glad to let the conversation move on to other topics.

Though Elizabeth could not like Mr Darcy, she was a little mollified by the efforts he showed at supper towards securing Georgiana's comforts. His conversation was ever bent towards her; he watched her with no little solicitude; the supper, from what Elizabeth had already learned of Georgiana's tastes, was exactly calculated to gratify them. The company, too, was well suited to her shy friend, for all were already known to her and eager to please. In Mr Bingley's case, this appeared to be his natural good temper rather than any of those aims which an unmarried man might have been supposed to have on the widowed and very wealthy sister of his good friend. In Caroline Bingley, Elizabeth rather thought they were not so selfless, for the meanest observer could have seen how desperately she wished to please Mr Darcy. Everything that he did was to be benevolent; everything that he said was clever; and anything that had the least bit to do with Pemberley was the finest of its type in the world. Elizabeth really almost blushed for her, particularly as Mr Darcy did not appear to appreciate the display in the least. On the contrary, he appeared to find it embarrassing, and to wish for its cessation.

For that, at least, I must admit I like him, Elizabeth thought with an inward chuckle. Like Georgiana, he appeared to find praise more embarrassing than gratifying. Or perhaps it was only praise so obviously ingratiating that he disliked.

In all, the evening passed off more pleasantly than Elizabeth had expected. She had seen Georgiana treated with real friendliness by Mr Bingley and his sister and real warmth by her cousin and brother, and Elizabeth herself had been well received by everyone except Caroline Bingley, who seemed to be at some pains to display her claim to Mr Darcy and her social superiority to Elizabeth. Though Elizabeth liked Miss Bingley too little to be hurt by her pointed slights, the wastefulness of it irritated her. Elizabeth did not want Mr Darcy, and it would have been too bad for her if she did. Surely nothing could be less likely than that he would marry a gentleman's daughter of such low means and connections that she was forced to work for a living.

No, the gentleman that Elizabeth would hope to one day fall in love with would be a rather different sort. He would be good tempered, intelligent, inclined towards books and reading without being lost to the real world. A man of judgement, and love of nature, and a good heart.

Such a paragon could not be real, of course. Or if real, he would not likely be inclined to marry a woman who earned her own keep.

Chapter Twenty

The supper at Mr Darcy's townhouse had also been of some practical use, for Elizabeth and Georgiana had been the last to leave. It was not until they were at the door that Mr Darcy had cleared his throat and suggested that Georgiana return at a time of her convenience to discuss her finances.

A meeting time two days hence was quickly suggested and quickly agreed upon; the only sour note in the proceedings was that Mr Darcy had looked rather displeased at Georgiana's mentioning that Elizabeth would be one of the party. Elizabeth was not slow in assigning a cause for his reluctance. It would be all too easy for Mr Darcy to have everything his own way if Georgiana came alone, for she was so little inclined to argue with her brother, he might have proposed risking her entire dowry on a game of chance before she would have protested.

If Elizabeth had disliked him less, she might have guessed the real reason for Mr Darcy's unease. Quite simply, he was ashamed. Not ashamed of having withheld Georgiana's dowry from Mr

Wickham — that choice had proved entirely correct, for in addition to the generous allowance with which he had provided them, Mr Darcy had from time to time settled debts of honour that Mr Wickham did not wish to share with his wife, and of which Mr Darcy was equally determined that Georgiana should remain ignorant. Her fortune would have been badly depleted or perhaps destroyed entirely, if Wickham had had free rein of it.

Nor was Mr Darcy ashamed of anything he intended to do, for his designs were as liberal as any man's could be. Mr Darcy was a man of rather simple tastes and £10,000 a year. Each year, when he had paid the vast sums necessary to run and maintain Pemberley, when he had laid out money to improve his lands and promote the welfare of his tenants, when he had donated to charity and indulged himself in the purchase of more books for Pemberley's library, there yet remained a sum to be added to his investments. It had not occurred to him that there could be any temptation to make free with Georgiana's money, for what could he do with it?

No, the money would be hers, as soon as she showed herself capable of managing it or married a man of any sense at all. But that Mr Darcy was confident in his decisions, both past and present, did not mean that he was at all content to discuss them before a third party. Who was Mrs Smith?

Georgiana had not known her a twelvemonth, and she was to be included in all their nearest concerns. If the rapprochement between the siblings had not been so new and fragile, Mr Darcy would have tried to dissuade her, but as it was, he did not wish to attempt it.

Georgiana's carriage arrived promptly at the appointed hour. Mr Darcy (who told himself that it was entirely a coincidence that he was standing at the window at the time, for he certainly was not watching for it) saw it arrive.

After an exchange of pleasantries and an offer of tea, which was declined, the little party settled down in Mr Darcy's study.

"If you will allow me," Mr Darcy began, "I should like to begin by informing you of what I have done thus far, and of how matters stand. We can then discuss what is to be done."

"Yes, of course," Georgiana said faintly. Elizabeth frowned. He might at least have softened his tone with her, for Georgiana's nervousness ought to be obvious to anyone.

"Very well, then," Mr Darcy said with a nod. "As I wrote in my letter, your dowry has grown considerably in the past three years. The Exchange has been kind to us."

"Brother, there is something I do not understand," Georgiana said, her voice carefully steady. "How can my dowry have grown so? The living allowance was quite generous."

"It was my choice not to release your dowry to Mr Wickham," Mr Darcy said shortly. "It was therefore my responsibility to furnish the allowance. The funds came from my income."

Elizabeth blinked in surprise at this. She would not have expected such disinterestedness of anybody, and it was not at all consistent with the image she had been forming of Mr Darcy. Georgiana had spoken of the house in Edinburgh, the arrangements which, if not lavish, were more than adequate. It must have taken a significant sum.

Georgiana was, if anything, still more taken aback. "Fitzwilliam, this cannot be. It is too much, entirely too much. You must allow me to repay you, or rather, take the money out of my dowry. It will still be a prodigious sum."

"No," Mr Darcy replied calmly. "That I shall not do, so let us not waste our breath discussing it. As I was saying, your dowry was once large, and is now still larger. You are a very wealthy woman, Georgiana."

"I have learned much about how to handle money these past three years," Georgiana said. She blushed. "I mean to say, I had an excellent teacher."

"I am pleased to hear it," Mr Darcy said carefully. Though it pained him to prevaricate, he could not risk losing Georgiana's confidence at so delicate a stage of their rapprochement. Later, perhaps, when they had developed some confidence in each other, he might tell her that Mr Tiller had not come to Edinburgh to be her tutor by chance, but in response to Mr Darcy's earnest pleas.

"If you would not object," Mr Darcy therefore continued, "I should like to set you a few problems of household organisation and management. Please do not be insulted, sister. It is only that I believe I would be irresponsible not to verify your competency. You do not object to my making a little test of your knowledge?"

Georgiana shook her head. "I have no objection."

His questions were reasonable, and as far as Elizabeth could judge, he seemed to be trying to prove Georgiana's competency, rather than prove the lack of it. That was an easy task, for Georgiana answered everything with alacrity and serene confidence.

Mr Darcy's expression was first surprised, then pleased, then rather proud. "That is well done, Georgiana. I do not think I could have answered so well at your age. You had an excellent teacher, to be sure."

"I am thankful to dear Mr Tiller — the Mr Tiller who used to work at Pemberley, you know," Georgiana replied eagerly. Elizabeth wondered at the strange expression that flashed across Mr Darcy's face. It had seemed rather like relief.

He was already replying. "Ah yes, Mr Tiller, a good man indeed. Your skill is not surprising with a teacher as capable as that. And I am pleased such is the case, for it is my intention to put your money into your own hands, if you wish it."

Georgiana drew in a quick breath. "I had thought I would have to persuade you."

"No," Mr Darcy said. "After all, under a more conventional marriage, the money would have left my hands in settlements long since."

Though Georgiana winced a little at the reference to her unfortunate late husband, Elizabeth was glad to see it did not cow her. "You are not afraid that I would choose poorly again?" Georgiana asked, a little defiantly.

Mr Darcy shook his head. "You are no longer sixteen, Georgiana. You have learned much of the world, and your judgement of character is no longer that of an innocent girl. I do not think you will be fooled a second time."

"No," Georgiana said, emotion bare in her voice. "No, I shall never make such a mistake again."

An uncomfortable silence stretched through the room. Though Elizabeth would have given much to ease her friend's heartache, she was at a loss for what to say. At last, Mr Darcy spoke.

"You will have a number of decisions to make, Georgiana, and I think it would be best for me to show you the resources available to you in more detail. I have, of course, kept extensive records…"

With this, Mr Darcy took out various ledgers and legal documents, and all looked relieved to see the conversation moving into a less emotional vein. Elizabeth hoped Georgiana had not envisioned her companion giving her detailed advice on the meetings the job posting had mentioned, for it was quickly apparent that both Darcy siblings were conversant in business to a degree of knowledge far beyond her own. The mysterious Mr Tiller was evidentially an effective teacher. Though Elizabeth listened carefully, she could not have hazarded an opinion on any of the more detailed questions they discussed.

After a half an hour, Mr Darcy called a halt to it. "If it suits you, Georgiana, I think we would to better to stop now, and resume again another day. I always find I make better decisions if I may first receive the facts, then let them sit for a little time before choosing."

"I would like that," Georgiana admitted. "I confess I have grown rather weary. Would Thursday next suit you?"

Mr Darcy nodded. "Gladly. And I shall call for you both on Tuesday for the concert."

"It is settled, then," Georgiana agreed, and, making their polite goodbyes, the two young women made their way from the house.

When they had gone, Mr Darcy returned to his study and collapsed heavily in his chair. It had gone well enough, and indeed better than he had hoped. There had been some bad moments. He ought to have known better than to speak of Wickham in any connection, and he had nearly given himself away in the matter of Mr Tiller. But she seemed to have forgiven him readily enough, and that was a true blessing.

Mr Darcy leaned his chin on his hand and considered the question that weighed so heavily on his heart, he had not dared to risk speaking it aloud. It was not yet time, he told himself. At the next meeting, it would — perhaps — be time to speak.

As a wealthy widow, Georgiana had the right to make her own establishment. In hiring Mrs Smith, she had shown that she had every intention of doing so. But while Mr Darcy would not dream of speaking against it, his heart could not be dissuaded from the vision of Georgiana again living at Pemberley. To once again hear the sounds of the pianoforte resounding through the halls and to have the privilege of requesting his favourite songs, to be close at hand to protect her and guide her in the choice of a second husband — it would be the closest he could ever come to erasing the pain of the past three years.

In point of fact, Mrs Smith might not prove an impediment to his plans. After all, Georgiana certainly would have had a companion in any case. While he would have hired a rather motherly lady, rather than the young and pretty Mrs Smith, it was at least workable. She appeared to be clever and personable, no bad addition to their circle at Pemberley.

Mrs Smith was indeed charming, more charming than he would have guessed at their first meeting. Though Mr Darcy had then deemed her no more than pretty, her sparkling dark eyes had proved difficult to ignore. Their loveliness really made her almost beautiful. And there was a quality of perception about her that was yet more than this. One had the sense that she was clever, that she saw more of people than a surface examination could reveal, and yet that she viewed the world with a friendly gaze. It was no wonder Georgiana had selected her as a companion, for she lifted one's spirits with no more than a simple word or a friendly glance.

Stop thinking of ineligible women, Darcy, he told himself, *and start thinking of eligible ones. Preferably before Caroline Bingley grows so obvious, you have no choice but to do something about it.*

With a shake of his head, Mr Darcy forced himself to stop thinking of the whole business. He opened his ledgers again and set to work.

Chapter Twenty-one

Short as the time was until Tuesday and the promised concert, it seemed long in anticipation. Miss Bingley called on Georgiana Monday morning, bringing fresh gossip about the performers and the news that she also intended to attend. Though the Bingleys had not been present when Mr Darcy suggested making it a general party, they intended to go likewise. Georgiana saw nothing odd in this, being extremely eager for the music herself, but Elizabeth thought cynically that Miss Bingley had not seemed much interested until she learned that Mr Darcy would attend. As Georgiana did not seem to have noticed the designs that lady had on her brother, Elizabeth said nothing. Mr Darcy could decide such things for himself. There was no need to create trouble and fuss where none were necessary.

Miss Bingley delicately sipped her tea and set down her cup on the little side table next to the sofa. She leaned forward. "I have heard that Mr Hummel will perform one of his own compositions," she said, with evident pleasure at knowing more than her listeners.

"How delightful!" Georgiana exclaimed. "Do you think it will be the Trio No. 3? Or perhaps one of the sonatas?"

It was rather amusing to watch Miss Bingley's look of consternation on finding Georgiana better informed than herself. "Well — that is — I am not quite certain," she replied, putting on a bright smile.

"Or perhaps he will even premiere a piece," Georgiana said eagerly. "Would that not be exciting?" she asked, turning to Elizabeth.

Elizabeth smiled at her enthusiasm. "Certainly it would," she said with a little chuckle, "but I must confess that I know nothing of Mr Hummel. I have never had the privilege of hearing his music before."

"Indeed, that is a shame," Miss Bingley said with a little sniff.

"Nor have I," Georgiana said. Miss Bingley looked rather crestfallen for a moment before resuming her social smile. "I have only heard of his work. But all I hear of this concert only increases my anticipation."

Though Miss Bingley hinted at wishing to attend the concert as one of their party, Georgiana would not have dreamed of issuing an invitation on her brother's behalf, and the lady went away disappointed. Elizabeth was not sorry for it. She liked Miss Bingley too little to regret her disappointment. Her company was by no means pleasant. If she was not giving Elizabeth herself some small set-down, she was making Georgiana uncomfortable with her over-generous praise; and if she was not praising Georgiana to the skies, she was flirting outrageously with Mr Darcy. But that was, of course, the least offense of the three. It was certainly no business of Elizabeth's if she did so.

On Tuesday evening, Mr Darcy's carriage came for them promptly, but the ladies equalled him in politeness by being already dressed and waiting. Seated in the carriage across from Colonel Fitzwilliam and Mr Darcy, Elizabeth felt herself to be unreasonably fortunate. She had never imagined that her 'sacrifice,' if so it could now be termed, of going out to work would turn out so well. She had hoped for genteel work that would not mar her reputation and a comfortable home. This she had, yet Elizabeth could never have imagined half the pleasant things that had come with it. She was vastly pleased with her new circle of acquaintance, excepting only Caroline Bingley. Colonel Fitzwilliam's charm, Mr Bingley's friendliness and good humour, even Mr Darcy's intelligence and generosity: they were a formidable group of men, and made for pleasant company.

And who could ever have imagined that her work would have her attending one of the most desirable concerts of the London season? It was a luxury of which she could not have dreamed.

Upon arriving at their destination, it took only a little time to present their tickets and be admitted to the hall. The Bingleys were already there, and the two parties found each other almost within the first moments.

After the first bows and greetings had been exchanged, Caroline Bingley placed herself next to Mr Darcy. Looking up at him, she said in a confidential tone, "We are seated in the same area, are we not? Our places are directly by the orchestra."

"No — I am afraid not," Mr Darcy replied. "We are a little farther off." Miss Bingley's face fell, but Mr Darcy could not bring himself to feel any regret. The seats nearest the orchestra were the seats of grandeur, where one went to see and be seen. Knowing well how little taste Georgiana had to be on display for all the *ton*, Mr Darcy was confident that she would prefer his selection of somewhat more modest seats, excellently placed to see and hear every detail of the concert while making rather less a show of themselves.

"Oh! That is a shame," Caroline Bingley said with a little pout. "We shall miss you prodigiously during the performance, but of course we may chat in the intervals."

Mr Darcy only nodded at this. Georgiana would not miss anybody during the performance, for he was certain she would not be thinking of anything but the music, and for his part, he had no wish to engage in any more of Miss Bingley's attentions than he must.

Turning to Mr Bingley and the rest of the party, he was just in time to see them laugh heartily.

"What is this? Come, you must share the joke with us," Caroline Bingley said.

Mr Bingley shook his head, still chuckling. "Oh, it is nothing, really. I cannot quite recollect what was so funny about it, only Mrs Smith is such a wit."

Miss Bingley turned to Elizabeth with an acid smile. "Oh, really? How delightful."

"It is nothing, only that we are all in such pleasant spirits in anticipation of the music," Elizabeth said. Really, her mild jest about how greatly she and Georgiana had looked forward to the concert was not so very amusing, and no joke could be funny when repeated a second time, out of the moment that had inspired it.

Thankfully, Mr Bingley noticed her disinclination and took pity on her. "Tell me, Mrs Wickham," he inquired, "did not you say that you thought Mr Hummel might play a new composition tonight?"

While Georgiana was pleasantly engaged in explaining that she did not think Mr Hummel would play a new piece, she only hoped he might, Elizabeth found herself wishing that Jane might have attended. There was the enjoyment of the music itself, of course, but much more than this, she wished her sister could meet Mr Bingley. Of course he was handsome and in possession of a good fortune, but this was all nothing compared to the kindly benevolence of his spirit. It put Elizabeth in mind of no one so much as Jane herself, and she felt confident that if only they could have met, they would have liked each other prodigiously. It was a shame, for she did not think it was within her power to arrange, or at least not without a degree of contrivance to which she would never descend. Elizabeth refused to be a schemer, common as the failing might be. Miss Bingley had certainly shown herself unblushingly ready to manoeuvre and contrive her way into catching her desired husband. But Jane would never wish to be involved in such manipulation, and Elizabeth had no desire to set her hand to such a thing. She would simply have to hope that, soon or late, the chance would come one day.

It was not long before it was time to take their seats. Not being familiar with Mr Hummel's work, Elizabeth could not have said whether the work was a new one. Looking at Georgiana, however, she felt confident that it was not. Georgiana seemed pleased with what she heard, rather than overcome with excitement, as she would have been upon being privileged to hear something entirely new.

By the time the intermission came, Elizabeth was glad to stand and walk around a little. All in their party seemed ready to stretch their legs, and they passed out of the concert room on their various errands, some to fetch tea, and others to speak with their acquaintances in the room. Seeing a small balcony that opened out on one side of the room, Elizabeth turned to Georgiana.

"Would you excuse me for a moment, Mrs Wickham?" Elizabeth murmured. "I should like to have a little fresh air."

"Naturally. Do you wish for some company?" Georgiana enquired.

Elizabeth smiled and shook her head. "No, I shall be perfectly all right. I would not want to cost you the opportunity to speak to any of the performers, if they are to appear." This being agreed, Elizabeth made her way out to the balcony, silently slipping through the elegant French doors that connected it to the hall. The night was cold, but not bitterly so, and the little distance from the crowd and hubbub inside was extremely pleasant.

—

Mr Darcy only wished that his enjoyment in the society to be found at the concert could be equal to the music. Though he had the pleasure of seeing Georgiana enjoy herself greatly and of speaking to his cousin and his good friend, Miss Bingley was being unusually teasing. She was not a fool, so why did she not accept his obvious lack of interest in her? Mr Darcy had long given her answers no more encouraging than bare politeness, and sometimes even less than that. If nothing else, he had to respect her determination.

That determination was highly inconvenient at the moment. "Do you not think, Mr Darcy, that an English or Italian pianist would be better?" Miss Bingley was saying brightly to him. "Oh, this Austrian is acceptable, I suppose, but I would not call his work truly elegant."

"That, I cannot judge," Mr Darcy said coolly. "I look to my sister for all questions of musical taste."

"And so you should," Miss Bingley agreed with alacrity. "Mrs Wickham is prodigiously talented. I am sure I do not know another lady half so gifted."

Mr Darcy could not help but soften a little at the praise, disingenuous as he knew it to be. "She is devoted, to be sure."

"How she practices! I am sure I shall never forget how diligent she was that spring we visited Pemberley. It was 1811, was it not? I do not know anything more delightful than Pemberley in spring."

Mr Darcy did not think he could bear to ignore her hints for much longer. "I thank you for the compliment — you are too good," he said, in a tone that carried as much finality as he could bring to it.

With that, Mr Darcy excused himself and walked briskly towards the French doors that opened out on to a small balcony. Despite the cold winter air, the night was crisp and fine, and he felt he must escape the hot crush of society for a moment, whatever the other guests might say about it.

Closing the door behind him, Mr Darcy breathed a sigh of relief. In the next moment, he stiffened. He was not alone in seeking the solitude of the night air. Another figure stood at the railing, looking up into the night sky, what little could be seen of it past the smog and streetlights of London. Hearing his approach, they turned to face him.

Chapter Twenty-two

"Mr Darcy!" Elizabeth said in surprise. She was breathing rather hard, for no reason she could fathom. Only she had been absorbed in feeling the beauty of the night and hated to leave her time among the stars.

"Forgive me for interrupting you, Mrs Smith," Mr Darcy said rather coldly. "I shall go inside directly."

"No — you need not go," Elizabeth said quickly. "I should hate to be the cause of anyone being deprived of the night sky. It can be a great relief when one has spent too much time among hustle and bustle."

Half surprising himself, Mr Darcy joined her at the railing. The situation was not too unsuitable, he thought. They could be clearly seen from inside, which ought to satisfy the demands of propriety, and after all, she was a widow, and did not need to be as careful as a young lady on the marriage mart.

"You felt yourself to be in need of it, then?" Mr Darcy asked her, and wondered if she would snub him with some reply that was no answer at all.

"In great need of nature, in whatever form I may have it," Elizabeth said softly. "I am a country girl at heart, Mr Darcy. London is magnificent, but I must own that I long to be in the countryside again. I should like to wake early and go on a long walk over the hills. I should like to hear the birds and feel the wind on my face."

Mr Darcy could almost see it as she spoke — though he supposed she must be picturing Hertfordshire, and he was certainly seeing the fields around Pemberley, and the magnificent hills of Derbyshire.

"I spend as much of my time as possible at Pemberley," Mr Darcy said at last. "I never feel so well as when I may look out of any window and see green things, and when every breath of air is free of soot."

She looked at him with a more gentle smile than he had yet seen on her face. Mrs Smith was always charming, and always honest even in her witticisms, but she had not given him such a look before. It was a look that one might give to a friend, or to someone one wished to make a friend.

"If you would allow me, Mr Darcy," Elizabeth said slowly, "I should like to speak rather plainly."

"Please do," Mr Darcy said, a little startled. She was so much changed this night, as though she had been holding up a mask of pretended civility, only to let it fall and reveal the real heart of her.

"Mr Darcy, I think I owe you an apology. I have not been quite civil to you," Elizabeth began.

"I was rather under the impression that you disapproved of me," Mr Darcy said, and cursed himself for his inability to hold his tongue.

Elizabeth let out a startled laugh. "That is certainly plain speaking, with a vengeance." She gathered her courage and went on. "That is not quite right, Mr Darcy. Say rather that I disapproved of the image I had formed of you."

He raised an eyebrow, but said nothing.

Elizabeth sighed. "I suppose you deserve an explanation. Georgiana was certain that you were furious with her, Mr Darcy. And so I thought you were the sort of man who would be furious with her. That, upon having his sixteen-year-old sister tricked into marriage by a scoundrel, would place the blame solely on her shoulders."

"She ought to have known that I would not blame her," Mr Darcy said, almost inaudibly. "There was no one to blame but Wickham...and myself."

"That is not quite right either, Mr Darcy," Elizabeth replied. He looked up at her in surprise. "From all that I have heard, Mr Wickham did not carry her off against her will. Yes, he acted as no honourable man would act, but you do Georgiana an injustice in supposing she had nothing to do with it. She is not a fool. She made a mistake, and she paid for it."

Mr Darcy smiled crookedly. "I wonder if you would be as sanguine if it were your little sister that Mr Wickham carted off to Gretna Green to marry over the anvil?"

"He certainly never would," Elizabeth replied, "for my sister has not a fortune of £30,000."

"I suppose that is true," Mr Darcy admitted. They stood for some moments in a silence more companionable than either could have anticipated.

At last, Elizabeth sighed. "I suppose I ought not to delay any longer. I was in the process of apologizing to you, Mr Darcy. I allowed myself to be carried away by prejudice until I formed an impression of you that was most insulting and entirely unfair to you. Please forgive me."

"I forgive you, since you ask it," Mr Darcy said, "but I am not entirely convinced that forgiveness is necessary. We are all so subject to error in our attempts to understand one another. I confess that I was at one time suspicious of your designs in working for my sister. It is a responsible post, when one's employer is so young."

"My designs?" Elizabeth inquired with a smile.

"An unscrupulous woman might have taken the post for the chance to find a rich husband, or worse still, for the influence it would give her over Georgiana. Perhaps you have heard of Mrs Younge."

"I have not," Elizabeth admitted.

Mr Darcy's face grew dark with fury, though

his voice remained even. "I blame her for what happened at Ramsgate nearly as much as Wickham. She was Georgiana's companion at the time. Colonel Fitzwilliam and I had exercised great care in selecting her, but we were unhappily deceived in her character. She was working with Wickham, and everything she did was designed to forward his chances at Georgiana's fortune. She admitted him to the house, encouraged Georgiana in believing every good thing of him, and at last encouraged her to go off to Scotland with him. When Fitzwilliam and I questioned her, she at last admitted it all."

As she listened to this recital, Elizabeth's face grew pale with shock and horror. "I have never heard of such a thing," she said at last. "This is infamy indeed. I cannot understand how Georgiana could have brought herself to trust me after suffering such a betrayal."

"She has always had a loving, trusting heart," Mr Darcy replied, "and you are not much like Mrs Younge."

"No," Elizabeth said, low. "No, I should hope not."

Though the lights of London almost obscured the stars, Polaris could be seen, twinkling nobly above them. Elizabeth watched it for a time, thinking.

She reached a decision. "In the interests of being as little like Mrs Younge as possible, Mr Darcy, I have another confession."

He did not look alarmed. "I am listening."

Elizabeth took a deep breath. "My name is not Mrs Smith. It is Miss Bennet. And I am working not due to the death of my husband, but due to the death of my father, whose estate was entailed away from his widow and daughters. I have never been married. Georgiana and I agreed I would pretend to be a widow, that I might better perform the rôle of companion to so young an employer."

Mr Darcy had grown rather pale. "You are an unmarried woman, and the daughter of a gentleman."

"I am," Elizabeth agreed.

Mr Darcy abruptly turned and made for the door. "We ought not to be alone together. It is bad enough for an unmarried man and a young widow, but for an unmarried woman, it is utterly unsuitable."

Elizabeth followed him, rather amused. "I am the same person I was a few moments ago, Mr Darcy. No one here but you and Georgiana knows the truth. I am not afraid for my reputation."

Mr Darcy whirled around. For an instant, he seemed almost about to take her by the shoulders, but he did not touch her. Elizabeth was suddenly aware of how tall he was. They had been repeatedly in company together, and she had been so accustomed to disliking him that she had almost forgotten how imposing a man he was, and how handsome. Looking deeply into his eyes, the magnetism of his presence was impossible to ignore.

"Perhaps you ought to be," Mr Darcy said heavily. He turned and was gone.

Elizabeth was frozen still, staring after him. Her breathing was strangely loud in her own ears.

It was the oddest thing. For just a moment, she had seen something strange in his eyes. It seemed almost as though he was about to kiss her.

She ought to have been frightened. She supposed she was. But at the same time, for just a moment, she had wanted him to.

—

Mr Darcy leaned against the wall, breathing heavily.

Which are you more, Darcy — a scoundrel, or a fool?

He shook his head. Even the sternest self-reproach seemed inadequate. He had almost kissed Mrs Smith — that is, Miss Bennet.

He would never have actually taken such a liberty. It would be utterly immoral to take advantage of so unprotected a woman. It had been his shock at realising her position that had done it — the shock of realising that the person he had thought to have some experience of the world was, in fact, an innocent.

He had wanted her to realise she needed protection.

It was almost amusing to realise that in other circumstances, he might have been the one at risk. It was all too easy to imagine what Caroline Bingley might have done under similar circumstances. With all the power of wealth and consequence, not to mention the deep debt of friendship and gratitude he owed to Mr Bingley, any compromise there would have had grievous consequences indeed. Marriage to Caroline Bingley, who saw his wealth and position and was utterly indifferent to his character, formed no part of his plans.

Mr Darcy did not believe for a moment that Elizabeth had intended any such thing, even apart from the fact that she lacked the connections to make him marry her if she were compromised. There was a clarity to her eyes, a will to understand others and to be understood herself, that belied any such designs. A less scrupulous woman might have applied for the position of Georgiana's companion to find a wealthy husband among her employer's connections, but if he were a betting man, he would stake a guinea that Elizabeth had only intended to work well and earn her keep.

With a sigh, Mr Darcy set off to rejoin the rest of the party. It was lowering to realise how much her apology — or rather, the change in her opinion — had meant to him. She was only the slightest acquaintance. Her opinion ought not to mean anything to him.

But he would be lying to himself if he said that it did not.

Chapter Twenty-three

Georgiana had not forgotten the meeting set for the Thursday following. On the contrary, she had been writing down columns of figures and making little notes of plans for the future in almost every free moment. Elizabeth watched her with mingled respect and amusement. Her earnestness was rather charming in view of her fortunate situation. Yet Elizabeth could not wish it otherwise. She felt she could hardly have respected anyone who did not take such a sum of money seriously.

When it came time for the meeting, her work seemed to have paid off. Mr Darcy looked prodigiously impressed with all her answers, and the conversation took a little turn to a discussion of how Mr Darcy's own monies were arranged.

"I should like a little more variety," Mr Darcy admitted. "Until last year, I had a sum invested with a merchant here in London, but upon hearing some disquieting things about his business practices, I withdrew it. I was only just in time, for I am afraid his next shipments did poorly, and there were some very unpleasant rumours. I have not yet found anyone to replace him."

"Have you considered Mr Gardiner?" Georgiana asked him. "From all Elizabeth has told me of her uncle, I would feel vastly confident in placing my own money with him."

"If you are looking for a more trustworthy partner in business, my uncle would certainly serve your purposes," Elizabeth commented. "The only other commendation I can offer is that he has given me some lace from his warehouses, and the quality is very fine. I am afraid I cannot comment on any other aspect of his business, for I am sadly ignorant of it."

Mr Darcy looked thoughtful. "I shall look into it," was all he said. The meeting went on pleasantly until at last it was time for Georgiana to look through the ledgers containing all the transactions made with her funds over the past years.

Remembering how his sister had always valued silence for deep concentration, Mr Darcy offered her the sole use of his study. "If you like, Georgiana," he suggested, "Mrs Smith and I may wait for you in the drawing room, so that you will not be every moment distracted by our looking at you and loudly wondering when you may be done."

Georgiana giggled at this. "Yes, I would appreciate it. Perhaps Elizabeth can play something for you on the pianoforte, for she is a charming performer."

Though protesting this compliment as too kind, Elizabeth did not allow it to delay her in leaving Georgiana to the solitude she so clearly desired for her studies. She meekly followed Mr Darcy to the drawing room, expecting him to take up a book and ignore her, or perhaps leave the room entirely.

"Would you be so kind as to play for me, Mrs Smith?" Mr Darcy asked her.

Elizabeth almost gaped at him before recovering herself. If his tone had not been so obviously sincere, she would have thought he was teasing her. "Certainly, if you wish it," she said at last, "but you must not be disappointed when you find me far from a capital performer. Your sister is too kind."

"Georgiana is kind, to be sure," he returned, "but not dishonest. Particularly regarding music. She would not say that your playing brought pleasure to her if it were not so."

"Well, then," Elizabeth said. "I suppose I will simply do my best." She walked away from him and went to the pianoforte. There were few pieces she knew well enough to play without sheet music. After a little thought, Elizabeth settled on the prelude to The Well-Tempered Clavier, the piece she had played at her interview with Georgiana. Whatever Georgiana found to admire in her rather imperfect style of playing must certainly be present there.

Elizabeth breathed out deeply, settling herself. She touched her hands to the keys and began.

After a few stanzas, she was startled almost to the point of missing a note by seeing Mr Darcy approach. She resolved not to stop until the prelude was complete. He had asked for her playing, and he would have it.

"Do you mean to intimidate me, Mr Darcy?" Elizabeth asked with a teasing smile as she played on. "However closely you observe me, I assure you I will only make as many mistakes as I should have done in any case. I do not lay claim to much courage, but I can certainly withstand such a test as this."

She rather wondered if she might offend him, but Mr Darcy only smiled at her. "Surely you cannot imagine that I wish to do any such thing. It is your rather playful wit which credits me with such a design." His eyes met hers. "My real purpose is much simpler."

Elizabeth thought for a moment that she would forestall him by refusing to ask, but in the end, she could not resist. "And what is your real purpose, Mr Darcy?"

"It could not be simpler," he replied. "Merely to enjoy your playing, which does indeed give me great pleasure."

"I thank you," Elizabeth said softly, and played on. At the conclusion of the piece, she stood up rather abruptly and closed the instrument. "I will not further test your patience," she said. There was something a little forced in her voice. Without waiting to hear any protest, she crossed the room and sat down on the sofa.

Mr Darcy stood opposite her, turning a carved soapstone lion that had rested on the mantlepiece over and over in his hands.

"There is something I have wished to say to you," he said at last. Elizabeth waited in silence. "I have wanted to thank you."

"To thank me?" Elizabeth repeated. "Whatever for?"

Mr Darcy looked down, seemingly fascinated with the figurine in his hands. "I have wanted to thank you — indeed, I am most grateful — for all you have done for my sister."

"That is little enough," Elizabeth said, half astonished. "It is rather I who owe thanks to her, for I was in need of work, and I had not expected to find anything half so pleasant. I intend to give satisfaction, but surely it is I who benefits more from the circumstances of my employment."

Mr Darcy did not answer at once. He merely looked into the distance, shaking his head a little as though in thought. At last, Mr Darcy met her eyes. "I can sometimes hardly believe how well Georgiana has overcome all the struggles of the past years," he said quietly. "I had the gravest fears for her happiness and even for her character before we met again. I am more relieved than I can say that they were proven false, but still I cannot credit it."

"For my part," Elizabeth replied, "I am inclined to believe that Georgiana overcame the years of marriage to a man who, by all your accounts, seemed to have been unworthiness itself due to the fortunate presence of two of the greatest blessings anyone can have under affliction. I mean the presence of good people about one and strength of character within."

"Surely strength of character is the greater of the two," Mr Darcy remarked.

Elizabeth slowly shook her head. "I am convinced we need them both — both friendship and fortitude, as we might call them. Oh, do not misunderstand me, Mr Darcy. I would never speak against the importance of character."

"I should hope not."

"No, no indeed. We are nothing without self-command and the will to be better than we are, and this is the fortitude that carried your sister through all her troubles. But there was more than this, was there not? I believe you helped her in no small measure."

"I did not do nearly enough," Mr Darcy replied hoarsely.

"Yet you did do much. Colonel Fitzwilliam told me you would not allow him to duel the late Mr Wickham. In valuing what was best for Georgiana over a foolish idea of honour, you dissuaded your cousin from taking an action that would have added greatly to her misery. You provided for her material comforts and preserved her fortune. Perhaps one never can do enough, in such a case, but you were a friend to her indeed."

He waved this away. "And what of you, Miss Bennet? I have learnt a little about your struggles. You have lost your father, your home. You have gone away from your sisters to earn your daily bread among strangers. Would this all not be utterly unsupportable without a great deal of fortitude?"

"I thank you," Elizabeth said. There had been a degree of admiration in his voice, a degree of understanding for the courage and effort of will it had taken, that made it rather difficult to speak. "Indeed, I thank you for the compliment, but this case proves my point quite neatly. I could have done none of this without friendship. Without my sisters encouraging me, without my uncle providing me the most material assistance and watching for my safety and comfort as a father would, without Georgiana being a friend to me as well as an employer...Mr Darcy, without all this, I should be a sad woman, indeed."

"Do not misunderstand me, Mrs Smith," Mr Darcy said earnestly. "I do not mean to set the value of friendship at nothing — of course not. It would be reprehensible to do so, when I have benefitted so greatly from having the sort of friend one can truly rely on. I only mean that it is a mistake to rely too greatly on friendship only. Without strength of character, true inner strength, what becomes of us as soon as we face a challenge and have no friend close to hand?"

"In essence, I believe we agree," Elizabeth remarked. "I have no more wish to dismiss the merits of fortitude, I believe, than you do of friendship. It is merely that I think each is but half a virtue without the other. No man can make his way in the world by strength of character alone, and yet it is a sad fellow who lives only for friendship, without the virtues of purpose and resolve."

"Yes," Mr Darcy said thoughtfully. "Yes, I suppose we do agree." He fell silent for a time. Elizabeth would not have intruded into his privacy for the world, yet even a less acute listener would have sensed that he wished to say something more. Patiently, Elizabeth said nothing, and let him make the choice to confide in her or to remain silent.

"What do you think was my failing, Mrs Smith?" His voice was so low, it was almost inaudible.

"I beg your pardon?" she said in surprise.

"When I failed Georgiana," he said bitterly. "Was it a failure of friendship or of fortitude that kept me from seeing her danger? That made me stay away all the years of her marriage, when I am now certain that she would have forgiven me for my failure straightaway?"

"There, you are a little mistaken," Elizabeth

said gently. "Georgiana never thought there was anything to forgive. And I join her in thinking you are rather too hard on yourself, Mr Darcy. I would not classify any of your actions then as a moral failing, but only that of a brother trying to fix a terrible situation."

"You are too generous," he said. "I feel my own failure too deeply for this. I believe I ought to feel it. I certainly ought never to forget it."

"Perhaps it is better not to forget," Elizabeth said lightly, "but I cannot believe it is better not to forgive. Certainly, whenever a person has intended no wrong, we ought to forgive them. Even if that person is — ourselves."

At that, he met her eyes, and a smile briefly flashed across his face. Elizabeth marvelled for a moment at the change it wrought. Mr Darcy was a very handsome man when he smiled.

"It is remarkable how much you have eased my heart," he said at last. "I believe you are correct."

"I am convinced of it," Elizabeth replied with a smile, "and if there are any other little matters that I may argue into complacence, I beg you will share them with me."

Mr Darcy shook his head, a little shamefaced. "I hope you will accept my apology, Mrs Smith. I can't think what came over me to speak so freely. It is most unlike me to press such a confidence even on a close friend, let alone an acquaintance of such recent standing."

"It is not entirely your fault," Elizabeth remarked, keeping her voice even with an effort. "I am afraid I may be partially responsible. You see, I have always drawn such confidences out of others, ever since I was a child. I do not recall a time before I was the recipient of other's secrets, and I assure you, I have never sought them. You see, Mr Darcy, you are only the most recent victim of this odd quirk, and there is no need for you to blame yourself."

"I am not surprised — at least, not entirely surprised," he said. "It is indeed something in you. One feels you are truly listening, and the words simply fall out. But I am sorry, all the same."

Mr Darcy looked into her eyes then and found he could not look away. They were beautiful, to be sure, dark and sparkling and remarkably clear. But even more than this, Mr Darcy found himself wondering if he had ever before looked into anyone's eyes and found such a remarkable degree of understanding.

"Then I accept your apology," Elizabeth said. Her smile was remarkably gentle, and he found himself smiling in response. "And as a fellow devotee of friendship and fortitude — not to mention a friend to Georgiana — I assure you, there is nothing to forgive. Let us shake on it."

Mr Darcy nodded and took her hand. "To fortitude, then."

"And to friendship," Elizabeth rejoined, and as they shook hands, their eyes met, and they found themselves irresistibly given over to laughter.

Chapter Twenty-four

It was strange that Elizabeth found herself thinking of her father more and more often as Yuletide approached. He had never been particularly fond of the season. It was always her mother who relished the decorations and parties, presents and balls. Yet to know that she would not see her father on Christmas Day brought it home as nothing else could that he was truly gone.

She had made up her mind not to say anything to Georgiana, who had cares enough of her own. It was rather hard to judge how the season might affect her. Her marriage had been troubled. Little as she spoke of it, that much was obvious. Yet to speak of it might still bring great pain, either in the remembrance of good times, or worse still, in the absence of them.

Georgiana was therefore the first to speak about celebrations for the holiday. They were sitting side by side on the pianoforte bench, trying to play four-handed and failing rather badly, when Georgiana turned to Elizabeth with a look of sudden decision.

"I have been thinking about Christmas day," she said, "and of how I should like to celebrate it."

"Oh?"

"Yes — I think I have made up my mind. You will wish to spend it with your sister and the Gardiners, will not you, Elizabeth?"

"I confess I should like that," Elizabeth replied, "but I had expected to spend it with you, and if you would like my company, you shall have it."

"Much as I should enjoy your company, I think I would be wrong to keep you from your family when they are so near at hand. I shall ask my brother to join me, and we shall both spend Christmas with our families."

"If you are sure," was Elizabeth's response. "In truth, I think the plan is an eligible one." She smiled a little to herself, thinking how cold a man she had believed Mr Darcy to be when they first met. If he had been such a man in truth, she would never have abandoned Georgiana to his society on Christmas Day. But his true nature had been revealed to her, and she would never again think him cold or unfeeling. If Georgiana wished to be by his side on Christmas day, that was where she ought to and would be.

As it happened, the plan took a little alteration. Elizabeth was indeed to join Jane and the Gardiners in Cheapside for Christmas, but while

Georgiana would spend Christmas with her brother, they were both to join Colonel Fitzwilliam at the home of his father, the earl.

—

Christmas day dawned clear and bright, with a little powdered-sugar coating of fresh snow on the ground. The Gardiner children showed their delight in loud yells and merry chatter, both audible quite an impressive distance from the nursery. Elizabeth felt all the cheer and gratitude of the season within her as she woke in Jane's bedroom. Their Christmas Eve supper had been delightful and had been surpassed only by the pleasure of talking with Jane late into the night. What had once been so common was now a rather rare enjoyment, but all the more treasured for it.

"Good morning," Jane said softly, seeing that her sister had awoken.

"Good morning, and Merry Christmas!" Elizabeth replied.

Jane smiled. "It is a merry Christmas, indeed. I am so glad you could spend it with us, Lizzy!"

"It is a wonderful thing to have an amiable employer," Elizabeth agreed. "I had discarded the idea of asking Mrs Wickham for the time, thinking it far too great an imposition to ask of her, but she proposed it herself, instead. She is a dear woman."

"Thank goodness for that," Jane said warmly. "I think we ought to prepare for church, do not you?"

Elizabeth agreed, and the two sisters prepared themselves for the day. Dressing and putting up their hair was quickly accomplished, and they went down to greet their family. The little Gardiners were already visibly eager for their presents, and only their parents' careful training in good manners made them ready themselves for church instead of clamouring for them.

The Gardiners attended services in a little church not a quarter-mile away. In all but the foulest weather, they walked instead of taking the carriage. It was a magical walk that Christmas morning, with the thin layer of fresh snow on the ground and the sidewalks already swept clean, the air fresh and crisp about them, with only a little bite to the December breeze.

In the time she had stayed in Cheapside, Elizabeth had grown fond of the Gardiner's pastor. He was a dear old man with thick grey whiskers. His voice had grown thin with age, yet he preached messages of such love and peace that it was a joy to hear. That Christmas day, he outdid himself, and even the little Gardiners forgot their impatient fidgeting and listened enraptured.

Mr and Mrs Gardiner, who were indulgent parents when they did not think their children would suffer any harm from it, did not further test their patience once they had all returned home.

They announced at once that it was time to open presents. There began a joyful noise. Elizabeth had fashioned paper dolls for the children, and Jane had made the clothes for them to wear. The sisters judged their own work as rather clumsy, but the children seemed to be delighted with it.

For her aunt and uncle, Elizabeth had made handkerchiefs — a manly, unadorned one of fine batiste for her uncle, and one trimmed with fine lace for her aunt. They surprised her with a present in turn. Opening it, Elizabeth stopped a moment in shock. It was a fine golden chain, plain but good. She had not expected them to spend half so much on her, but could not, of course, say so.

"It is delightful," Elizabeth declared instead. "I am already looking forward to when I shall have an occasion fine enough to wear it, and indeed, I cannot thank you enough."

"I am pleased you like it, Lizzy," Mrs Gardiner replied. She wrapped an arm around her niece's shoulders and lightly squeezed her. "You are dear to us, you know."

"I do know, aunt," Elizabeth said softly. Jane was opening her present. It was a gold chain like Elizabeth's, but shorter and with a looser, wider weave.

"I shall wear it with my amber cross," Jane declared, and put it about her neck at once.

It was a scene of such merriness and family feeling that Elizabeth could forget for a moment that it was not her home. She was a working woman now, and would leave the next day. It was folly to pretend that all was as it had been in the past. She was no longer a gentleman's daughter come to London simply to enjoy its culture and society. That life was gone, as irretrievable as though it had never existed.

It was not so bad, after all. She had a happy life and was more fortunate in having Georgiana as her employer than anyone could well expect to be. Compared to the dark fears she had after her father's death, she was blessed indeed.

And if she were still Miss Bennet of Longbourn, she might never have come to know Mr Darcy, and that would have been a shame. From the most unpropitious beginnings, he was coming to be dear to her. Elizabeth told herself that he was only a friend, almost like a cousin to her, but the thought was unconvincing.

There was more. In the way he spoke to her, the flashes of understanding that seemed to pass between them, the connection that she felt when their eyes met.

It was impossible. It was foolish of her to even think of it. Yet it was so.

—

"My father knows how to celebrate, or my

name is not Fitzwilliam!" the Colonel declared, laughing.

Mr Darcy laughed too. "I cannot deny it. We often celebrate in a milder vein at Pemberley, as you know, but nothing can beat the Earl for a more — festive — celebration."

When Georgiana had asked Mr Darcy if they might spend Christmas Day together, he had been delighted, yet the suggestion had also presented him with a problem. Not wishing to impose on her, he had already accepted Colonel Fitzwilliam's invitation to join his family, as had been their custom for the past two years.

Thankfully, it was the work of moments to add Georgiana to the celebrations. Indeed, the Earl and the Countess were as delighted by the suggestion as he could have wished.

"My sister has brought her companion with her almost everywhere. I hope that will not be an imposition," Mr Darcy told them.

"No, certainly not," the Countess reassured him at once. "Mrs Smith seems a genteel, pleasant sort of person. We shall be glad to have her."

Mr Darcy thanked her and told himself that his gratitude was for Georgiana's sake. His little sister seemed much less shy when bolstered by the high spirits and friendly conversation of her companion. If he was also happy in the anticipation of Mrs Smith's company for the holiday, that meant nothing. She was merely a pleasant person, whose society anybody might have looked forward to enjoying.

It was not until the celebration itself that Mr Darcy learned his mistake.

"Mrs Smith is not with you, I see," he remarked to Georgiana, with an attempt at casualness.

"No — she is with her sister, and their aunt and uncle. I thought it would be a terrible shame for her to spend Christmas so near them, and yet with strangers."

"That was kind of you," Mr Darcy commented. His mind seemed strangely blank. It was kind of her, no doubt about it. He ought to be grateful that Georgiana had thought of doing such a thing. Indeed, he ought to be embarrassed not to have thought of it himself. It was absurd for him to regret her absence.

Mr Darcy was rather quiet that Christmas Day. Thankfully, amid the general gaiety, it went unnoticed. His present to Georgiana was at least a success. While he had considered buying her jewellery, he had at last settled upon buying her sheet music for the pianoforte. The gift had been far less costly in pounds sterling, but more so in time. He had first taken every opportunity of visiting her to ascertain what pieces she had already, and how her skill and tastes might have altered over the past three years. That being done, he had presented the list to a skilled maestro of the instrument and paid him to select the most suitable pieces for such a performer.

If Mr Darcy had any doubts about the success of his present, they were swept away by Georgiana's reaction upon opening it. The maestro had selected well indeed. It transpired that some pieces were ones Georgiana had heard performed and wished to acquire, while others were beyond her knowledge. She thanked him again and again.

Though Mr Darcy had not really expected a present in return, Georgiana had no sooner finished her earnest thanks for his than she was pressing a small package upon him. Mr Darcy almost gasped upon opening it. It was a little watercolour of middling skill, showing a pleasant scene of trees and a lake. Though pretty, it was not artistic appreciation that had taken his breath away.

"I hope I have remembered it rightly," Georgiana murmured.

"You have," Mr Darcy said. "Indeed, you have remembered everything perfectly."

Georgiana had painted the lake and grounds of Pemberley as seen from the southern drawing room where her piano had always stood. The likeness was remarkable. Each detail of the scene must have been engraved on her heart, to have been remembered with such clarity three long years later.

"I shall treasure it always," Mr Darcy told her. "I do not know what would be better — to keep it here in London, so that I may look at it whenever I am homesick, or to put it up in the drawing room, so that I may look out the window, and then to this painting."

Georgiana giggled. "In London, please, brother. I am sure my little likeness would not stand up to such a comparison as that."

"For my part, I am by no means certain," Mr Darcy told her. "Fitzwilliam! Look at this and tell me what you see."

Colonel Fitzwilliam came over with a good will. "It is the view from Pemberley, to be sure," he said at once. "Did you paint this, then, Georgiana? It is an excellent likeness."

Georgiana smiled and thanked him. It was not long before they were all called away to join the others, and the festivities went on.

Mr Darcy had taken Georgiana to their uncle's house in his carriage, and likewise took her back again. Georgiana was chatty on the ride back. Her brother was grateful for it, for he was attempting to make up his mind. It was not until they were almost at her door that he did so.

"Perhaps you might give this to Miss Bennet for me," Mr Darcy said, almost under his breath. "I had thought she would attend, and did not wish for her to be without anything to open." He handed Georgiana a parcel wrapped in brown paper. Its size and shape, not to mention the slight smell of paper and good leather that came from it, pronounced it to be a book.

"That is kind of you," Georgiana said, looking at him in surprise. Her brother was always kind, to be sure, but this present called forth other ideas to her mind. "Yes, of course I will give it to her. Or if you like, perhaps you might come in a moment, so that you might hear her thanks yourself."

"No, I had better go," Mr Darcy said shortly. He told himself he did not wish her to feel any sense of obligation or awkwardness. That was true, and yet, if he was entirely honest with himself, there was more. He felt obscurely that it would be dangerous to go in. He wanted to see Elizabeth Bennet's smile upon opening her present too much.

Brother and sister then said their goodbyes, and Georgiana left him and went inside. Elizabeth had already returned and was ensconced comfortably in the drawing room with a novel from a lending library.

"Welcome back, Georgiana," Elizabeth said laughingly. "And a merry Christmas to you as well."

"Merry Christmas, Elizabeth," Georgiana replied. Seeing Elizabeth's eyes lighting curiously on the wrapped present, she handed it to her.

"What is this?" Elizabeth asked. "Are you giving me a Christmas present? I am sorry to say I did not think to make one for you."

"There is no need to be sorry, for it is not from me," Georgiana told her. "It is from my brother." Though Mr Darcy might have preferred her to add his explanation of not wishing Elizabeth to be the only person present at the Christmas celebration who did not receive a gift, Georgiana kept her own counsel and remained silent.

Elizabeth's eyebrows had raised in surprise, but she said only, "That is kind of him. I had no idea that Mr Darcy would give me a present."

"Are you going to open it?" Georgiana nudged her.

"Certainly." Elizabeth carefully untied the twine that held the wrappings closed and eased back the paper.

On beholding the package, no one could have been surprised to learn that it contained a book, but the book was at least surprising in its beauty. Bound in the finest leather, it bore the title 'A Traveller's Account of Derbyshire.' Curiously, Elizabeth opened the cover, and was surprised to find an inscription.

—

Presented to Elizabeth Bennet on Christmas 1815 with my best regards. I hope this account may prove instructive before the spring visit to Pemberley.
Sincerely, F. D.

—

Elizabeth had been surprised enough by the intimacy of giving her a present, yet to inscribe it seemed more daring still. And yet...and yet... truly, it was nothing more than he might do for a distant cousin. Surely it was only his kind wish of considering her, as Georgiana's companion, as almost part of the family. Yes, indeed, that must be it.

"I shall thank Mr Darcy with all my heart when next I see him, and I shall give better thanks in the form of reading this with great attention. It is kind of him, to be sure."

"I think the compliment of reading a book chosen for you is the best thanks you could give my brother," Georgiana said. Her tone was light, yet there was something in her eyes that made Elizabeth look away for a moment, afraid that she was blushing.

"Well, good," Elizabeth said briskly. "It is a compliment I am glad to give." Then, with a smile only a little forced, she began to ask Georgiana about her Christmas celebrations, what everyone had said and done, and what presents had been given. Georgiana answered with a good will, and if she noticed the rather deliberate change of subject, she did not remark on it.

Chapter Twenty-five

As though Christmas and New Year's had taken up all the gaiety everybody had and left none behind them, the period after Twelfth Night seemed rather dull and undistinguished. The weather must have agreed. It was one grey, clammy day after another, with neither sun nor snow nor even sparkling frost to distinguish them. One morning, Georgiana came to table wearing a gown Elizabeth had not seen before. It took Elizabeth a moment to understand why the difference should look so striking.

"Ah, it has been six months, then," she said at last.

Georgiana nodded. "It shall be a relief to wear half-mourning now," she said softly. "I shall not feel nearly so conspicuous."

"It looks remarkably well on you," Elizabeth said. The lavender touches on the black dress were far more flattering to Georgiana's colouring than unrelieved black. "The timing is rather fortuitous as well."

"I suppose you mean the Dalrymple's ball," Georgiana replied. "It will feel rather strange to go to such an event again. I hope I shall not be thought too forward."

Privately, Elizabeth thought there was little danger of that. As Mr Wickham had been so little known to London society, not to mention so little loved by Georgiana, she might have gone into half-mourning after the six weeks that were the least one might decently observe. Still, Georgiana was perhaps wise to give Mr Wickham more remembrance even than he had deserved. One would always rather do too much than too little.

"No, I think there is little danger of that," Elizabeth replied instead. "After all, your aunt thinks it entirely appropriate for you to attend, and if a countess thinks you ought to go, who can gainsay you?"

Georgiana's shoulders dropped their tension as she let out a great sigh. "Yes, you are right. And besides, my brother encouraged me to come as well."

"It is settled, then," Elizabeth said lightly, and the two ladies set to breakfasting. It was fortunate that Georgiana did not seem inclined for more conversation, for Elizabeth could not leave her own thoughts long enough to attend properly. Her own mourning was as real as Georgiana's, though for a father and not a husband. It was strange indeed to face the prospect of a London ball with so little excitement. The companion of Mrs Wickham would not be likely to be asked to dance, and though there might be some conversation, she would have no friends there beyond Georgiana's circle, for Jane certainly had not received an invitation. There would be the same pointless sparring with Miss Bingley, the same polite nothings shared with chance acquaintances. It was all rather tiring.

If Elizabeth was not quite honest with herself — if there was, in fact, one gentleman she rather wished to see at a ball, rather wished to know how he might dance — the lapse was all too pardonable. She felt her hopes, modest as they were, to be greater than the event might justify.

Her hopes were exceeded in at least one respect, for she was to present a better picture at the ball than she could have imagined. Georgiana had offered to purchase a new gown for her — or rather, as Elizabeth had initially demurred, thinking the offer far too generous — had absolutely insisted that she be allowed to purchase a new gown for Elizabeth. At last, Elizabeth had been forced to give in. The defeat was not a bitter one. Weighty as the purchase of a ballgown would have been for Elizabeth's purse, she well knew it was nothing at all to Georgiana's fortune.

When the gown had at last been completed and delivered, Elizabeth had almost sighed at its loveliness. Georgiana's fashionable *modiste* was far more skilled than the tailors of Meryton. The fabric alone was beyond comparison. Tinted the soft lavender of half-mourning, the silk was as soft as a dream. The richness and lustre of the fabric alone would have made it one of the finest gowns Elizabeth had ever owned, but its detail made it truly extraordinary. The silk bore a fine woven pattern of wisteria vines that appeared and disappeared as the light hit it, and the dress bore a delicate trim of real Brussels lace. Looking at her reflection in the mirror, Elizabeth could not help but smile. Her supposed status as a poor widow and a lady's companion might well make her a wallflower, but at least her appearance would not be the cause.

Georgiana had selected white and black for her gown, livening the black silk of the skirt and bodice with a broad trim of white lace. Only the expression on her face did not fit the image of an elegant, confident young widow, for her trepidation was obvious.

Elizabeth looked quickly at the clock. Thankfully, there was still a quarter of an hour before they need call the carriage.

"Georgiana," she said softly.

Georgiana looked rather startled. "What? Please excuse me, I was not attending."

"No, I believe you were busy worrying," Elizabeth agreed.

Georgiana sighed. "I confess I was," she said. "It is only — well, I have never been to a London ball before. I was yet not formally out when Mr Wickham and I married."

Elizabeth repressed all the condemnations of the man that such a sentence could not help but inspire. It would not help Georgiana's nerves to spend time criticising her late husband, however much the man might deserve it.

"I hope you will enjoy yourself," Elizabeth said instead. "I imagine there will be fine music to enjoy, and I am sure you will not lack for partners. But even if you do not care for it, Georgiana, it will not be so bad."

"You do not think so?" Georgiana said. "Oh, I know a ball is nothing terrible. But to be under the eyes of so many people, after so long away, and with many of them knowing how foolish I was —"

"I am convinced that we believe others think about us far more than they ever do," Elizabeth replied calmly. "We are all of us rather selfish creatures, far too wrapped up in our own concerns to spend so much time worrying about others. Let alone to spend much time harshly judging them. Why, look at me. I will admit that I have always made a kind of game of trying to understand others, to make out their characters. Yet even I do not stand about at a ball and think of flaws for which I may judge them."

Georgiana laughed. Elizabeth was relieved to see how her spirits were improving. "You are much too kind to do any such thing."

"I am certainly much too busy, and so, I believe, are we all." Elizabeth paused a moment.

"Come now, Georgiana. Really, you must listen to me. Truly, I do not believe you have done anything for which you ought to be so harshly judged."

"But I —"

Elizabeth interrupted her to go on, gently but firmly. "Now then. Your reputation is not a bad one. Yes, you were married young and imprudently, but you were married. Worse happens every day. And —" here Elizabeth smiled rather grimly — "and besides, Georgiana, you are a wealthy widow, and likely to become an influential one. Do you really think anyone will judge you? They are more likely to court you."

Georgiana seemed to have been stunned into silence. "I suppose…you are right," she said at last.

Elizabeth nodded. "I know I am. And, Georgiana — if you are going to have this power, perhaps you ought to think about how to use it."

"Yes," Georgiana said slowly. "Yes, I believe I should."

It was a quiet but companionable ride to the ball, for Georgiana was clearly thinking furiously. Elizabeth did not attempt to converse with her, but left her to her thoughts. She was rather preoccupied herself, and not sorry to be left alone to think for a time. If she could help Georgiana realise how much she might do in society, she would be doing much to benefit her young patroness. It was an odd relationship in some respects — the one dependent on the other for her bread and butter and so far below her in wealth and consequence. Yet Elizabeth was older, more assured, more confident in society. The natural deference that one might expect her to have for her employer had quickly shifted into something more like the fond protectiveness she had for her little sisters, mixed with the friendliness and ease of confiding in one another she enjoyed with Jane. The change might be surprising, but it was by no means unwelcome to Elizabeth.

Greeting their hosts was characteristic of the welcome Georgiana might expect from London society. Lady Dalrymple was all that was warm and welcoming, mentioned the Countess her aunt and how they had recently met at the opera, and implored Georgiana to enjoy herself. With amusement, Elizabeth saw that Lady Dalrymple was rather transparently considering which of her sons might be most likely to succeed at tempting the young Mrs Wickham and her vast fortune to the altar a second time.

Mr Darcy and the Bingleys found them not long after they left their hostess. They were accompanied by a couple Elizabeth had never met before. Noticing the woman's resemblance to Caroline Bingley, Elizabeth strongly suspected them to be sisters.

Mr Bingley performed the introductions with his customary cheerfulness. His first words confirmed her impression. "Sister, you of course know Mrs Wickham. This is Mrs Smith, her companion. Mrs Smith, this is my sister, Mrs Hurst, and her husband, Mr Hurst."

"Charmed, I am sure," Mrs Hurst said languidly, as though she were not quite certain why she was being introduced to a mere companion.

"A pleasure to meet you, Mrs Hurst, Mr Hurst," Elizabeth replied evenly.

"Yes, a pleasure. Quite a charming evening," Mr Hurst replied with hearty civility and little interest. "I say, Bingley, are those the card tables? You must excuse me."

And with that, he hurried off. Elizabeth rather wondered at his poor manners, but his wife did not look at all surprised to be deserted in the middle of a ball.

"Tell me, Georgiana, are you spoken for in the second set? I should very much like to dance with you," Mr Bingley said with as much calm friendliness as though he knew of her nerves. Glancing at Mr Darcy and the care with which he was watching his sister, Elizabeth rather thought he might.

"I am not engaged, and I should be delighted to dance with you," Georgiana said with a smile. It was easy to see how much at ease she felt with her brother's friend. Without further ado, she wrote his name down on her dance card by the second set.

"Delightful!" Mr Bingley replied. Without a moment's pause, he turned to Elizabeth. "And what of you, Mrs Smith? Perhaps you might oblige me in the third."

From the looks on everyone's faces, it was evident that this action had not been prearranged. Caroline Bingley and Mrs Hurst looked appalled, while Mr Darcy changed colour with shock.

Elizabeth supposed they had not thought her fine enough to dance with — at least, not for a man of such fashion and fortune as Mr Bingley. She did not hesitate with her reply. "Thank you, Mr Bingley. That would be pleasant, for I am fond of dancing," Elizabeth said mildly, writing down the engagement.

"As am I, as am I!" Mr Bingley returned. His high spirits seemed completely unaffected by his friend's surprise and his sisters' disapprobation. Elizabeth felt a great respect for his particular blend of kindness coupled with self-confidence. Few men would have thought of asking Georgiana's companion to dance and thereby raising her status and giving her a far greater stake in the enjoyment of the ball. Mr Bingley had not only done so, but had asked in a most gracious, gentlemanly way, as one asking for a favour rather than conferring it. Elizabeth felt she liked him prodigiously. She could see why Mr Darcy might have wanted him for Georgiana's husband, even as Elizabeth herself did not think their personalities would quite suit. Mr Bingley was the sort of man anybody would be glad to see married to one of their nearest relations.

It was not long before the group was separated, for the dancing was soon underway, and all had some engagements. Even notwithstanding Mr Bingley's invitation, Elizabeth would not have been such a wallflower as she had supposed, for Colonel Fitzwilliam was also present, and solicited her for the honour of a dance.

The evening was passing off far more pleasantly than Georgiana had feared. It even exceeded Elizabeth's more rational expectations. The pleasure of joining in the rhythm of the dancing, of conversing pleasantly with a good partner and feeling the exhilaration of the steps, was an enjoyment Elizabeth had almost forgotten. It had been such a long time. Not since before Mr Bennet's last illness had she attended a ball.

When Elizabeth's dance with Colonel Fitzwilliam ended, they said their goodbyes and went to look for different companions. Elizabeth thought it her duty to see how Georgiana was enjoying the ball, and Colonel Fitzwilliam said jokingly that if he did not drag Mr Darcy to the dance floor, he would stand in a corner glowering half the evening and give everyone a fright. Elizabeth laughed heartily at this image and bid the Colonel farewell. She stood to the side, where she might be out of the way while yet commanding a good view over the room, and scanned for her employer.

Suddenly, Elizabeth gasped. Her eyes had fallen on a very different figure.

Chapter Twenty-six

It could not be. She must be mistaken. Yet Elizabeth was afraid she had recognised the man rightly, for his figure and bearing were all too deeply impressed on her memory.

The next moments of observation made it a certainty. His tall but ungainly figure; his odd posture, which seemed to combine haughtiness and humility in equal measure; the coarse sound of his laughter from across the room, sounding, as ever, as though he had not quite understood the joke.

It could be none other than Mr Collins. No doubt he had come to enjoy the London season and triumph in his new status as the master of Longbourn. It would be like the man.

There was, however, still hope, for surely he would have no more wish to meet with Elizabeth than she with him. If there were any circumstance more humiliating to a man than to be rejected after much thought by one sister and after no thought by the next, Elizabeth hoped she might never learn of it. Surely he would remain as far from her as possible and, if they could not avoid the introduction, at least they might refer to each other as acquaintances and a distant family connection.

Alas, all of Elizabeth's careful reasoning and self-reassurances were in vain. No sooner had Mr Collins chanced to glance across the room than a look of recognition came over him, and no sooner had he recognised her than he approached her. His expression was an odd mixture of parts. There was triumph there, to be sure, a measure of disdain, and, as he drew nearer and chanced to hear her called "Mrs Smith" by a passing acquaintance, no small measure of surprise.

Elizabeth sighed and walked towards him in turn. If Mr Collins were to inflict new conversational absurdities on her, she would rather not subject her companions to them.

"Mr Collins," she addressed him as they exchanged bows. "It is a pleasure to see you here, cousin."

"Likewise, I am sure," he said. "I had not thought to see you so far from home, cousin. But perhaps you are staying with your mother's brother, whom I understand resides in London."

"I was, when I first arrived here," Elizabeth said evenly. "But now I am employed as a companion to Mrs Wickham, and naturally, I live with her."

"Mrs Wickham — I do not recollect the name," Mr Collins remarked with a frown. "Well, if she is not a well-connected or well-to-do lady, cousin, you must not repine. We all of us have our lots in life, some more fortunate," (here, Mr Collins assumed a look of self-satisfaction quite revolting to behold), "and others less, and if one later comes to regret a decision one has made, it is best to accept Fate, and resolve to be wiser in the future."

Mr Collin's tone of noble rebuke as he delivered this last remark was too much, even for Elizabeth's sense of humour. She lost her temper and said more than was perhaps wise.

"Why, cousin, I assure you I have no cause to repine," Elizabeth said sweetly. "I could not wish to be companion to a sweeter-tempered or more generous lady. Nor, indeed, a better connected one, for Mrs Wickham's name before her marriage was Miss Darcy."

This announcement fell upon Mr Collins with the force of a thunderbolt. "The Darcy family!" Mr Collins cried. "Why, I congratulate you, cousin. That is a fortunate post indeed. You could not do better. Certainly no one could do better. The Darcys are a very well-connected family, you know, and your Mrs Wickham must be niece to my former noble patroness, Lady Catherine de Bourgh."

"That is so," Elizabeth replied. "I can confirm it, for Mrs Wickham has mentioned her aunt to me on a number of occasions."

"Well, cousin, perhaps things turn out for the best after all," Mr Collins announced ponderously. Slowly, a cloud passed over his face. "Did I not hear you called Mrs Smith?" he asked.

Elizabeth would have given much to omit a response, but could think of no way to do so. "As you may know, cousin, Mrs Wickham is rather young. It sounded better to have a Mrs Smith as her companion than a Miss Bennet."

Mr Collins shook his head furiously. "That cannot be. Lady Catherine de Bourgh would never accept such a thing. I wonder I did not see it before. Indeed, you are too young — far too young — to truly provide protection and companionship to a young lady from such a family. You must forgive me, cousin, but it cannot be. I have no choice but to make this known."

"I appreciate your scruples," Elizabeth replied with careful patience, "but I assure you, there is no need. Mrs Wickham is fully aware of my real name. Indeed, it was her idea in the first place, for I presented myself to her as Miss Bennet at our first interview."

"I do not doubt your truthfulness, cousin," Mr Collins replied, though his expression contradicted him. "Yet this is not sufficient. I understand that Mrs Wickham is a very young lady. She cannot be expected to choose for herself. Indeed, we have already seen what foolish choices a young lady of nineteen or twenty may make."

Elizabeth chose to ignore the latter statement, pointed as it was. "Your concern is admirable, cousin, but this really is not necessary."

"Oh, but it is," Mr Collins insisted. "I could never face my former patroness, Lady Catherine de Bourgh, if I had left her only niece so unprotected. It is nothing less than my duty to see that the truth is known."

In her wildest imaginings, Elizabeth could not have suspected that an encounter with Mr Collins would go so poorly. It would be a scandal indeed if he pronounced in the middle of Lady Dalrymple's ball that Georgiana's companion was using a name and title not her own, and such a scandal would present them with a hideous choice. She might take much of the sting from Georgiana by taking all the blame onto herself, inaccurate as it would be to pretend the idea had been hers. But if she did so, the cost to herself and, worse still, to her sisters, would be terrible.

There was yet one card that Elizabeth might play. "The truth is known, Mr Collins, by everyone concerned in the affair. I have already told you that Mrs Wickham knows my true name, and if that is not enough for you, allow me to inform you that her brother, Mr Darcy, knows it, too. You can hardly believe that you know better than Mr Darcy does what is best for Mrs Wickham. He was her guardian before her marriage, and he raised her after their father's death."

"No, indeed I would not go against anything that Mr Darcy might say," Mr Collins began. Elizabeth felt a ray of hope, only to be dashed when he continued. "However, cousin, I cannot believe for a moment that Mr Darcy knows of this. It is a sin to lie, Elizabeth. You must pray to be forgiven, for certainly Mr Darcy would never permit his sister to have an unmarried woman as her companion, if he knew of it."

Elizabeth could see it in his eyes — say what she might, Mr Collins was determined to divulge her secret before everyone present. Indeed, she really believed he relished the trouble that it would bring her.

Yet in the next moment, a look of shock came over Mr Collins's face. Elizabeth turned to see what had surprised him and stood open-mouthed as she recognised the man who stood there.

Chapter Twenty-seven

"You must allow me to contradict you," Mr Darcy said with a bow. "I assure you, I am well informed of the matter."

"Surely you have not thought, Mr Darcy —" Mr Collins began.

Mr Darcy smoothly interrupted him. "Forgive me — we have not been introduced." His significant look at Elizabeth jarred her into action.

"Mr Darcy, allow me to present my cousin, Mr Collins," she said. "Mr Collins, this is Mr Darcy. As you know, he is the nephew of your former patroness, Lady Catherine de Bourgh."

The two gentlemen bowed, Mr Darcy gracefully, and Mr Collins looking as though he might fall over, from excitement if not from lack of balance.

"It is a pleasure to meet you, Mr Darcy, such a pleasure," Mr Collins gushed. "And this is a very fortunate meeting, very fortunate indeed, for I maintain a correspondence with Lady Catherine de Bourgh to this day, and it is actually within my power to assure you that she was in very good health as of my last letter, perhaps one month ago."

"I thank you for your kindness," Mr Darcy replied. "Perhaps it may interest you to know that she remained in good health as of last Thursday, the postdate of my most recent letter from her."

"That is indeed a relief," Mr Collins replied warmly. Elizabeth closed her eyes for a moment. The man was too much of a fool even to be embarrassed.

Any concern for him she might have felt vanished at his next words. "Really, Mr Darcy, we must discuss the matter at hand, unpleasant as it may be. I appreciate your concern for my cousin, indeed I do. But this cannot continue. I must make the unpleasant truth known."

"No, Mr Collins," Mr Darcy said steadily. "You must not."

"But Mr Darcy, if you were to only consider the view which your aunt would certainly take of the matter —"

"I am rather better acquainted with my Aunt Catherine than you can be, Mr Collins," Mr Darcy said quietly. "Now, I insist you let me handle this matter. It is, after all, one in which my family, my sister, is primarily concerned."

Mr Collins drew himself up. "My conscience will not allow it, Mr Darcy. I must speak."

Mr Darcy gave him a look of such contempt

that Mr Collins cringed back. Mr Collins was forced to look up in order to meet Mr Darcy's eyes for, though Mr Collins was a tall and rather weighty young man, Mr Darcy was of still greater stature. Mr Darcy gave him a long stare, looking down his nose at the unfortunate Mr Collins. At last, he spoke.

"It is evident you do not yet understand the rules of London society, Mr Collins," Mr Darcy said icily. "It is a failing sadly common among those who are only newly raised to the standing of a gentleman."

"Why — that is —" Mr Collins sputtered.

Mr Darcy did not wait for him to complete his thought, even supposing that such might have been within Mr Collin's powers. "I have already assured you, Mr Collins, that Mrs Smith's history is known to me. She is employed by my sister with my blessing, and Georgiana is deeply attached to her. As such, Mr Collins, I would take a dim view of any attempt to interfere with my sister's happiness."

"I should never dream of — but perhaps you have not considered —" Mr Collins stammered.

Mr Darcy looked at him with a gimlet eye. "Mr Collins, I consider everything that is essential to my family's welfare. Perhaps you have not considered to what extent you will be received by society — or, to express it more accurately, will not be received by society — if I were to make it known that your presence is unwelcome to me."

Mr Collins gulped, evidentially picturing how

quickly the doors of London would be closed to him. Though her fright had not yet passed off, Elizabeth could not help but be amused by his look of horror. Clearly, he could imagine no worse fate. "Yes — yes, I understand," he said faintly. "Please excuse me, Mr Darcy. Naturally, I shall say nothing about this matter to anyone."

"Naturally," Mr Darcy answered with some emphasis. He did not trouble himself to return the abortive bow that Mr Collins gave before he fled.

When Mr Collins had disappeared into the crowd, Mr Darcy's eyes met Elizabeth's. The humour of the situation was too much for them, and it was some moments before both could entirely subdue the laughter that overcame them.

"It is too much, entirely too much," Elizabeth laughed. "He was so confident, and then you —" She made a gesture that seemed to encapsulate Mr Collins's discomfiture and flight, and they both laughed anew.

"I do not think the gentleman — if so he may be called — will trouble you any further," Mr Darcy remarked.

"Perhaps we may term him an oddity, if not a gentleman," Elizabeth sighed. "I hope you are correct. My sister Jane and I turned down his marriage proposals, and I am afraid he has never forgiven us."

"I beg your pardon," Mr Darcy said slowly. "Do you mean to say he proposed to you both?"

"I suppose a lady ought not to speak of her proposals," Elizabeth replied, "but yes, he did. He proposed to Jane, and she thought it over with all her might, for though she could not bear the thought of being married to such a man, she thought it might be her duty to do it, to save us all from poverty. In the end, though, her good sense prevailed, and she refused him. He proposed to me the same day, and I refused him the next instant."

Mr Darcy was sputtering with laughter, though he could not help being appalled. "I would say I could not believe any man would act in such a way, but having met your cousin, I am afraid I do believe it."

"And so you ought, for it is nothing but the truth," Elizabeth said wryly. "I am heartily relieved he did not go on to propose to our younger sister Mary, for, having rather less sense than either Jane or myself and placing still greater value on a woman's duty, she might have accepted him."

This provoked them both into a fresh fit of laughter.

Mr Darcy was the first to calm himself. "I should like to ask you something."

"Please do," Elizabeth invited him.

"Mrs Smith — or, as there is no one nearby to hear, I shall say, Miss Bennet — are you engaged for the next dance?"

Chapter Twenty-eight

For a moment, Elizabeth only looked at Mr Darcy in disbelief. It was not long, however, before good sense and manners reasserted themselves.

"Why, no — I am not engaged," Elizabeth said slowly.

"Would you be so good as to dance with me, Miss Bennet? I feel greatly inclined to join in the dance."

"I should be delighted," Elizabeth replied steadily. She could not seem to make him out. What on earth could Mr Darcy mean by it? Elizabeth could only follow him to take their places in the line, for the floor had already emptied out on the conclusion of the last, and the dancers for the next set were taking their places. It was fortunate that she and Mr Darcy were quickly separated and had not the opportunity of talking, for it gave Elizabeth the chance to arrange her thoughts. By the time they were reunited, she had made up her mind.

"I believe I understand you now," she announced merrily, though in an undertone that would not carry to the other dancers.

Mr Darcy raised an eyebrow. "Is that so?"

"Yes, indeed, for I could not at all make out why you would ask me to dance. But I believe I have it now. Mr Darcy, you find Mr Collins as impossible as I do, do you not? And I believe you have chosen this method to show him you do not regard his opinions in the least, and that he ought to hold his tongue."

"That is only partially correct," Mr Darcy amended, "for I certainly do not regard Mr Collins enough to allow any of his actions to determine mine. I asked you to dance because I thought I would greatly enjoy dancing with you. And indeed, the event has proven me correct."

At such praise, Elizabeth could not help but blush. Mr Darcy watched her with a smile, admiring the rosy flush of colour on her cheeks. Though Elizabeth almost dropped her gaze, she refused to be so easily routed. Gathering her courage, she instead met Mr Darcy's eyes.

"I must then thank you twice over for this dance," she said with a little laugh. "Firstly, for my own enjoyment of it, which is certainly great enough. And secondly, for the discomfiture it has given Mr Collins. After the set-down you gave him, he certainly will not dare to speak against me."

"You must not thank me for either," Mr Darcy replied. "My enjoyment in the dance is certainly as great as yours, for your grace and lively spirit have brought me pleasure beyond what I am accustomed to experiencing in a dance."

"Very well," Elizabeth laughed. "We have now suitably established that we are both equally pleased by the dance, and neither deserving nor desiring thanks."

Mr Darcy chuckled. "Indeed. But you must not thank me for dealing with your cousin either, for there, too, I was acting entirely selfishly."

The dance separated them for a long moment, during which Elizabeth's heart beat wildly and her mind worked furiously. There had been such particular meaning in his voice. It had held a depth of emotion such as she had never heard before. Yet he could not mean — he could not possibly mean —

They were reunited, and Elizabeth looked up at Mr Darcy with a smile, as best as she could make it, merely of friendliness. "I suppose you mean you would not wish Georgiana to be touched by any scandal if Mr Collins were to reveal that I am a Miss Bennet and not a Mrs Smith."

Mr Darcy smiled a little crookedly. "I should indeed do anything within my power to protect Georgiana against scandal, but I did not think of this at the time."

"Then perhaps you meant simply that Georgiana and I have become great friends, and she would miss me if she were forced to dismiss me from her employment."

"That is certainly true, but I am afraid it was

far from my mind as well," Mr Darcy said quietly. "Perhaps it makes me a fool, but I confess I thought only of you."

The next strains of music separated them again, as it was time for each to step down the long row of dancers. Elizabeth would have been surprised to know how generally admired she was then, and how many people at the sidelines spoke to their companions, inquiring as to the name of the graceful dancer with the dark hair and bright smile.

"Ah — that is Mrs Smith," Mr Bingley told a group of admiring young men. "She is a companion to Mrs Wickham, who is sister to my friend Darcy, you know. A remarkably pleasant lady."

"I could not say that I know her, for she is hardly anyone to know," Caroline Bingley told the gentleman bringing her some punch, in a rather different style. "She is the hired companion of Mrs Wickham. There is some mismanagement there, to be sure, for a mere companion to put herself forward in such a way. But Mr Darcy has the best heart in the world, and no doubt he took pity on her."

Georgiana was dancing herself, and smiled to see her friend come down the line. For, even-tempered and good natured as she had always found her companion to be, she had rarely seen a look of such open joy on her face.

By the time she rejoined Mr Darcy, Elizabeth had composed herself a little. She supposed she had been foolish to put so romantic an interpretation on his words as she had done. For a little time, she had danced and laughed as though she had been Miss Elizabeth Bennet again, a gentleman's daughter who would not dream of working to earn her own keep. A young woman with worries enough, to be sure, but one for whom marriage with Mr Darcy would be possible, if rather a triumph.

But she had remembered herself in time. That young woman was gone. Necessity had made her a Mrs Smith as surely as marriage to a Mr Smith would have done. And if she thought that Mr Darcy would flirt with a Mrs Smith, a mere hired nobody, she was dreaming.

Mr Darcy would never fall in love with his sister's hired companion. They were friends — indeed, they were becoming good friends — and for that, she would be grateful.

Elizabeth told herself firmly that it would be wrong to dream of more.

—

Thank goodness she has more sense than you do, Darcy, Mr Darcy told himself with disgust. For a moment, he had allowed himself to forget everything — his station, what he owed to his family, what he owed to Georgiana — and speak only the truth.

She was Elizabeth in his private thoughts, not

Mrs Smith or even Miss Bennet. And Elizabeth was stunning.

It was not her face, though that was certainly pretty enough. It was those eyes, so deep he might drown in them. It was the expressions that crossed her face almost too quickly to see, and his knowledge of the mind working quickly behind her polite social smile.

She was someone he might have loved. Mr Darcy could at least admit that much to himself. Elizabeth was someone he might have loved, at any rate, if it were only possible.

A gentleman's daughter of no connections or fortune would have been bad enough. Mr Darcy could not pretend that he would have ever congratulated himself on the prospect of acquiring relations whose condition in life was so decidedly below his own. But he was a gentleman, and she a gentleman's daughter. There would at least have been nothing the *ton* would have remembered longer than a season in it.

But to marry a working woman — to marry his own sister's hired companion — that was a story the *ton* would never forget.

Mr Darcy sighed. It was perhaps easier that matters were so simple. That the choice before him was really no choice at all. He would remember what he owed to his sister, to his family, and if he could not help but think that Elizabeth was the woman he might have loved, he would endeavour to forget it.

Chapter Twenty-nine

Much to Elizabeth's relief, Georgiana had informed her she intended to sleep late the morning after the ball. They had both done so, and thereby risen late but rested.

The morning's first post had already arrived before either Georgiana or Elizabeth rose for the day, and by the time they met at the breakfast table, the butler had already delivered it there, no doubt thinking that his mistress might wish to read her letters over breakfast.

As it happened, the results were somewhat mixed. While Elizabeth had received a single slim letter from her sister Mary, the postman had brought her friend three letters of different types, and which were destined to be very differently received. Georgiana eagerly seized upon two of her letters, a missive from an old school friend from whom she had last heard before her marriage, and a thick sheaf of paper from Edinburgh.

"It is from Mr Tiller, who was a good friend to me there," Georgiana explained. "He was a manager at Pemberley ever since I was a girl, and by great good fortune, he happened to move to Scotland not long after I did. I benefited greatly from his advice, for he taught me all I know about budgeting and managing property."

"That is fortunate indeed," Elizabeth commented mildly. "It is lucky that such a good friend was close at hand."

Though Elizabeth did not choose to say what she was thinking — that it was likely not good luck at all, but rather Mr Darcy's signature combination of benevolence and high-handed interference that had caused Mr Tiller's presence — Georgiana was too quick-witted and had grown to know her too well.

"Elizabeth," she said quietly. "You have noticed something I have not. Come now, I have learned to know that look on your face. Please tell me what it is."

Elizabeth sighed. "Oh, very well. I was just thinking that it would be rather like your brother to send Mr Tiller to Scotland for you."

Georgiana gave her a long look, though she said nothing, clearly reviewing the past in a different light.

"How right you are," she said at last. "It would be like him. I wonder I did not think of it before."

"Don't be angry with him," Elizabeth urged mildly. "You know what I once thought of your brother, and how wrong I was. I am convinced that if he did indeed do so — for you must remember, this is the merest conjecture on my part — then, high-handed as the gesture may have been, he did so only out of love and concern for you, and because he feared that more direct help might have been rejected."

"I am not angry," Georgiana protested automatically. After a little more thought, she went on. "No, truly, I am not angry with him. How can I be angry over something that had such good results? But I must own I do grow tired of always being his little sister to be controlled and protected, but never to be confided in."

"I do not blame you for that," Elizabeth said frankly. "I have come to believe your brother is a good sort of man, but he is still a man. It is only natural for him to want to help and protect you, and sometimes forget that you would like to be helping and protecting him, too."

"I suppose I shall have to remind him, then," Georgiana said with a small smile. "I may well have my chance now, for this letter is from my Aunt Catherine de Bourgh, and Lord knows my brother may need some protection from her."

Elizabeth laughed. "From your aunt? Whatever do you mean?"

Georgiana smiled a little grimly. "My aunt has wanted Fitzwilliam to marry her daughter Anne almost since the day she was born. She is really almost irrational on the subject."

"And your brother does not wish to marry her?" Elizabeth inquired, with what she told herself was idle curiosity.

"No, indeed, for while Anne is a good sort in her way, she is not in the least what Fitzwilliam would like in a wife. I am afraid she is sickly and pale, and due to her health, she has never been able to gain any accomplishments."

"I suppose Mr Darcy would be the sort to want an accomplished wife," Elizabeth said with a chuckle.

"Oh, no — not so very accomplished, I mean. But I do not believe he would consider any woman who did not wish to improve her mind through reading, and for my part, I do not think he would be happy unless his wife had a rather lively, happy sort of mind. My brother sometimes wants a little cheering up, I think."

"You ought to select a wife for him," Elizabeth replied with a slightly forced laugh, "for I am certain you understand what would make Mr Darcy happy rather better than he does."

Georgiana waved this away. "Be that as it may, my aunt will not listen, no matter how many times Fitzwilliam and Anne say that they will not marry, for Anne does not want him any more than he wants her."

"I wonder that your aunt is so stubborn, for Anne is her heir, is she not? She could surely find a husband with ease, as long as his name need not be Darcy."

Georgiana sighed. "That is Aunt Catherine all over, I am afraid." She slit open her letter and read its contents. "Oh, dear."

"Please, do not leave me in suspense," Elizabeth requested.

"She is coming to town, and she informs me she will stay here, as I cannot possibly use so much space, and she cannot think what Darcy was about, renting this place for me instead of having me join him in his townhouse."

"That is rather rude of her," Elizabeth commented.

Georgiana nodded. "It is a terrible thing to have an indomitable aunt." She continued scanning the letter. "She has a few affairs to settle before leaving — telling her pastor and her neighbours how they ought to manage their affairs, if I know my aunt — but proposes to join me in little more than a week."

"Will you put her off?" Elizabeth inquired.

"I do not think I could. Even rudeness or flat denials cannot deter Aunt Catherine."

"Oh dear, indeed," Elizabeth replied.

Georgiana sighed. "I suppose she cannot force Fitzwilliam to marry Anne or me to go into a convent — or whatever she thinks appropriate for a young widow who did not marry sufficiently high —

and we will simply weather the storm."

"From what you say, I do not believe we have any choice in the matter," Elizabeth replied.

As both women were happy to forget what they could not affect, the conversation quickly turned from Lady Catherine de Bourgh and the difficulties she might represent. Between talking over the ball and their plans for the coming days, then going out on their morning visits, Elizabeth all but forgot that she had a letter of her own.

Chapter Thirty

Mr Darcy was to join them that evening for a small family supper. For once, even Colonel Fitzwilliam would not be present, as he was dining with his father and mother.

Supper passed off pleasantly, between talking over the ball yet again, and exchanging news of their letters from Lady Catherine de Bourgh, for Mr Darcy had also been favoured with a missive from their aunt.

"Do not worry, Georgiana," Mr Darcy instructed her firmly. "If Aunt Catherine is too much, you may send her to me. I will not have her worry you."

Georgiana exchanged a rather speaking glance with Elizabeth, who had all she could well do to restrain her mirth. It did her good to see Georgiana viewing her brother as a mere mortal, rather than something akin to a divine being.

"I thank you, brother," Georgiana said, "but surely you will have all you can do convincing Aunt Catherine that you do not intend to marry Anne, whatever she may have to say about it. Certainly Aunt Catherine will try to arrange my life to her satisfaction, but I fear she may bring still greater determination towards directing yours."

Mr Darcy coughed. "I hope our aunt will be sensible, and accept that there never was such an arrangement."

"I certainly would like it if our aunt were sensible, and accepted that she cannot arrange everything in the world as she might like it," Georgiana said in a thoughtful tone. "I wonder how likely that is to occur?"

Mr Darcy glanced askance at Elizabeth. "You are a terrible influence on my sister, Miss Bennet. She would never have dared to tease me before you came to her."

"I confess it, I am known for inspiring impudence everywhere I go," Elizabeth said lightly. She could not help being rather moved by the sincere gratitude that shone from Mr Darcy's eyes, however reproachful his words might be. It was clear that the elder brother wished his sister to be confident in his love and regard for her, and was more than willing to accept some impudent wit in testimony that it was so.

After supper, as was his custom, Mr Darcy earnestly entreated Georgiana to play the pianoforte. As he wished to listen, Georgiana wished to play, and Elizabeth was happy in their happiness, it was quickly arranged.

It was not until the first concerto was almost complete that Elizabeth remembered her letter. Turning the pages for Georgiana required her to remain in place, but she determined she would read it at the first opportunity. Such an opportunity was sure to arrive before long, for Georgiana was always careful not to overtire her audience, however earnestly Mr Darcy might request her to play and play again, and they were sure to spend a time talking over the newest music together.

When the piece concluded, Mr Darcy and Elizabeth applauded from the heart, for Georgiana's playing was always a joy to hear. Elizabeth then requested that they excuse her.

"I have just recollected that I received a letter at breakfast," Elizabeth explained, "and I should dearly like to know the latest news of my sister."

Georgiana gasped. "That is right — I talked so much over my letter from Aunt Catherine that you had no opportunity to read yours. Of course you must read your letter."

After the appropriate protestations that it was not Georgiana's fault, Elizabeth retrieved the letter and retreated to the desk at the far side of the room to read it, that she might be better prepared to answer it at once.

She had not read many words before she placed the letter gently on the desk in shock. It seemed impossible — it must be impossible.

Yet it must be so, for Mary would never joke about such a matter. Indeed, she had never known Mary to joke at all.

—

Lyme, January 17, 1816
My dear sister Elizabeth,

I have such news for you — such news I never could have imagined I would have to relate. But I am afraid I may be alarming you. What I have to relate is joyful news. Indeed, I am well, and all the world is more wonderful than I ever thought it could be.

What I have to tell relates to the Admiral. I did not dare to say before how much I really like and admire the man. After all, who could have thought that he would ever return my feelings? I am only Mary Bennet, after all, with neither dowry nor looks to recommend me.

Elizabeth, I am delighted to say that Admiral Pellew requires none of these. He has proposed to me, and I have accepted. He loves me, Lizzy — he says he believes he fell in love with me the first time he heard me playing Bach on the pianoforte. The first banns will be read this Sunday, and the wedding will take place in Lyme four weeks hence. I have written to our aunt and uncle Gardiner to ask that they may come if they are able. I do not expect that you could leave your work, but naturally you would be welcome if I am wrong.

Your work relates to the other thing I wish to tell you. My dear Admiral suggested that if any of my sisters wished to live with us, they would be welcome. Unfortunately, we will sometimes have little room in shipboard quarters, and I cannot invite more than one. I will not make the invitation to Kitty and Lydia, for I do not think I could check them in the mischief they would be sure to seek out. But if you are not happy in your place, Lizzy, you have only to write to me. The Admiral and I are coming to London soon, to stay a little time before he is sent on his next mission, and I with him. Though we would be travelling all about and often aboard ship, John assures me that there would be room enough for one more, and you would be very welcome. I would see to it that you have a comfortable home and as much opportunity to mix in society as I can arrange.

You need not decide at once, Lizzy. Though I would gladly take Jane if she wished, I rather suspect the little Gardiners could not spare her.

With joyful and loving regards,
Your sister, Mary Bennet

—

At first, Elizabeth's surprise was too great even to allow joy. Of all her sisters, she had worried most about Mary. Lydia and Kitty were safe with their mother, at least for the moment, Jane with their aunt and uncle, and Elizabeth felt so well-settled in her place with Georgiana that her worry for herself had all but subsided. Mary alone had remained uncertain, and whenever Elizabeth recalled her evident admiration of the mysterious Admiral, and thought of how unlikely a chance it was that he would return her regard, she had the gravest fears.

But all was well, all was safe. Elizabeth had never been so grateful to be wrong in her life. Admiral Pellew would make Mary happy. Indeed, the cheerful tone of her letter showed he was already making her happy, for Elizabeth had never imagined receiving so light and joyous a letter from her staid, sometimes over-serious sister. It was a blessing unlooked for, but deeply appreciated.

"I do not wish to pry, Elizabeth," Georgiana remarked from across the room, "but I am becoming dreadfully curious about your letter, for your face has really been a study. Now, you must tell me to mind my own business if it is anything private, but if it is possible to satisfy my curiosity, I should greatly enjoy it."

Elizabeth smiled at her employer, for she had not the least hesitation in sharing such good news, and it was delightful to observe how much freer and more open Georgiana had become over the course of their acquaintance.

"No, I do not mind," Elizabeth said. "It is a letter from my sister, Mary. I believe I have spoken to you of her before. She lives in Lyme with the Calder family and is governess to their two children."

"Yes, I recollect her well," Georgiana agreed. "And there is good news?"

"Very good news indeed. In a previous letter, Mary told me of a guest to the house, a certain Admiral John Pellew of the White. I thought even then that she had the beginnings of a *tendré* for him, though I must own I did not think a man so situated would consider marrying a mere governess. But I am happy to say I was entirely wrong. The first banns will be read this Sunday, and they are to be wed four weeks hence." Elizabeth laughed a little and held out the letter to Georgiana. "You may read it if you like, for my sister is delightful in her happiness, and I am sure she would not object."

"Oh, yes," Georgiana agreed, and took it. She scanned the lines rapidly, and her face fell, though she attempted to recover the cheerful expression she had only moments before. "Elizabeth, your sister has offered you a home. You need not work anymore, if you do not wish it."

Elizabeth took her friend's hand and squeezed it tightly. "But I do wish it. It is kind of Mary to offer me a place, but I have greatly enjoyed being your companion — I hope it is not too bold of me to say, being your friend — and I should like to stay longer. Only if you wish it, of course."

"I do indeed," Georgiana said eagerly. "I hope you will stay a great deal longer. As my companion... and as my friend. Now that I need have no fear of losing you, I may feel twice as much joy for your sister!"

Elizabeth laughed. "I am glad to hear it."

With that, the two young women began to talk and surmise over the wedding, deciding on a basis of no facts whatsoever what sort of bouquet the bride might carry, whether Mary would wear one of her old dresses or have a new one, and what the Admiral might look like. Mr Darcy looked on without attempting to join a conversation. He was glad of the opportunity to lose himself in his own thoughts.

Admiral Pellew was known to him as a man of great fortune and reputation, one who had already come far and was likely to go farther still. And he was to marry a younger Miss Bennet, one with little more than hard work and some skill at the piano to recommend her. He had ignored all the dictates of society, passed over all the young ladies of better birth and greater fortune that had no doubt been presented to him, to make a choice that would please no one but himself and the lady in question.

Mr Darcy knew he ought to feel concern for the man, or perhaps a little amused contempt, but he was afraid that his feelings might better bear the name of envy.

Chapter Thirty-one

By February, all the gaieties of the London season seemed a little tired and threadbare. Nobody seemed to want anything but the blossoms and green leaves of spring, and these were not yet to be had.

"I think I feel the February doldrums even more than I did in the country," Elizabeth remarked to Georgiana one day. "Oh, we were dull enough in Hertfordshire, to be sure, particularly when it had been a little long since the last assembly. Yet one still saw more of nature, even of a rather grey and tired nature, and I believe this makes winter in London even more wearying."

"I think you have the right of it," Georgiana said slowly. She closed her eyes a moment, remembering. "I do not think winter seems longer in London than it did in Edinburgh. They are, after all, both great cities. But when I try to think back to winter at Pemberley, I do think it was easier when I might look out and see our woods, even if the branches were bare."

"Perhaps we might walk in Hyde Park one day, if the weather permits it," Elizabeth suggested.

"The weather will be the troublesome part," Georgiana said with a smile. "I do not think we have had a day without rain for the past week."

"We shall not plan, then, but perhaps we may hope."

Their hopes proved to be more effective than hopes typically are, for they were favoured with unusually clear and clement weather only a few days later. Neither had forgotten the conversation, and so it was that Georgiana and Elizabeth dressed for a winter's walk and set out in the carriage with hardly any discussion at all.

It would have been folly to walk on the grass, for the ground must have been half mud. Yet there were so many well-gravelled paths and dry walkways that it did not much matter, and Georgiana and Elizabeth were not five steps away from the carriage before they felt they were enjoying their outing prodigiously. Half of London seemed to have had the same idea. Mr Bingley was escorting his sister along the paths, and they walked and talked together for a full quarter of an hour. Caroline Bingley then made an excuse that she had seen an acquaintance to whom she desperately needed to speak across the park, but Elizabeth thought wryly that she was leaving because Mr Darcy was not with them.

Elizabeth had hardly had the thought before

she saw Mr Darcy himself, standing and talking with his cousin. It would have been hard to miss them, for they were both uncommonly tall, well-dressed men. Mr Darcy had the handsomer face, to be sure, but Colonel Fitzwilliam would have cut a fine figure on any ballroom floor.

She touched Georgiana's sleeve. "Look there. It is your brother and your cousin."

"So it is," Georgiana said happily. "Let us go to them."

The men noticed them before they had covered half the distance and came to meet them.

"Well met, cousin," Colonel Fitzwilliam greeted them. "Good day, Mrs Smith. As always, it is a pleasure to meet you."

"Likewise," Elizabeth replied, smiling warmly at him. The Colonel was one of the most charming men of her acquaintance, and his society was always enjoyable. "Good afternoon, Mr Darcy."

He smiled at her, a sudden flashing smile that left her taken aback at how it transformed his face, normally so stern. "Good afternoon, Mrs Smith. Georgiana, how delightful to see you." She smiled at him in reply, a smile that twisted Elizabeth's heart in how much it resembled her brother's. The two Darcy siblings, both so shy and so kind, so quick-witted, yet sometimes strangely diffident. Georgiana with her astonishing talent on the pianoforte, and Mr Darcy, one of the most intelligent men she had ever known. Elizabeth did not think she could ever bear to part with either of them.

"Do I understand correctly that our aunt is coming to visit?" Colonel Fitzwilliam was asking Georgiana.

"I am afraid so — I mean, yes, indeed, that is correct. We shall have the pleasure," Georgiana replied, stumbling a little over her words.

Thankfully, Colonel Fitzwilliam only laughed. "I cannot fault you for that, Georgiana. I too have little taste for being taken to task and told exactly what I ought and ought not to do. Our relation is not an easy visitor. Shall we take the path along the stream?"

This suggestion was taken up at once. The gravelled path to which Colonel Fitzwilliam led them was remarkably dry, considering the season and the recent rains, and uncommonly charming for its near views of the little brook. Elizabeth delighted in its music, formed as the water rushed and gurgled over stones and around logs. The whole party stayed some minutes at the peak of a bridge over the stream, watching the water flow by. It was as grey as the winter skies overhead, but remarkably beautiful. At last, Georgiana confessed to the beginnings of a chill, and they walked on.

"I grow more curious to meet Lady Catherine de Bourgh every day," Elizabeth remarked to Mr Darcy. They fell into step together, trailing a little behind Georgiana and Colonel Fitzwilliam. Elizabeth smiled to see silver-scaled fish flashing through the creek. How delightful it would be to swim through such clear water, like flying.

"My aunt is an excellent woman in her way," Mr Darcy remarked, "but I am afraid she sometimes speaks when she ought to listen."

Elizabeth laughed. "It is a common failing, to be sure. I think that half of everyone one meets shares it, and certainly I do myself."

"No — that is not so," Mr Darcy contradicted her. "It is a common failing, but you do not share it. I have never known anyone who listens the way you do."

He had spoken with uncommon feeling. Elizabeth stayed silent a moment, feeling the compliment of the words. "I thank you," she said at last. "I have long found a value for listening — truly listening, I mean, listening with care. But not everyone troubles themselves to notice it."

"I could not do otherwise," Mr Darcy said earnestly. "Our conversations have been too precious to me. You have shown me too much to ignore, both in your listening and in your speaking. And even were it not for this, I could not thank you enough for what you have done for Georgiana."

Surprised that he would speak of it with her so near, Elizabeth looked to her employer. She and Colonel Fitzwilliam had now outdistanced them by a considerable margin, and were laughing and talking cheerfully together. Mr Darcy had not misjudged. As long as they did not raise their voices, there was no danger of their conversation being overheard.

"Georgiana has done more for me than I for her," Elizabeth therefore said. "I could not have hoped for a better employer, or, indeed, for a better friend."

"I am glad indeed of your friendship, for it is through this that you have helped my sister. She has been so happy in your company. I had never known her to jest with me, even before her unhappy elopement. She was very serious and shy as a child."

Elizabeth smiled. "Perhaps I ought to apologise, then, if I have taught your little sister to make a mockery of you."

"Never," Mr Darcy vowed. "I have little care for my dignity, not when such jests show me my sister smiling again. I have rarely been more grateful for anything."

"I am sure you give me too much credit," Elizabeth protested. "Surely I do not have the power to raise anybody's spirits, at least not more than for a moment. Anyone might do as much with a witty answer or a friendly word."

"You are mistaken," Mr Darcy told her. "I know that you have the power to show a person that the world is a beautiful place, for all its flaws, for you have done the same for me."

Elizabeth looked at him, astonished. There had been a depth of feeling in his voice that made it impossible to protest further. His naked honesty demanded an equal return.

"It is strange to hear from you," she said slowly, "for it is weeks now since I have thought of you as one of the most insightful men of my acquaintance, and the kindest."

The compliment touched him to the heart — that much was apparent at a glance. He turned almost white, as though it had been a deadly insult rather than the dearest truth of her heart, and did not speak for a little time. There was joy in his face, and yearning, but it was not untouched by pain.

"I thank you," he said, his voice low. "With all my heart."

They walked on through the crisp February air, warmed by the weak sunlight. There was not so much as a crocus blooming; not yet the least promise of spring. By and by, they talked of lighter things, of literature and the spring visit to Pemberley, but Elizabeth felt almost dizzy with the weight of what had passed between them. She reminded herself that they had spoken no words of love. He certainly had made her no proposal, no promises.

Even so, everything had changed in an instant, for she could no longer deny that there was something between them. And nor, she thought, could he.

Chapter Thirty-two

It was growing late one evening when the rattle of a carriage was heard outside the window. On the streets of London, this was no uncommon occurrence, but to hear the wheels slowing to a stop outside the townhouse doors was an event of more note.

"Perhaps it is my brother, arriving for an evening visit. He knows I do not stand on ceremony with him," Georgiana remarked hopefully.

"Perhaps," Elizabeth said. "Or perhaps it is your aunt, arrived a little earlier than expected. Would it be like her?"

"Indeed, it would," Georgiana admitted reluctantly. "She likes to keep people on their toes."

In the wake of that alarming information, Elizabeth moved to the window and looked out. "It is not Mr Darcy, for I do not recognise the carriage," she reported. "It is large, rather fine, done up in shades of navy and dark wood."

"That is Aunt Catherine," Georgiana said

a little grimly. Elizabeth looked at her with a reassuring smile, for it would do Georgiana no good at all to behave as though she were a child that an older relative might scold and chide into better behaviour.

It was not long before the lady swept into the room with an imperious air. "Lady Catherine de Bourgh," was the butler's announcement.

"Very well, very well," Lady Catherine told him, "I am sure my niece has not forgotten who I am, and mind you do not forget to tell the stableboy my horses are to be rubbed down well, and he is not to omit checking their hooves!"

Elizabeth was astonished to hear a lady concern herself with such minutiae, not to mention by Lady Catherine's brash manner of expressing herself. She quickly schooled her expression as the lady turned to them.

"Aunt Catherine, please allow me to present my companion, Mrs Smith," Georgiana said a little faintly. "Mrs Smith, this is my aunt, Lady Catherine de Bourgh."

"It is a pleasure to meet you, Lady Catherine," Elizabeth said.

"Likewise, I am sure," Lady Catherine returned with a somewhat dubious gaze. "You are full young to be a companion to my niece."

Georgiana looked horrified at this early evidence of Lady Catherine's disapprobation.

Elizabeth said smoothly, "Indeed I am, Lady Catherine, but perhaps there may be some benefits to my age, as well as disadvantages. As two young women, Mrs Wickham and I may have thoughts and experiences in common, which perhaps a companion of greater age could not share with her in the same manner."

"I suppose that is so," Lady Catherine allowed, with an air of shelving the matter only for the moment. "Now then, I am tired, and I should like to be shown to my rooms."

"Of course, Aunt," Georgiana said quickly, and rang for the housekeeper. Lady Catherine was shown to the best guest chamber without delay, though her voice lingered a little way behind her, instructing the housekeeper as to the arrangement of her luggage, and commenting on the narrowness of the stairs and Mr Darcy's folly in letting such a house, and for that matter, letting a house for his sister at all.

When the last hints of her voice had faded away, Georgiana dropped heavily into a chair with a sigh. "Elizabeth, if you must leave me to go to your sister, please, do not leave me now."

Elizabeth sat next to her and chuckled. "I must admit, it does appear that you are in need of reinforcements. Will she try to arrange your life as much as she is attempting to direct your household, do you think?"

"More so," Georgiana said with grim certainty.

"She will want me married off as quickly as possible to a gentleman as staid, well-connected, and rich as possible. And ideally one rather older than myself, for she has informed me in her letters that I 'want a steadying influence'."

"Oh dear," Elizabeth said faintly. "She would think of remarriage so soon? You are still in half-mourning."

"She informs me it is the only way to ensure everyone will forget the disgrace of my first marriage, and thus repair the harm I did to our family's reputation." Georgiana's voice was as hard as iron.

Elizabeth laid a hand lightly on her arm. "Do not listen to her, my friend. And try not to fret so much. She cannot force you to marry."

"No, but she can try," Georgiana said.

"Much good may trying do, when you have your brother on your side," Elizabeth told her. "Mr Darcy would not have you marry one instant before you truly wish to. I am certain of it."

At that, Georgiana seemed to ease a little, and heaved a quiet little sigh of relief. "You are right. If she importunes me too much, Fitzwilliam will tell her to stop."

Elizabeth looked away. The trust and confidence in Georgiana's voice was too much. It reminded Elizabeth too woundingly of all she had once felt for her father — and all the trust and confidence she too was coming to feel for the gentleman in question.

—

As was his frequent custom, that gentleman waited on them in the morning hours the next day. Colonel Fitzwilliam came with him. It was evident that the two were true gentlemen, for there was no other explanation for the dedication with which they drew their aunt's fire to give Georgiana and Elizabeth some respite.

"Mrs Smith, I hope you do not attempt to advise my niece," Lady Catherine de Bourgh said severely. "I cannot abide persons who are always officious and attempting to influence others, and though you are somewhat the elder, you must remember that you are a companion, not a governess."

"Naturally, Lady Catherine," Elizabeth replied sweetly. "I should not dream of it. I am quite of your mind that people who try to run other's lives for them rarely do any good, and often much harm."

Thankfully, Lady Catherine did not understand the full meaning of these words. As she was drawing breath to go on, Colonel Fitzwilliam intervened.

"Tell me, Aunt, how does my cousin Anne? Is she well?"

He had chosen well, for the lady quickly seemed to lose all interest in Elizabeth.

"Anne is very well indeed," she said, "and as my former clergyman Mr Collins told me not long ago, she is blooming like an English rose. Though I am sad to say she still suffers from the megrim, and she is not as strong as I would like."

"I am pleased to hear it," Colonel Fitzwilliam replied, choosing to concentrate on what was positive in his aunt's response and ignore all that was nonsensical and contradictory in it.

"Darcy, I say, Darcy," Lady Catherine called out, instead of responding to him. "You ought to attend to me. I am certain you would like to hear what I have just told Fitzwilliam about Anne."

Mr Darcy, who had been quietly telling Elizabeth about a book he had lately read, gave her a smile of apology and crossed the room without delay. "Yes, certainly, Aunt Catherine. How is my cousin?"

"She is grace and elegance itself, and wants only your presence at Rosings to lend her a little more liveliness," Lady Catherine informed him in a meaningful tone. Even with the evidence of discourtesy that Lady Catherine had already given her, Elizabeth rather wondered that she could hint so shamelessly. But Mr Darcy seemed to find nothing unusual in the exchange.

"Perhaps I might visit you in the early

summer," he replied. "What think you, Fitzwilliam? Would you be inclined to spend a little of the summer in Kent?

"Certainly," he replied. "It is a pleasant time for the countryside around Rosings."

"That is exactly what I say myself," Lady Catherine interjected. "Just as I have always said, there is nowhere half so lovely in summer as Rosings Park."

"You will have to excuse me, Aunt Catherine," Georgiana said, making everyone look at her in surprise. "Indeed, I have fond memories of Rosings, but I must admit that I find summer at Pemberley to be more lovely still."

Mr Darcy looked at his sister with surprise almost as great as his appreciation, for the Georgiana of three years ago would never have dreamed of contradicting their aunt.

"Yes, indeed," he said. "I hope you will forgive us, Aunt Catherine, for thinking that Pemberley is the loveliest of all. It may not be so in point of fact, but it will ever be so in the heart of anybody born a Darcy."

Observing the smile exchanged by the siblings, Elizabeth blinked back tears composed equally of joy and pain. Joy there was most of all, for in that exchange and that smile was all the promise of confidence and sibling love renewed, of a bond perhaps stronger than ever. Yet in the very beauty of the moment, a pain seized her heart. Her home lost; her sisters housed under four different roofs; her father gone forever. For all Elizabeth devoutly considered herself to be a fortunate woman, these were still griefs that would sometimes come upon her as freshly as though they were newly made.

Colonel Fitzwilliam chuckled and joined their rebellion. "I am afraid it is not only those born a Darcy, Aunt Catherine," he said. "I confess I too think Rosings Park all that is lovely, and yet Pemberley lovelier still."

Though Lady Catherine sputtered and protested, she gave way and changed the subject rather sooner than Elizabeth would have guessed. She smiled to herself. It seemed the indomitable Lady Catherine would have to learn to brook disappointment after all.

Chapter Thirty-three

Mr Darcy was perhaps thinking as much of his sister's relief as his aunt's enjoyment when he arranged a little supper party not long after her arrival. His invitation to Mr Bingley was couched in terms more honest than appealing.

"I should be heartily glad if you could attend," Mr Darcy said frankly as they rode early one morning. "My aunt can be rather...forthright, shall we say, and I think my sister and Mrs Smith would benefit from an evening of more varied company. But I shall not attempt to convince you it will be a pleasant evening, for I have not known evenings in Lady Catherine's presence to often be so."

"I shall attend no less out of curiosity than the desire to oblige you," Mr Bingley said with a laugh. "I have always wanted to see a dragon."

"Your wish shall certainly be granted," Mr Darcy said. "I only hope you enjoy the experience as much as you might suppose."

Mr Bingley chuckled. "I am sure I shall enjoy an evening in your company, my friend. Do you intend to extend the invitation to Caroline as well?"

"I had thought to. And the Hursts as well. They are staying with you still, are they not?"

"Yes, indeed," Mr Bingley said. "I believe they shall stay all the rest of the season."

Not for the first time, Mr Darcy marvelled at his friend's patience and good temper. Ever since his sister had married Mr Hurst, a man of much fashion but little fortune, they had lived with Bingley more often than in any home of their own. Mr Bingley did not seem to object, merely remarking from time to time how pleasant it was that Caroline should still have the company of her sister, and he should benefit from the society of both his siblings. Mr Darcy had sometimes wished his friend's complacency a little less, at least where his sisters were concerned. Miss Caroline Bingley had made no secret of her enthusiasm for her brother's friend — or, at least, for her brother's friend's fortune and his estate.

The match was not entirely an unreasonable one. For all the late Mr Bingley had been in trade, he had left his daughter with so generous a dowry and so refined an education that she was reaching only a little above herself. It mattered not, for the lady was so ill a fit for him, it was a wonder she had not seen it for herself. If Caroline Bingley had spent so much as a moment attempting to truly understand his character, rather than merely offering fulsome compliments and empty adoration, she would have known that not all their mutual fortune could have ever made them happy together.

Nonetheless, Bingley enjoyed having his sisters included in such invitations, and it was little enough to grant his friend.

"I shall include you all, then," Mr Darcy said lightly. "Shall we gallop?"

As they had just come to a rather tempting path, fringed by trees on both sides and with a good line of sight that rendered the suggestion not too dangerous, Mr Bingley readily agreed, and the two men urged their horses into a gallop, enjoying a morning's exercise under the weak winter sun.

—

Mr Darcy was as good as his word. The invitations were written and in the post that same day, as soon as he had returned from his ride, had his bath, and found the time to write them. Showing the efficiency of the English postal service, it was not long before the letters had been carried across London and delivered to their various recipients.

"What do you have there, Georgiana? Show me at once," Lady Catherine commanded peremptorily.

Elizabeth was shocked and appalled at the lady's rudeness, but her employer did not seem struck by it.

"It is an invitation from my brother, aunt. He asks us all to dine with him," Georgiana said mildly.

"Very well, then. That is fine. That is the gentlemanly behaviour I would expect of him. Let me see it. Few young men know how to write an invitation these days," Lady Catherine said.

Georgiana gave her the letter without making any objection. Lady Catherine pounced on it and looked it over rather as though she were a schoolmaster and Mr Darcy, her star pupil.

"Good handwriting — quite out of the common way. The phrasing is well done, and the invitation is well thought of. Yes, my nephew certainly is one of the few who does things properly." Lady Catherine said, with a sniff.

Elizabeth turned away to hide her smile. Lady Catherine seemed to enjoy first proposing the existence of a problem and then discovering the removal of it, but for her part, she thought it would be rather simpler to avoid inventing the problem in the first place.

"You must send your acceptance at once," Lady Catherine told Georgiana.

"Yes, aunt, I think so as well," Georgiana agreed calmly.

Lady Catherine turned to Elizabeth. "I suppose you shall be glad to have an evening free, Mrs Smith."

"I have generally gone with Mrs Wickham to such events," Elizabeth replied. "A companion may be particularly welcome at such a time, ma'am. One may then have the amusement of recounting the evening once one is home again with a friend who has shared in all that passed. I remember well that for my sisters and I, half the fun of a ball or a supper out was always to be found in talking it over afterward."

Lady Catherine's expression grew increasingly stormy as this little speech progressed. "You are very young, Mrs Smith, and perhaps you are not familiar with the way things are done in fine families," she said in cutting tones. "I beg you do not take advantage of my niece and nephew. You must not be grasping, nor putting yourself in where you are not wanted."

For a moment, Elizabeth was too insulted to speak. Worse still, the comment had been nearly as insulting to Georgiana as it was to Elizabeth herself, for it made it clear that Lady Catherine saw her niece as a child and an incompetent.

"No, Lady Catherine," Elizabeth said at last. "I certainly shall not do so. Mrs Wickham has been a splendid employer to me. I shall be glad to go anywhere she asks me to go and stay any time she wishes me to stay."

Georgiana gave her a look of gratitude. "I wish you to come to supper, Elizabeth. Indeed, you must, for I know my brother greatly enjoys conversing with you."

"Then it is settled," Elizabeth replied, "and I

beg you would excuse me a moment, for this has reminded me I owe more than one of my sisters a letter of my own."

"Naturally," Georgiana replied.

With a bow to her employer and to Lady Catherine, Elizabeth left the room. As she closed the door behind her, she could hear Lady Catherine's querulous voice beginning to lecture Georgiana on the impropriety and danger of addressing her paid companion by her first name.

—

By the time the supper arrived, almost everyone invited had begun to look forward to it with no common degree of anticipation. Mr Bingley was the sole exception, for, while he was always glad to keep company with his dearest friend and enjoy pleasant society, he had no shortage of opportunities to do either. Caroline Bingley anticipated the supper as a chance to recommend herself to Mr Darcy, while Mrs Hurst intended to assist her, and Mr Hurst looked forward to enjoying the work of Mr Darcy's French chef. Georgiana's two guardians had not yet lost a sense of joyful wonder at having regained her in their family circle. Lady Catherine de Bourgh could never find any society as pleasing as that of her nephews, nor would she miss any opportunity to further her daughter's suit. Elizabeth and Georgiana were simply grateful for the opportunity to share their difficult guest's conversation with a rather larger circle.

Though Georgiana and Elizabeth were dressed and waiting in the drawing room a quarter of an hour before the carriage was to be called, Lady Catherine found it necessary to lecture them both on the solemn importance of punctuality.

"Punctuality is the politeness of princes," Lady Catherine said. "Mind you, Georgiana, there is nothing more rude than to arrive late to an engagement. I cannot abide people who have no mind to the comfort and convenience of others, but simply do what they like with no regard for the inconvenience they may cause."

"That is quite right, Lady Catherine," Elizabeth commented. "You pay your niece a kind compliment, for as you see, she is dressed and ready to step into the carriage. Mrs Wickham is the soul of punctuality."

Lady Catherine wished to disagree with this, but knew not how. In the end, she settled for lecturing them on how conversation ought to flow at a supper party and how best to put others at their ease until the carriage arrived at the front door to take them to supper.

Despite their punctuality, they were not the first to arrive, for it transpired that Colonel Fitzwilliam had spent the whole of the day with his cousin. With kind courtesy, he whisked Lady

Catherine away to a comfortable chair in the corner of the room, earnestly entreating her for her advice on a question of tenantry that had lately come before the earl.

"I hope you have both spent the day pleasantly," Mr Darcy said to Georgiana, leading the two younger ladies a little apart from his aunt.

"Very pleasantly indeed," Georgiana replied. "I have been learning a new piece on the pianoforte, quite fiendishly difficult. It is extremely diverting. The arpeggios alone..." She laughed. "I suppose I should say that *I* have had an extremely pleasant day, for it would not be surprising in the least if Mrs Smith had grown rather tired of my playing."

"No, certainly not," Elizabeth reassured her. "And you were so good to play 'Sleepers, Awake' when I happened to think of it and longed to hear it again. It is a particular favourite of mine."

"No wonder, it is so lovely," Georgiana told her. She turned to her brother. "Do you still care for Bach, Fitzwilliam?"

"Indeed, I do," he said. "I have not forgotten how you used to play the Goldberg Variations. They were always a particular favourite of mine, and you the pianist I should prefer to hear above all others."

Georgiana coloured a little at the compliment. "You are too good to me, brother."

Lady Catherine de Bourgh must have caught something of this, for she called across the room,

"Pray tell, of what are you speaking? Is Mr Darcy giving in to some indulgence? It is the worst of having given charge of a child to so young a man. They are forever after saying yes when they ought to say no."

All her audience felt the injustice and the oddity of these remarks, but none could think of any way to refute them that would not lead to still greater awkwardness. At last, Colonel Fitzwilliam said a meaningless, "Yes, perhaps so, Aunt Catherine. I suppose there is something to what you are saying," and led the conversation another way. It was a profound relief when the butler entered to announce the arrival of the Bingleys and the Hursts.

After they had exchanged their formal bows, the party broke up into little knots of conversation here and there. From her position with Georgiana and Mr Bingley, Elizabeth could not help having her attention drawn a little elsewhere. She was watching Lady Catherine de Bourgh watching Caroline Bingley. That lady was certainly being a little assiduous in her attentions to Mr Darcy, but there was nothing unusual in that. They were never in company together without her making it known to all that his house was the best in all London, his person all that any gentleman could aspire to, and his opinions the last word on every subject. Elizabeth thought wryly that it was good her own first opinions of the gentleman had proven so entirely wrong. If he were the self-centred, arrogant coxcomb she had first thought him, so much praise surely would have puffed up his head with vanity until he floated away entirely.

It was strange that Caroline Bingley wished to marry him without understanding him in the least. The Mr Darcy Elizabeth had come to know, the quiet man with a wicked sense of humour, keen intelligence, and a measured judgement, had no interest in such empty compliments. Elizabeth could so easily picture the words that would move him. They would be simple, but from the heart. For such a man, words sincerely felt are everything.

Elizabeth shook herself out of her reverie and chided herself for being absurd. It would be much better to attend to what was transpiring around her. Lady Catherine de Bourgh seemed to view Caroline Bingley with, if anything, a still more critical eye than she did Elizabeth. Thankfully, supper was called before the lady could make any more shattering pronouncements.

Supper was superb, to no one's surprise. Each remove offered to them was light and pleasing to the palate, balanced expertly between luxury and restraint. Elizabeth breathed a little easier, enjoying the company of good friends and forgetting all that was uncomfortable in the meeting. Mr Darcy was seated at one head of the table. Lady Catherine de Bourgh was seated at the other, which served both to honour her rank and to insulate her from Georgiana as much as possible. Knowing Mr Darcy for a caring brother, Elizabeth was certain he had done it intentionally. After all, he was not wrong. Lady Catherine was a rather tiring house guest.

With Georgiana seated at his right hand, Mr Darcy could talk to her of spring at Pemberley and their plans for the visit to his heart's content. Caroline Bingley, seated a little further down the table, chimed in often to praise the estate and the whole county of Derbyshire to the skies.

Unfortunately for that lady, her renewed praises had not escaped the attention of Lady Catherine de Bourgh. She seemed to grow increasingly offended as she observed Miss Bingley's extravagant flirtations and Mr Darcy's acceptance of them, even though it was an acceptance offered, as far as Elizabeth could see, without the least encouragement. As the meal progressed, the lady's face darkened, but she held her tongue.

Like all good things, it could not last forever. The pudding course was before them, half eaten, when his aunt at last lost her patience. "Mr Darcy," Lady Catherine called out.

Mr Darcy had entirely forgotten Lady Catherine for a time, being occupied with Georgiana and Elizabeth's amusing tale of learning to play a four-handed piece on the pianoforte together. He looked at his aunt with rather the air of having been caught out. "Yes, Lady Catherine?"

"We have not yet heard from you on the subject. Pray tell us your thoughts on marriages across lines of class. Can they ever truly be for the good of those involved, do you think?"

Though Lady Catherine was undoubtedly thinking of Caroline Bingley, well-dowered but still daughter to a man who had made his fortune by trade, Mr Darcy's thoughts were elsewhere. "It is a subject on which much care ought to be taken, to be sure," he replied. His own thoughts on the subject were such a muddle of hope and caution, duty and desire, that he did not think he ought to be answerable for them. To state publicly what he had not yet fully understood for himself seemed an impossibility.

"True, very true," Lady Catherine approved. Though Mr Darcy hoped this could bring an end to the matter, he was doomed to disappointment.

His aunt went on. "But what about you yourself, my dear nephew? Would you ever consider proposing to a woman of means and connection decidedly below your own?"

Though Lady Catherine spoke these words with a gimlet eye on Caroline Bingley, as though to be certain she did not miss the import of the conversation, Mr Darcy did not notice. His thoughts were all for Elizabeth.

She had become a true friend to him, as dear as Bingley or even Georgiana. Her eyes, her wit, the lightness of her step — all were entrancing to him. For some time now, it had been impossible to picture any woman as his future wife, if she were not a brunette of great compassion and intelligence, sparkling eyes and quick wit, a bright spirit despite all she had suffered. If she were not, in fact, Elizabeth.

Yet that his heart was already given changed nothing. He had responsibilities that were weightier than any desire could be. There was Georgiana to think of. To marry her paid companion would make a scandal and a mockery of her. In the eyes of the *ton*, her reputation could be badly damaged, linked to a story that was only a hair's breadth from a scandal.

In the end, Mr Darcy supposed it was as simple as that. To propose to Elizabeth would hurt Georgiana. Therefore, he could never do it.

"No, I certainly never would," Mr Darcy replied at last. "I hold it to be every man's first responsibility in selecting a wife, that she be no one who might prove an unpleasant connection to his family, or who might lower them in the eyes of the world. Respect there must be, and mutual admiration, but these are secondary qualities that may be searched for only after the first test has been passed."

Lady Catherine looked satisfied with this answer, as well she might. Her expression soured a little, however, in the wake of Caroline Bingley's quick commendation of Darcy's speech. It was obvious that whatever Lady Catherine might think, Miss Bingley considered a wealthy and well-educated woman such as herself to be entirely suited as Mr Darcy's wife. Mr Bingley was protesting a little, and saying that surely love and respect ought to outweigh even the importance of good connections, but Mr Darcy hardly heard him.

He had met Elizabeth's eyes and could not look away. By one person in the room, at least, his true message had been received. The soft curve of her lips and the pain in her eyes made that much clear, for the mix of joy and pain in her expression showed she had understood it all. She had heard his confession of respect and admiration — put its true name to it: of love — and she had also heard his declaration that marriage between them was impossible.

Chapter Thirty-four

The last days of Lady Catherine's visit were rather quiet. Lady Catherine was occupied with planning her journey back to Kent and giving Georgiana all the last pieces of advice she considered so essential. It left her little time or attention to spend on correcting and guiding her niece's companion, a blessing for which Elizabeth was decidedly grateful. At a time when her spirit was sunk with pain, it would have been almost too much to bear.

In an instant, she had learned that what she most hoped was true — and so was what she most feared. Mr Darcy felt for her that combination of friendship and regard that most promised lasting felicity. He felt the same connection, the same attraction that she did. It was all quite real.

Elizabeth almost wished it had not been, or that he did not have the firm resolve that was such an essential part of his character. He had made up his mind. It was done, and only misery could come from attempting to undo it. If he were not willing to look below himself for a wife, even to secure the blessings of mutual admiration and respect, it was not within her powers to convince him otherwise.

Yet knowing there was little to be done about it did not make it easier for Elizabeth to regain the composure of her spirits. It seemed impossible that she could ever come to feel tolerable acceptance of such a circumstance. If he had not loved her, it would have been quite different. She would have quickly learned to accept it, and in time, regained her heart. But to know him anything but indifferent, to meet each week in London and almost every hour when the time came to visit Pemberley — it seemed to her impossible to endure.

When they had seen Lady Catherine handed in to her carriage, both young ladies breathed a sigh of relief. There are few things more wearing than a constantly critical observer, and Lady Catherine was one still more tiring than many, as being unusually willing to speak her mind whether or not anyone would benefit from hearing it.

"I think I should like to rest in my room a little," Georgiana murmured. "And you?"

Elizabeth breathed a sigh of relief. "I shall do the same."

Though she had no intention of sleeping, Elizabeth truly was relieved to spend a little time in the quiet of her room. Her thoughts had grown badly tangled of late, and however painful the results might be, it was time to untangle them.

The crux of the matter: was it wise, was it even right to remain so often in the society of Mr Darcy?

Elizabeth had no fears for her reputation or her virtue. She had too much confidence in both her own morals and in Mr Darcy's for that. Her fears were all for peace of mind, both his and hers. If the decision had been made, if it was a settled thing that two who loved each other would never be together, then it would surely be the wiser course for them to part. They might then begin to regain their equilibrium. Mr Darcy would one day marry, and Elizabeth only hoped he would find a woman truly suited to his spirit, rather than an Anne de Bourgh or Caroline Bingley suited only to his family's convenience or the conventions of society. And though Elizabeth would lose her post and her dear friendship with Georgiana by such an action, she would at least know herself to be acting with all prudent care.

To lose Georgiana and Mr Darcy at a stroke — even imagining it caused a deep pain in her heart. She, the friend and employer who had become another sister to her. He, the only man she had ever loved. Every choice seemed equally impossible, unendurable.

At last, Elizabeth came to a decision.

She left her room to seek out her employer. Though Georgiana was no longer in her bedchamber, it was the work of moments to find her. It was rarely difficult to find Georgiana in the few times they were apart. One simply went to the pianoforte. Elizabeth waited until Georgiana reached the end of the piece and turned on the bench to face her.

"Elizabeth!" Georgiana exclaimed happily. "I did not hear you come in. I have almost captured the timing in the second movement. Another week of practicing, and I will have it."

Elizabeth smiled weakly. "I must admit that I am a little distracted. Listening simply from enjoyment and without an eye for potential improvement, I did not notice anything wanting."

Georgiana gave her a warm smile. "I thank you. But you look as though you have come seeking me. I have not forgotten anything, have I? Are we late for an appointment?"

"No, nothing like that," Elizabeth reassured her. "But I do need to speak to you."

Georgiana's face fell. "This sounds rather serious," she said softly. "Shall we go into the drawing room?"

Elizabeth nodded and followed her there. There was a brief silence, made all the more difficult to break by Georgiana's look of half-fearful anticipation.

"I suppose I must begin," Elizabeth said heavily at last. "I have so greatly enjoyed being your companion, Georgiana. I had not thought that

I would find a position half so pleasant — still less that I might find a true friend. But I have thought more about the offer my sister Mary made to me, and I have decided to take it. I must therefore give you my notice."

Georgiana drew in a quick breath. "Will you not tell me why?" she asked. "We have had such a pleasant time together. I shall miss you terribly. Of course, you need not have any reason in the world, but I should like to know why you changed your mind."

Elizabeth hardly knew what to say to this. The truth could only cause more pain, and in any case, she felt she could not bear to speak it. Yet surely Georgiana deserved a reason for this sudden desertion.

"It is not your fault — it is nothing you have done," Elizabeth said at last. "I have been very happy here. But I must look to my future, and I believe that after all, I shall do better to live with Mary and the Admiral."

"It is because of my brother, is it not?" Georgiana asked gently. She waited for a reply, but Elizabeth had been shocked into silence. "You are leaving because you love each other, and he will not marry you."

Elizabeth felt the tears well up in her eyes. With an effort, she kept her voice level. "I cannot deny it. I will only say I am sorry that I have been so indiscrete. More than this, I have been a fool even to dream of him."

"You have not," Georgiana cried out. "He is far from indifferent to you. I have seen it."

"I do not say you are wrong," Elizabeth replied. "But he has made his choice, and I must make mine. It would be madness for me to go to Pemberley with the two of us feeling this way. I must not do it. Luckily, Mary has given me another choice."

Georgiana was silent for a long moment. "I wish I did not see so much sense in what you have said," she breathed at last. "But I cannot argue with you. As to the notice period, do not think of it. Have the Admiral come for you when suitable, be it soon or late, and stay with me until then. For my part, I shall hope it will not be too soon."

"As shall I," Elizabeth said, looking at her dear friend whom she was soon to leave. A quaver came into her voice, and at last, her tears spilled over. But it was not of much matter, for as soon as she could look up again, Elizabeth saw that Georgiana's eyes were no dryer than her own.

Chapter Thirty-five

After a day of such upheaval, sleep could only be elusive. Elizabeth tossed and turned in body and mind. She could not repine her decision. She had made it with too much care. But neither could she rest in confidence of its being the correct one. She had only chosen prudence and grief over imprudence and the risk of still deeper pain.

At last, her weariness grew until she subsided into sleep. It seemed too little a time until the sunlight through her window and the chimes of the hall clock announced she must rise for breakfast.

Breakfast was a rather quiet affair. Afterward, Elizabeth and Georgiana settled down to a little quiet reading by silent and mutual agreement. Their peace was disturbed by Benson the butler, coming in with a visiting card on a silver tray.

"It is your sister and the Admiral," Georgiana said in surprise. "Shall we invite them up, Elizabeth?"

"Yes, that would be for the best," Elizabeth replied. "I cannot imagine why they have come with so little notice. In Mary's last letter to me, she wrote they had not even left for London yet. I hope there is nothing the matter."

Georgiana instructed Benson to bring in their visitors. He bowed and departed. It was not long before Mary and Admiral Pellew were entering the room and making their formal bows.

Elizabeth liked her new brother-in-law at once. She was sure she would have liked him in any case, for he had a hearty, open, manly aspect and a kind twinkle in his eye. Yet Elizabeth liked him still more for the alteration in Mary's looks and expression. She was blooming with happiness and good health, and her cheeks held roses such as Elizabeth had never seen there before.

"You are looking marvellously well, Mary," Elizabeth observed as soon as the conversation allowed. "I need not ask how marriage agrees with you, for I can see the answer for myself."

"I shall answer all the same," Mary said with a small smile. "It is delightful, quite delightful to have such a companion by one always."

Hearing this, Admiral Pellew beamed in pleasure and lightly squeezed his wife's hand. "I am a lucky man, if I do say so myself," he remarked. "I knew from the first time I heard her play the pianoforte that my dear Mary would change my life, and I am pleased to say she has."

The two were so smiling and confident in each other's love that it almost made Elizabeth forget her own pain in her happiness for them.

"I am glad that you both came to visit me today," she remarked. "I had not expected to see you so soon."

At this, Mary and the Admiral exchanged a significant glance. "In fact, we have a particular reason for coming today," Mary admitted.

Admiral Pellew took up the tale. "I am afraid it is my fault, my dear," he told Elizabeth. "I have received new orders weeks before I had believed it was possible. Mary and I will leave London tomorrow. We cannot delay even a day, for I am being sent for with unusual urgency. You will always be welcome if you wish to make your home with us, sister Elizabeth. But if you wish to do so any time this year, I am afraid it must be now or never."

It took a moment for the full import of the words to sink in. "Oh," Elizabeth said, feeling words to be badly inadequate to her feelings, particularly when the Admiral was only so slightly known to her. "Yes, I see. I am grateful to you for coming to tell me, for indeed I would like to go with you."

"I shall be glad to have your company," Mary said at once.

"Delightful! Delightful! I shall not worry half so much for my Mary whenever I am away, if she has a sister by her side," was Admiral Pellew's response.

Mixed as Elizabeth's emotions were, their enthusiasm could not be otherwise than pleasing.

Yet the thought of leaving so abruptly brought all the pain of the separation before her as fresh as ever.

Elizabeth turned to Georgiana. "I am dreadfully sorry to leave with so little notice," she said.

Georgiana shook her head, a few tears sparkling in her eyes. "Do not think of that. I insist upon it. You are not to give it another moment of worry. I shall miss you terribly in any case, so it does not much signify whether there is much notice or little."

"You are very good," Elizabeth said, her voice low. Before company, she could not say more, and yet it seemed impossibly little for all Georgiana was to her. For a moment, she almost could have wished away her love for Mr Darcy, that it might be possible to stay. But as soon as the thought had entered her head, she knew it for an absurdity. Though that love might be doomed to go forever unfulfilled, she could not wish it away. It would be tantamount to wishing herself a different person, or wishing away all in Mr Darcy that had led her inextricably to admiration and love.

The rest of the visit was entirely consumed with practical matters, for there was much to arrange and little time in which to do it. When Elizabeth saw her guests to the door, she was torn between gratitude and love for all the care they had given her, and a shameful wish that they had never come.

Chapter Thirty-six

It was all the better that Elizabeth had brought only what was most necessary from Longbourn for her new life in London — it made packing everything within a few hours an arduous task rather than an impossibility. Georgiana bid the housemaid to help Elizabeth and really intended to help as well, but the disturbance of her feelings made this impossible. She was instead to be found at the pianoforte, giving relief to her emotions in the form of great, rolling chords and works composed in minor keys.

At last, all was in readiness. Elizabeth looked at the tidily packed trunk with satisfaction and dismissed the housemaid with thanks. Suddenly feeling the weariness of all her exertions, she sat down heavily on the bed.

She could hardly believe that she would be gone from Georgiana's house and from London on the morrow. London had seemed so foreign at first, so cold and dirty compared to the countryside. So gradually she had not noticed it, the strangeness had all worn away. Now she would leave again, and she did not know when she might come back.

Time would not admit visiting Jane to say goodbye in person. It would have to be left to the cold comfort of a letter. Elizabeth sighed and made her way to the desk. She would not attempt to write cleverly, nor to explain her real reasons for going. The letter must be made to serve as thanks to her aunt and uncle, too, for all they had done for her. The relief of telling her dear sister all would have to wait until they might speak together in private — though no one could say when that might be.

At last, Elizabeth forced herself to begin writing. It would be better to send any letter, however imperfectly it expressed her feelings, than to send none at all.

—

London, 3 March, 1816
My dear Sister,

I write with surprising news: I will be leaving London tomorrow to make my home with our sister Mary and the Admiral. How I wish I might say goodbye to you in person! But the decision was made only today, and I have not a moment to spare, I am so hurried in my attempts to arrange everything.

Please tell my aunt and uncle how much I love them and shall miss them, and how grateful I am to them. I have never known a moment's fear since our father's death, thanks to their kindness, for I knew I was never alone, nor friendless. I wish everyone were so fortunate as to have such kind friends.

I will look forward to our next meeting with impatience, though I do not know when it shall be. I will write to you again at our next destination, and whenever I have an address to share with you, I beg that you write and tell me of all you do, and think, and feel. Write enough that I may imagine I am speaking with you, my dear Jane.

With all my love,
Elizabeth Bennet

—

With a sigh, Elizabeth sealed her letter. She sat back in her chair and played with her quill, thinking.

Ought she to write a note of explanation to Mr Darcy?

It would not be accompanied by much social risk for either of them. Georgiana knew all, and she could carry a letter to her brother without hazarding it to the postal system. It would, perhaps, be a courtesy. He would know where she had gone, and why, and that he need not be concerned for her. It would save Georgiana from having to explain anything when Mr Darcy came to call, as was his frequent habit, and found that Elizabeth was not there.

Yet Elizabeth did not think it was cowardice that held her back from wishing to attempt it. She thought it rather a species of courage. He had made his decision; she had made hers. What their hearts wanted was of less importance than what their rational minds had decided would be the case. If there was an end to it, then let it be an end, quick and clean.

That was not quite right, either. If it was not cowardice that held her back, neither was it prudence. If anything, it was the knowledge that she did not think she could write the letter without including the words "I love you."

And to write those words, knowing she would never have any reply, was more than she could bear.

—

The next morning dawned chill and clammy, smothered in a low fog. The Admiral's carriage arrived for her punctually, and her trunk was loaded into it in a moment. Elizabeth might have wished it had all been done with less timeliness. In this case, the rudeness of delay might have been a blessing.

"Write to me as soon as you have arrived," Georgiana urged her as they stood clasping hands before the door. "I should like to know that you are well."

"Of course," Elizabeth said. "Georgiana —" She fell silent a moment, struggling with herself. At last, she went on. "Georgiana, I am so sorry. I shall miss you terribly. I said once that you were a friend to me, as much as an employer. But I think of you now rather as a sister."

Georgiana gave a short, choked sob and threw herself into Elizabeth's arms. "You nearly were my sister in truth," she mumbled. "Oh, I cannot bear it."

"If I were wiser, you would not have to bear it," Elizabeth said, half under her breath. Self-reproach could be bitter indeed.

"No — it is not you who is the fool, Elizabeth. It is not you," Georgiana cried. "I only wish—"

At the look of reproach Elizabeth gave her, she fell silent. "It is better not to speak of it, I think," Elizabeth said gently. "He has made his decision, and so have I."

"It is goodbye, then," Georgiana said heavily.

"It is goodbye." With that, they clasped hands one last time, and Elizabeth went out of the house and climbed into the carriage. Though reproaching herself for her weakness, she could not help but look back at the elegant little townhouse where she had spent so many happy hours as the horses picked up speed and trotted away.

Chapter Thirty-seven

It had been several days since Mr Darcy had last visited Georgiana. Though he desired and feared to see Elizabeth in equal measure, it was of little matter compared to the duty of waiting on his sister. Tomorrow, he must and would go. Though there might and likely would be something of pain in the meeting, there would at least be the joyful occupation of talking over the plans for visiting Pemberley in the spring, plans which were every day coming closer to fruition. Mr Darcy did not know how he would bear it, seeing Elizabeth there, feeling that she ought to be the mistress of it, and knowing it could never be. It did not much matter. He would have to bear it.

Though the hour was late, Mr Darcy made no move to rise from his chair and leave his study. The candlelight gleamed off the rich leather of the books that lined the walls and cast strange shadows in the corners, but he hardly noticed it. Mr Darcy was thinking, and trying not to think.

On the whole, he thought that his relations

with Elizabeth — with Mrs Smith — were tenable. Yes, all his attempts to lie to himself had failed, and he could no longer deny that his feelings towards her were not merely those of friendship. He had tried to turn away his eyes, to ignore how ardently he admired and loved her, and he had failed. That much did not admit of a doubt.

Yet it would be enough — it must be enough — that he would have the advantage of her society, her listening ear and quick wit, and if they were to part, he would at least see her happy. Any woman as handsome and charming as a Mrs Smith was not likely to remain single forever, were she ever so bereft of dowry. But, safely ensconced with Georgiana, Elizabeth could have the luxury of choice, and if she ever made one that removed her from the Darcy family's circles, he would at least have the comfort of knowing her to be well.

Mr Darcy firmly told himself that any other outcome of greater personal felicity was impossible. To offer her any kind of irregular establishment was out of the question, and he would not risk Georgiana's position in society, still less the fragile rapprochement between them, by offering her the insult of marrying her hired companion. All this had been decided, reconsidered, and decided again many times over since he had fallen for Elizabeth. It was the height of absurdity in him to regret the impossible once again.

Mr Darcy abruptly sat bolt upright, looking

around him. He was certain that he heard a bustle of footsteps and clamour of voices actually within the house, and even coming towards him. As he was on the point of rising to investigate them, he was suddenly able to recognise the voices that approached him. One was that of his butler, explaining that the master was not at home to visitors. Strangely, the other was that of a young woman. More strangely still, it was Georgiana.

In the next moment, she had flung open the door and stamped into the study. Mr Darcy was speechless with astonishment. His gentle, loving, forgiving sister, the elegant little woman who had survived three years of marriage to a fortune-hunting scoundrel without the least stain to her morals or coarsening of her opinions, was openly fuming at him.

His poor butler looked badly harried. "I beg you will forgive me, Mr Darcy, but Mrs Wickham insisted —"

Mr Darcy dismissed him and his apology with a wave. "Not to worry, Rogers, I quite understand. You may leave us now."

Though with a slight look of concern for his master, Rogers bowed and did so, closing the door behind him.

Mr Darcy firmed his resolve with a quick breath and turned to his sister. "Georgiana. You are furious. That much is obvious. Please explain."

"Elizabeth is gone, and you are a fool,"

Georgiana spat. She paused a moment. "No. That is too generous. I mean to say, Elizabeth is gone because you are a fool."

"Because I —" Mr Darcy sputtered. "Georgiana, you cannot mean it. I have never offered Mrs Smith the least insult or suggested any improper interest in her. Surely you do not believe I would say words of love to a woman so far below us in consequence, particularly one actually in your own employment. I would never insult you in such a way."

"I know very well that you have offered no words of love to Elizabeth," Georgiana said. "What I want to know is, why not?"

"Georgiana, how could you…I am sure I do not know what you mean," Mr Darcy said with an attempt at firmness.

"Do not trouble to deny it," Georgiana replied impatiently. "Anyone who has been in the room with the pair of you these past weeks could not mistake it. She has eyes only for you, and the depth of your regard for her could not be more obvious. From the first occasion of our meeting, I knew that Elizabeth's light-hearted wit would be a balm to my own spirits, and I can see you have found it so as well. I learned only after many days that her spirit and compassion are equal to her wit, and this too I believe you have found out for yourself. Do not lie to me, brother. You love her."

"Yes," Mr Darcy said almost in a whisper. "Yes, I love her. I cannot deny it."

"Then I have only one question for you," Georgiana went on, and Mr Darcy steeled himself to hear her. "Why have you never spoken to me about what transpired at Ramsgate?"

Mr Darcy looked at his sister rather as though she had grown a second head. "I beg your pardon?"

A pang shot through his heart as he saw her eyes were filled with tears. With difficulty, she kept them from falling. "Ramsgate. I spent three years fearing that you would never forgive me. It was not until Elizabeth, until she became more a friend than an employee, that I learned to look at those events rather differently. Yet even once you and I were reunited, we have never spoken of it."

"I did not wish to speak of it. I did not think you would wish to speak of it," Mr Darcy protested.

"You were wrong," Georgiana said simply. "Tell me this, brother. Do you forgive me?"

"Of course," Mr Darcy said hoarsely. He drew a ragged breath. "Georgiana. There was never anything to forgive. The fault was not yours."

"If not mine, then whose?" Georgiana asked implacably.

"Mine," Mr Darcy said. He cleared his throat. "Mine. The fault was mine."

Georgiana looked at him, as stern as a judge. "And if that is so, why have you never spoken of it to me? Why have you never asked *me* to forgive *you*?"

Mr Darcy looked at her with all his clear,

logical reasons on his lips. It was better to forget the past. They ought to let all that which was unpleasant fade away. Why waste their breath on what was shameful to speak of?

Looking at Georgiana's face, at the pain in each taut muscle, Mr Darcy knew them for a lie. He drew a deep, shuddering breath and told the truth. "Because I was afraid you could not forgive me. Because I did not think I deserved forgiveness."

"Go on," Georgiana said, almost gently.

"It was my responsibility to protect you. I chose Mrs Younge as your companion — I might as well have dropped you into a nest of vipers. I left you alone and unprotected. And I told myself that I ought not to go to you afterward, or allow Colonel Fitzwilliam to duel Wickham. I told myself that it would be better for you to avoid the scandal." Mr Darcy would have wished to hide his face at the hideous recital, but Georgiana deserved better than that. He kept his voice steady and his eyes fixed on hers to the last, and awaited her reply.

Her face softened, and she went to him, leaning her head against his shoulder. When she spoke, her voice was muffled. "We are both such fools, brother. I do not believe you had any more reason for shame than I did. We both of us made only honest mistakes. But do you understand why I have finally spoken of this, tonight of all nights?"

"Because it was time," Mr Darcy said at last, raggedly. "It was time, and past time, for there to be no more lies or secrets between us."

"Yes," Georgiana said. "That much is true. But also because Elizabeth is gone. She has left my home to live with her sister and the Admiral, because you love each other and you will not have her, and she is too wise to remain so close to a blighted love. And if you let her leave, brother, it will be the second time that you have chosen to do nothing, when you would have done better to speak the truth, whatever came of it."

Mr Darcy kept his voice level, though it cost him a painful effort. "The situations are hardly the same. I ought to have spoken to you directly and told you of my regret. That much is true. But to speak of love to Elizabeth — to marry Elizabeth — do not you see, Georgiana, that it would materially affect all our reputations? She is your hired companion, and I am your brother. At best, the *ton* would laugh behind their hands. At worst, it might make it impossible for you to marry a man of any consequence."

"I would not want a man who could be dissuaded by such a thing," Georgiana said. "I will never again suffer the shame of being unable to respect my partner in life, Fitzwilliam. Anything would be better. And I beg you would not force me to watch you go on without your chosen partner in life, simply because of imaginary concerns on my account. The *ton* may well laugh, brother. Let them."

Mr Darcy laughed a little at that. "Georgiana. I have been such a fool. I have treated matters of no significance at all as though they were of the first importance, and come closer than I like to think to a fatal error." He frowned, running his hand nervously through the thick waves of his hair. "It may already be too late. Georgiana...do you think she will still have me?"

"My dear brother, you will never know unless you ask her."

"No," Mr Darcy said. "No, I suppose I never would."

Chapter Thirty-eight

The night was no longer young by the time the two siblings had at last talked themselves out. After so long a time of estrangement followed by many weeks of polite nothings and conversation before a roomful of other guests, they could not soon exhaust all the topics of shared interest, all the memories both sweet and painful that were such an exquisite relief to communicate.

At last, however, even the joy of brother and sister at being once again able to share all the closeness of family could not outweigh their weariness, and Georgiana elected to stay in one of the many guest rooms, rather than remain awake even for the short carriage ride home. A word to the housekeeper, and a particularly nice room was made ready for Georgiana, while her coachmen were dismissed home to their beds.

"After all," as Georgiana remarked, "you may easily take me back tomorrow in your carriage, and I am sure the poor men want their sleep." As Mr Darcy had no objection, these arrangements were made, and it was not long before they could at last seek their rest.

"Goodnight, brother," Georgiana said to Mr Darcy with a last squeeze of his hand. She covered a yawn as she closed the door of the guest bedroom behind her.

"Goodnight, my dear sister," Mr Darcy replied, hopelessly fond. Just so had she looked as a little girl, half-asleep in her chair while insisting she was not a bit tired. He went to his own room, expecting to fall asleep at once.

Yet once his valet was dismissed and the candles blown out, thoughts of Elizabeth returned, making sleep impossible. Only now did Mr Darcy truly feel how deep the pain of pretending not to esteem Elizabeth, pretending not to love Elizabeth, had been. He now realised he had fooled no one — not even himself. Yet if the pain had been so severe for himself, the one with all the power of forwarding their relationship and asking her that all-important question, the one with all the benefits of wealth and consequence on his side, what had it been for Elizabeth?

What was between them was not one-sided. Of all the doubts and fears in his minds, that was not one. She had wanted as much, felt as much as he. That much was certain. What was uncertain was how much it had cost her, in tears shed and opportunities lost.

At last, Mr Darcy admitted to himself the

truest, most naked shape of the question that tormented him and kept him from sleep.

Could she ever forgive him?

Slowly and half unwillingly, Mr Darcy rose from his bed. He drew on his dressing gown, lit a candle, and sat down at the desk by the window. Drawing the curtain a little open, he could see the faint gleam of moonlight on the cobblestones and hear the distant call of a night watchman. To arrange paper, quill, and ink before him was the work of moments. With a long, slow sigh, he dipped the quill in ink and slowly began to pin down his heart upon the page.

Chapter Thirty-nine

The Darcy siblings set out the next morning in rather different tempers. The full expression of her feelings must have been a considerable relief to Georgiana, for she looked happier and more at peace than Mr Darcy had seen her since Ramsgate. For his part, he could not be so much at ease. It might be too late, entirely too late. For all Elizabeth's quick wit and soft heart, she was not without her prejudices, and whether she would choose to judge him by his present actions or his former cowardice was far from clear.

Mr Darcy carried his letter inside his coat, next to his heart. He would see Georgiana safely home, sit with her for perhaps a quarter of an hour, and deliver the letter to a receiving house before he returned home. If his valet ever learned of it, he would be surprised not to have been commissioned with the task himself. Mr Darcy felt firmly that if he were to commit the solecism of sending a letter to an unmarried woman, he would do it with as little publicity as possible.

"I shall not keep you long, but I admit I should be glad of a short visit," Georgiana said as they entered the house.

"If you will excuse me, ma'am, there is a visitor in the drawing room," Benson informed them as he held the door.

Georgiana frowned. "Really, Benson? And you admitted them when I was not at home?" Though her tone was mild, her surprise was obvious.

"It is Mrs Smith, ma'am," Benson said as though no further apology or explanation were required, and to judge from the reaction of the Darcy siblings, correctly so.

Georgiana said, "Oh!" and a look of surprise and brightness came into her face, but Mr Darcy said not a word before striding to the drawing room and throwing open the door.

Elizabeth was indeed seated there, and she rose and turned at his entrance. The sight of Mr Darcy seemed to shock her into speechlessness, and they stood for a long moment, staring at each other and saying nothing.

"You are not Georgiana," Elizabeth said at last, and though Mr Darcy was still beyond speech, his returning rationality was at least able to note that she seemed as affected as he knew himself to be.

In the next moment, Georgiana hurried into the room. She held her arms out to Elizabeth like a sister. "I am so glad to see you again," she told

Elizabeth, as though they had been parted for weeks instead of days. "But how comes it that you are here? I thought you would be in a different county by now!"

"Last night, I was," Elizabeth said, a little shyly. "But I found that I had left matters sadly unfinished here. When at last I realised it, I took the public stagecoach back at once. Mary and the Admiral did not like to see me go alone, but I would not allow them to persuade me out of it, and as the Admiral was under orders, they had no choice."

Mr Darcy shuddered at the thought of Elizabeth travelling alone. It was not at all the manner in which he would have chosen to be reunited with her, however satisfactory the results. She was here, however, safe and unharmed, and it was unwise to quarrel with success.

Elizabeth cleared her throat and went on. "I confess I have come to ask you for a favour, Georgiana. I should like to stay here for a few days, until I can arrange for an interview with your brother. I have something particular which I should like to say to him."

Though Georgiana was saying something in warm assent, Mr Darcy interrupted her without a second thought. "You may speak to me now," he said, and was surprised at the roughness of his own voice. "Let us not wait. I have something which I should like to say to you."

Georgiana cleared her throat. "Of course you

may stay with me, Elizabeth, for as long as you wish," she told her friend. "I shall be glad to have you. For the moment, however, I shall go into the other part of the room and leave the door ajar, as you are an unmarried woman under my roof. I hope I shall not forget myself and play a concerto on the pianoforte, for you know I shall not be able to hear anything if I do."

Having in this pleasant way given her brother and her friend both chaperonage and privacy, Georgiana left them. It was only a handful of moments before the sounds of Bach's "Goldberg Variations" could be heard from the next room.

"I had not expected my opportunity to come so soon," Elizabeth admitted, a little ruefully. "I hope you will consent to listen to me."

"Of all things, yes," Mr Darcy said fervently.

"I thank you. Mr Darcy, what I have to say to you is not sensible or polite. It is in every way reckless, and I hope you will forgive me. I wish to begin by saying that you owe me nothing. If I have misjudged your feelings, we shall say no more of it, and you shall never hear from me again on the topic.

"It is in every way absurd for me to propose that we ought to marry — in every way except for one. I know well that it is absurd in me to speak first to any man, let alone when the difference in our consequence is so great, and I, in a prudential light, have nothing to offer.

"I left thinking this, and thinking not that I

ought not to speak, but that I could not speak. But I was terribly angry at you, Mr Darcy — angry and sick to my heart, for all the time, I have felt certain that you love me as I do you, and chose not to speak of it. And I have come back to tell you I love you and that I always will, for I cannot be angry with you for keeping silent when I had not spoken of it myself."

Here, Elizabeth looked at Mr Darcy and laughed a little, as though at the absurdity of what she intended to say next. "I suppose what I am saying, Mr Darcy, when one strips it of all the verbiage and comes at last to the point, is this. Mr Darcy, will you marry me?"

His arms were around her, his lips pressed to hers, almost as soon as the words were spoken. There had been no conscious thought involved — Mr Darcy had not intended to take any action so utterly beyond the bounds of propriety — yet, in the first moment of exquisite surprise and relief, he did so. He felt a deep sigh run through her body as he held her and remembered at last what he was about.

Mr Darcy released Elizabeth and stepped back, clearing his throat. "I ought not to take such liberties until we are formally engaged," he apologised, though it was evident from the look of dreamy happiness in her eyes and the soft smile on her lips that his love was not at all inclined to reproach him. "And yes, Elizabeth, I shall marry you, for you have all my heart."

Though she smiled at him, the turmoil of

emotion in her heart was so great that bright tears stood in her eyes. "I am glad to hear it, for though I thought so, I was not certain. And even if it were so, I confess I feared you would be unwilling to overlook the difference in our wealth and consequence, even for love."

Mr Darcy winced, but he was too honest to reproach her. "After what I was so foolish as to claim before all the world, I cannot blame you. But if you will have patience with me, Elizabeth, I would like to show you some proof that I am not so hopeless as all this. I was coming to find you, just as you were coming to me."

"To hear of this will require no patience at all," Elizabeth steadily replied.

"Then I should like to give you a letter that I had intended to deliver to the post immediately after leaving Georgiana's home. I had pictured you reading it some days from now, and I was uncertain whether I dared to hope that you would grant me the permission I sought to come to you. Indeed, I was not sure whether it was more likely that you would never reply at all."

"Never," Elizabeth declared. "No matter how angry I might have been with you, I could never have simply left you awaiting a reply."

"I am glad to hear it. But enough of my delay. I shall give it to you now." With these words, Mr Darcy removed the letter and handed it to Elizabeth, gesturing that they might sit while she read it.

Elizabeth broke the seal and complied.

—

London, 5 March, 1816
Miss Elizabeth Bennet,

Forgive me. I have been, in every way, a fool. I know not what is worse — that I would have held consequence and wealth to be more important than the truest fidelity and affection, or that I was unblushingly ready to avail myself of your friendship and companionship while withholding the only worthy return I could make. I am ashamed to think of it.

It has not been a week since we parted, but I am already certain that a longer separation would be entirely unsupportable. Each time we have been in company together, it has grown more and more impossible for me to take my eyes from you, from your lovely face, from the enchanting sparkle of your eyes. Each time we have spoken, I have known that with no other woman could I find the happiness and ease I felt simply from conversing with you. Each time I did not tell you I loved and wanted only you, I made a liar of myself.

Please give me another chance. Do not say that such precious feelings are gone forever. In my heart, they will never go. I shall not know a moment's peace until you consent to be my wife.

With all my heart,

Fitzwilliam Darcy

—

Wordlessly, Elizabeth folded the letter and held out her hands to him. Mr Darcy clasped them firmly, seeing in her eyes a depth of love that left him shaken to his core.

"Oh, I am glad," Elizabeth said at last. "I am glad indeed that you would not have allowed us to simply part, had I not brought myself to confess my heart to you."

"No," Mr Darcy said. "No, I am deeply grateful that I came to my senses and realised how precious you are to me." He cleared his throat. "Elizabeth, my darling, would you object to a short engagement?"

"I should prefer it. For all I am concerned, we may be married as soon as the banns can be read."

"I am glad to hear it, for though I ought not to have kissed you, I do not think I could bear to wait through a long engagement until I might do it again."

It might be that at this juncture, Elizabeth gave him a look of such love and longing that Mr Darcy was moved to forget himself again. It is possible — it would be understandable in a newly engaged couple, particularly one that had so lately feared their love might be lost — if they again fell into each other's arms like a homecoming, if their lips again met in a tender kiss. But if it were so, it would surely have been only a moment before propriety and good sense reasserted themselves.

Elizabeth looked up at Mr Darcy. Her smile, though radiant, was still a little fragile after all the recent pain of separation and loss. "Shall we go and inform Georgiana of our happy news?"

"Without delay." Mr Darcy offered Elizabeth his arm. She took it readily, and they went to share the joy that they had so lately gained with she who had no insignificant part in bringing it about.

Chapter Forty

It was fortunate that Georgiana was not tired of Elizabeth's company, for she was fated to have a great deal more of it. The two dear friends were, of course, soon to become the dearest of sisters, but until that event might take place, it was desirable that she should go on staying in Georgiana's London townhouse. To stay with Mr Darcy would have had an odd appearance, however many chaperones they might provide themselves with, and while the Gardiners were always delighted to see their niece, their guest chambers would be needed so that Mrs Bennet and the youngest girls might come to see Elizabeth wed. The wedding breakfast was bidding fair to be a merry party, with so many delighted guests to come to it. Only one dear friend was to be missing, for Mr Bingley was detained elsewhere by the illness of an uncle who had been almost a father to him. The letter of regrets he sent Mr Darcy was as smudged as most of that gentleman's communications were fated to be, but no less from the heart.

"And I am the more vexed," Elizabeth told Jane as they sat together one morning, "for I am determined that you shall meet him one day, Jane. Mr Bingley is Mr Darcy's oldest friend, and I do not know when I have met a pleasanter man, or one with happier manners. I think you will like him very much."

"I am sure I shall, if you and Mr Darcy like him," Jane said softly, but with a quelling look. When Elizabeth gave her a shrug and a smile, the look grew stern. "No, really, Lizzy, you must not be matchmaking for me and supposing me discontented with my lot. I am fortunate indeed, you know. I have a happy home with our aunt and uncle. I know myself to be of use. And better still, with you and Mary so well married, I know I shall never have to fear for myself, or for our dear mother and sisters. Do not suppose me to desire any change in my circumstances."

"You are hard-hearted," Elizabeth replied with a gentle smile, "for you have not thought about what Mr Bingley might desire, or how much that gentleman might wish for a change in his circumstances. Jane, I have never met a man who so clearly had a heart to give, and yet I believe him to have a natural taste and judgement that have not yet been satisfied by any woman in his acquaintance. I am convinced it is because his acquaintance does not yet include the sweetest-tempered woman I have ever known."

Jane's attempt to conceal her blush was not entirely successful. "I give up, Lizzy, for you always could talk circles around me. But one day, this Mr Bingley and I shall meet, and you must promise me not to be disappointed if, after all, we are nothing more than common and indifferent acquaintances."

"I promise," Elizabeth replied without hesitation. "Now then, I am to have a new dress for the wedding. What think you — ought I to have this Spanish lace, or perhaps the Brussels lace that Uncle Gardiner showed us the other day?"

Pleased to talk of anything other than beaus, Jane gave her opinion decidedly for the Brussels lace, and in pleasant talk of lace and ribbon, the rest of their visit flew swiftly by.

—

In later years, Mr Darcy found it almost impossible to remember the period between his proposal to Elizabeth — or, to be strictly accurate, her proposal to him — and the wedding. It seemed at once to have disappeared in a flash and to have lasted an age. Though a courtship at last acknowledged and brought into the open may have its charms, Mr Darcy found himself so ardently wishing to have Elizabeth securely his wife that he could not wish for its continuance. That they met every day was a delight, but that they must part at the end of each, if not before, was every day a fresh grievance.

Though the period of waiting felt long to those most concerned in the matter, it was as short as it might be. Mr Darcy spoke with Mr Gardiner about the settlements. As there was on one side every desire to reach an equitable agreement and on the other every intent to be generous, there was no disagreement to delay the proceedings or mar the happiness that surrounded them. There was then only the three weeks of waiting for the banns to be read before their marriage might take place. In bad moments, Mr Darcy could almost imagine his Aunt de Bourgh daring to protest them, but thankfully, neither familial harmony nor his nerves were put to such a test.

The morning on which they were to be wed dawned full of rosy and golden light. Elizabeth could attest to it, for she was awake to witness every delicate ray of sunshine. Sleep had eluded her. It was strange, she thought, that something that made one so happy might at the same time be utterly terrifying.

She would be his wife; in not even a full day, she would be utterly changed. From Miss Bennet to Mrs Smith; then back to Miss Bennet and on to Mrs Darcy. The mind and heart that she had at first understood so little would be given into her keeping forever; she would be in every way his.

A soft knock came on the door. Elizabeth

granted permission to enter, and a maid came in holding a letter and a small parcel in her hands.

"This just came for you, ma'am. From Mr Darcy!" the maid said excitedly. "If you please, ma'am, I told the messenger to wait, in case you had a reply."

Elizabeth drew in a sharp breath. "Thank you," she told the maid with a smile. "I imagine I shall."

The maid bobbed a curtsy. "Of course, ma'am."

Turning her attention to the letter, Elizabeth broke the seal and read it eagerly.

—

My darling Elizabeth,

I do not believe I have ever looked upon a day with such joyful anticipation as this one. You are my heart, my love, and in a few short hours, I shall be able to indulge in the happiness of writing, "my darling Wife." Until then, I beg you would indulge me by wearing this.

Yours forever,
F.D.

—

Turning to the little parcel, she undid the knotted string that held it closed and slowly unfolded the paper. The breath caught in her throat as she slowly lifted the necklace it contained.

It was a most exquisite piece, and perfectly suited to wear with her new gown. The delicate little circle was made to fit closely around the neck. Though from a small distance, it appeared to be a broad chain, closer observation revealed it to hold a cunning pattern of leaves and vines. Set among them were small, sparkling stones. Their brilliancy and small size proclaimed that they were not of paste — they were real.

"Thank you, I shall write a reply," Elizabeth informed the maid, and hurried to the room's desk, which was thankfully well supplied with ink and paper. If she had allowed herself to agonise over it, a fitting response might have taken hours. It was fortunate, Elizabeth thought, that she had only moments if the response was to reach Mr Darcy before he left for the church.

—

My dear Fitzwilliam,

I would treasure anything given by your hand, were it even a vine of ivy or a few oak leaves. How much more, then, the most beautiful necklace I have ever seen? Of course I shall wear it when I am made most formally Yours.

With all my heart,

E. B.

—

It was the work of a few moments to blot and seal the letter. "Please give this to the messenger," Elizabeth told the maid, who curtsied and was gone.

Alone, Elizabeth at last fastened the love token about her neck and looked into the mirror. Beautiful as it was, she was yet more surprised by the look she found in her own eyes.

"Oh, it is terrifying to be so happy," Elizabeth murmured. "How can it be that I love him more and more each day?"

When they were children, Elizabeth and Jane had sometimes whispered to each other fantasies of what their wedding days might be like. Elizabeth had always pictured being married in Meryton church, with a wedding breakfast at Longbourn. She had never imagined being married at St. George, Hanover Square. Even when she stepped into the carriage to go there, it seemed half a mistake.

Yet by the time the horses drew to a stop outside, Elizabeth had all but forgotten her awe in anticipation of the event itself. It did not much matter where she married Mr Darcy, as long as she would be his wife. Meryton Church or St. George or even over the anvil in Gretna Green: what was a few hours of one day compared to all the years of their lives?

Alighting from the carriage, Elizabeth looked over the church with a smile. Over the months of her residence in London, she had often passed it. The square bell tower rising above the main body of the church was a familiar sight, as were the tall columns that adorned the front of the church.

The morning light poured through the east window, made of magnificent stained glass depicting the Tree of Jesse. On the floor, its patterns of coloured light turned strangely abstract, yet all the more beautiful for it. Elizabeth looked up at the figure of Mary most prominently depicted and felt her lips curve into a gentle smile. The beauty of the sacred space around her and of the promises to be made seemed fused into one.

She met Mr Darcy's eyes, and her heart was wrung again by the love she saw there. They spoke in turn as the pastor asked his questions, weaving their lives together, never again to be parted.

—

An excerpt from The Courier *and* The London Times, *7 April, 1816*

At St George's, Hannover Square, Mr Fitzwilliam

Darcy of Pemberley to Miss Elizabeth Bennet, spinster of the town of M— in Hertfordshire, lately of London. The bride was attended by three of her sisters, Miss Bennet, Miss Catherine Bennet, and Miss Lydia Bennet. Mrs Pellew, nee' Bennet, was also in attendance with her husband. The groom's family was well represented, with the Earl of Matlock and Lady Catherine de Bourgh being of particular note. London will miss the happy couple, as they intend to take up residence in Derbyshire immediately following the wedding.

Epilogue

Springtime at Pemberley

Mr Darcy's plans for a spring visit to Pemberley were to come true after all, though with a little alteration. Elizabeth was now his wife, and Georgiana joyously settled into Pemberley as her home, yet there were still visitors to his beloved corner of Derbyshire. To his wife's delight, the Gardiners had agreed to bring Jane for a visit, leaving their children in Meryton under the care of their elder cousins. Though such a plan would have once been highly ineligible, Kitty was grown ever more steady and able of late, and professed herself eager for the responsibility.

The carriage arrived late of an evening. The travellers were drooping with the weariness of their long journey, but full of smiles.

"My goodness, Lizzy," Jane said warmly. "You described Pemberley often enough in your letters, and yet I never imagined anything like this. I could hardly believe the size of the estate as we were arriving, and now I cannot believe how charming it is."

Elizabeth laughed and embraced her sister where they stood next to the Gardiner's carriage. "It is lovely, is it not? I shall enjoy showing you around most prodigiously. Though I confess you could have a far more able guide, for there is still much I do not know myself. Perhaps we shall have Mrs Reynolds, the housekeeper, guide us both instead."

"Any method of discovering this lovely place shall be vastly agreeable to me," Jane said with a smile. She slowly turned in a circle, looking all about her. "Elizabeth, how wonderful. If I had designed an estate for you to be mistress of, I could not, in all my wildest imaginings, have pictured this."

Elizabeth acknowledged the compliment with a nod. "Shall we go to your room? I imagine you must be tired after the long ride."

"Yes, I should like that of all things," Jane said gratefully. Having carried Mrs Gardiner along with them and deposited her in her own room, the sisters sat down in the guestroom assigned to Jane for a long overdue chat.

"Married life seems vastly agreeable, for both you and Mary are simply blooming," Jane remarked.

Elizabeth laughed. "I certainly find it so. It is a remarkable thing to have the person one likes best always close at hand. Fitzwilliam is so dear to me now, Jane. It is strange to think that the two of you have hardly met."

"I am sure I shall like him, since he has brought you such happiness," Jane replied.

"I am sure you shall, for he has the kindest heart. And I rather wish our father could have known him, for I think he greatly would have enjoyed Fitzwilliam's intelligence."

Jane squeezed her sister's hand. "I know he would have."

"But enough of that. Tell me something of you, Jane. Are you still happy in London? Have you any beaus?"

"Yes and no, Lizzy. I like London as much as ever, but I do not think I shall ever marry. I am growing rather old for it, you know. I am fully five-and-twenty."

"That is not so very old," Elizabeth protested. "And you are as lovely as ever. Any man would be lucky to have a wife half so beautiful as you are."

Jane shook her head with a sad, resigned smile. "Now, do not fuss, Lizzy. You are as bad as all newly married people are, wanting everyone else to be married too. I have great joy in my life, and it does not signify if I am not meant to have the joy of marriage, too."

"No, of course there are many other joys in life," Elizabeth readily agreed, though she would have felt more comfortable if only she could have felt that her sister minded rather less.

"I shall probably end an old maid," Jane went

on with her best attempt at cheerfulness, "but that is not so bad. I am lucky indeed to have our Aunt and Uncle Gardiner, and you, and Mary, for I may always be sure of having a pleasant home."

Elizabeth covered her sister's hand with hers. "Of course you may, Jane. Of course you may."

Though both felt as though they might have talked forever, Jane's weariness soon grew too pronounced to ignore. After the third time she covered a yawn and protested that she was not tired in the least, Elizabeth would take no more excuses.

"I shall leave you now," she said, "for we shall surely see each other in the morning, and all the days of your visit. Sleep now, Jane. I am convinced you are half asleep already."

"I must own I am rather tired," Jane admitted. With that, and with an exchange of 'goodnights,' both sisters went to their rest.

Elizabeth woke rather early on the morning after their arrival, for her pleasure in the visit and her desire to see her sister again as soon as possible were great. However, she would not have disturbed Jane after such a tiring journey for anything. It would be much better to pass the time in her own way. Finding such a pastime required little thought; she would walk through the grounds and enjoy the sunshine and fresh air. Under their mellowing influence, Elizabeth could almost forget her impatience. Thankfully, she had not long to wait. Upon seeing her older sister emerging onto the terrace, she hurried forward and hailed her. Jane came to meet her, looking all around her in astonished admiration.

"The grounds are every bit as fine as the house, Lizzy," Jane said. Her warm admiration was highly gratifying. "I am no such walker as you are, but I think I could walk in them forever."

"I know I could never grow tired of them," Elizabeth replied. She laughed a little. "When I think of how I used to disdain Caroline Bingley for pursuing Fitzwilliam so shamelessly! It becomes a little more understandable when one has seen Pemberley."

"Oh, Lizzy," Jane said, with an attempt at scolding that ended in a laugh. "I shall be curious to make her acquaintance after all you have told me of her. She will be one of the party on this visit, I think you told me in your letter?"

"Yes, she and Mr Bingley, too," Elizabeth replied. "In fact, we expect them to arrive this afternoon."

"I am sure they will be pleasant company," Jane said in her usual happy confidence.

"Yes, I think they will," Elizabeth replied. The sisters walked on through the gardens, talking of everything and nothing, until thoughts of the time recalled them to the house.

In the afternoon, Mrs Gardiner spoke of wishing to see more of the park than her own feet would allow, and the wish was hardly spoken before it was arranged that all four of the ladies would do so. By placing Elizabeth and Mrs Gardiner in the phaeton, and mounting Georgiana and Jane, who were considerably better horsewomen, on mares from Pemberley's stables, the four women might all go together. Mr Darcy felt he ought to keep near the house to welcome the Bingleys when they arrived, and so proposed that he and Mr Gardiner might try a little fishing instead. This suggestion was quickly taken up, and everybody set off on their day's amusements with a good will.

To ride through the gentle spring air together was delightful, and when the little expedition had ended, the only complaint anybody could make was that there was so much more of Pemberley that they had not had time to see.

"But that is of little matter," Georgiana said earnestly, "for we may go out again often, and in the end, we will view it all."

The others laughingly agreed, and it was with great mutual satisfaction that they returned to their rooms to rest a little and refresh themselves before supper.

Elizabeth came down for supper rather early, but she had not been waiting in the drawing room above a quarter hour before her husband and Mr Bingley joined her.

"It is such a pleasure to see you again, Mr Bingley," Elizabeth remarked after the formal bows and first greetings had been exchanged. "I hope your journey from London was not too tiring?"

"No, I am pleased to say we made good time," Mr Bingley answered with his customary smile. "It is always so refreshing to visit Pemberley that I daresay I would be feeling better now even if we had been delayed."

Elizabeth laughed. "It is quite something, is it not? My father's estate in Hertfordshire was pleasant, but it is nothing to Pemberley."

"I cannot think of many estates that would bear a comparison with it," Mr Bingley agreed. "Indeed, that may come to be a difficulty to me. I am interested in buying an estate of my own, you see, but all the properties I view suffer in comparison with what I know an estate in Derbyshire can be."

"You are looking in the neighbourhood, then?"

"My plans are far from settled, but there is much to recommend it. After all, I would then have the advantage of my friend's society rather more than I might otherwise."

"I should like to see you settled nearby," Elizabeth said, "and I am sure that Mr Darcy would as well."

"Nothing would please me more," Mr Darcy confirmed. "As you know, Bingley, I have been thinking seriously on the subject. I have just heard of an estate that is expected to come to market. It is not ten miles from here."

"I should like to see it," Mr Bingley commented.

Their conversation was then interrupted a little, as the Gardiners, Miss Bingley, and Georgiana all came to the drawing room in quick succession. In the flurry of bows, introductions, and greetings, little of any significance could be said.

After a time, they settled back into small groups, seated comfortably around the room. Mr Darcy and Mr Bingley had treated Mr Gardiner with every attention upon his arrival, and the three of them were now intently discussing the Exchange. Caroline Bingley had attempted to lavish excessive compliments on Georgiana, but with a little help from Elizabeth, Georgiana had led her into a technical discussion of the pianoforte instead. Elizabeth smiled to see them. As Miss Bingley truly was skilled, if not quite so much as her sister-in-law, the conversation appeared highly engaging to both of them.

"Jane is rather late coming down, do not you think?" she asked her aunt.

Mrs Gardiner smiled reassuringly. "I believe she was a little fatigued by so much riding, but I am sure she will be here soon. Jane is always so careful not to incommode anybody. She would not be late."

"Yes, of course you are right," Elizabeth said, shaking her head. "It is silly of me to fret."

Still, she could not help looking now and again at the doorframe and wishing her sister would appear in it. Her private curiosity and wish to observe a certain meeting had grown almost too strong to bear.

At last, her patience — which might, perhaps, better bear the name of impatience — bore fruit. Jane appeared at the door, walking as always with a quiet and graceful step.

She had not wasted the interval. When Elizabeth saw her last, her hair had been half falling out of its coiffure thanks to their little adventure. Her practical riding habit had grown mussed, with numerous horsehairs appended to its skirts. Jane never looked less than lovely, but her appearance certainly was not polished.

It was now. Jane had rarely looked lovelier. She did not have the advantages of a new gown or fine jewels, but every other refinement was hers. It was not only the perfection of her face and figure, but the goodness and unselfconsciousness shining from her eyes that made her a pleasure to behold.

"Jane, I think you have not yet met Mr Bingley," Elizabeth said innocently. "Come, let me present him to you."

Jane came smilingly and without hesitation at her sister's request. "I shall be glad to meet any friend of yours and Mr Darcy's," she said in her low, sweet voice.

In the next moment, she at last looked properly at Mr Bingley, and he at her.

Elizabeth was pleased to note that of the two, Mr Bingley's reaction was the more poorly concealed. His eyes widened in surprise and admiration, and the smile that customarily ornamented his handsome face disappeared for a moment, only to reappear even broader than before.

Jane nearly succeeded in concealing her sensibility. The first sight of Mr Bingley only caused her to turn momentarily white, then slightly flushed. She had regained her composure by the time the introductions were complete. In no more than a quarter of an hour, they were talking together like old friends.

Elizabeth had not omitted to seat them opposite each other during supper, and she was pleased to observe their absorption in each other continuing. Jane and Mr Bingley were both notably pleasant people and unusually easy to talk to, but she had never seen either so deeply engaged with a new acquaintance. Indeed, both only spoke enough to their other neighbours to be civil. By the time supper ended, they had established their similar tastes in music and dancing and matching disinterest in cards. Elizabeth thought wryly that the satisfaction of having guessed rightly was almost as enjoyable as her satisfaction in her sister's enjoyment.

She was not the only one who had noticed

their absorption in each other. Caroline Bingley had done all she could to prevent it with pointed comments and reminders of heiresses, but as she did not wish to take the risk of losing the privilege of visiting at Pemberley, she could not go far in deprecating the sister of its mistress. Mr and Mrs Gardiner seemed by their looks to have noticed their niece's preoccupation, but they merely forwarded the conversation going on around them.

While Caroline Bingley was playing a rather long and highly technical concerto and the others were variously listening and carrying on quiet conversations, Mr Darcy came over to his wife and spoke low into her ear. "Will you join me on the terrace for a moment, Elizabeth? The night air is remarkably fine this evening, and the stars are brilliant."

"I should be delighted," Elizabeth replied, and followed him out.

No sooner had the door closed behind them than he turned to her and took her hand, leading her out to the railing. The sky was velvety dark and sparkling with stars, and the night air soft with the warmth of spring. They stood together in silence for a long moment, looking at the beauty around them. The warm glow from the windows of Pemberley shone past them, sparkling off the trout stream and only just touching the edge of the trees opposite before fading away. Elizabeth squeezed her husband's hand, feeling a happiness that was too deep for words. Simply being together was enough.

At last, Mr Darcy turned to her and spoke. "You anticipated this, did not you, my love? You did not look the least surprised to see my friend and your sister so struck by each other."

Elizabeth laughed playfully. "I am sure I have not the slightest notion what you mean," she replied, though her teasing tone said quite the opposite.

"You suggested I ought to invite Mr Bingley to join the visit," Mr Darcy said wryly. "You were thinking of a match with your sister even then, isn't it so?"

"I confess, I have long wished for them to meet," Elizabeth said. "Now, if my mother were here, you would see what conniving and matchmaking really are. I assure you I will do nothing of the sort. They have met, just as I wished, and only time will tell if anything may come of it. It is out of my hands."

Mr Darcy laughed. "My darling wife, this is too much disinterestedness, to be sure. Confess it, you would be very pleased to have your sister so well married."

"Married to a kind and pleasant man who intends to settle near us, so that my dear sister would be always close by? I confess it. I am already a happy and fortunate woman, but I would not find it at all amiss if this happiness were also to be mine."

"Then may it be so," Mr Darcy said softly. He

drew her into his arms and softly kissed her hair. "My dearest Elizabeth, I hope you shall always have every happiness in life."

"I have," she said softly. "Or, at least, I have every happiness that matters, here in your arms."

"Oh, my dear," he said softly into her hair. "I had not thought I could be so happy. I do not know what to say."

"Nor I, except — I love you."

"My darling wife, my dearest Elizabeth," he breathed. "I love you with all my heart."

THE END

Thank You

Thank you so much for reading Friendship and Fortitude! If you enjoyed it, please review it on Amazon. Each review makes a big difference!

Claim Your Free Stories

Amelia's newsletter subscribers get free copies of her short stories, "A Letter for Mr. Darcy" and "A Valentine for Mr. Darcy". They also receive exclusive access to news and giveaways from Amelia and other Song Sparrow Press authors.

Subscribe at: songsparrowpress.com/authors/ amelia-westerly/newsletter/ and recieve your free stories today!

Other Books by Amelia Westerly

If you enjoyed Friendship and Fortitude, look for Amelia's other Pride and Prejudice variations, available in print, as ebooks, and on Kindle Unlimited through Amazon.

Discretion and Daring: A Pride and Prejudice Variation

Mr Darcy's surprising invitation to Pemberley conceals a hidden motive. But can Elizabeth save Georgiana from the danger that threatens her?

Sweethearts and Snowflakes: A Christmas Pride and Prejudice Variation

Elizabeth's first Christmas as the mistress of Pemberley will be full of joy and laughter...and a surprising romance for Mary Bennet!

Other Books from Song Sparrow Press

Beatrice Langford delights in writing sweet and wholesome Pride and Prejudice variations. Her works celebrate witty banter and good friendships.

The Parson of Kympton: A Pride and Prejudice Variation

Mr Darcy has no choice but to give Mr Wickham the living of Kympton…but if Elizabeth doesn't learn to understand her heart in time, the choice may end in disaster!

Fine Eyes and White Lies: A Pride and Prejudice Variation

A little white lie makes Mr Darcy believe that Elizabeth loves him…but when an untimely confession of the truth badly hurts his pride and his heart, can they ever find their way back to each other?

About the Author

Amelia Westerly lives in the Pacific Northwest with her two lordly cats, Edmond and Wentworth. She likes walking on rocky beaches and thinking about times gone by. Her other passions include tea, music of all kinds, and Jane Austen's wonderful novels.

Printed in Great Britain
by Amazon